TALES OF ELSINORE

TALES OF ELSINORE

EMILY WYNNE

BALANCE OF SEVEN
Newport, VT

Tales of Elsinore

For information, contact:
Balance of Seven
www.balanceofseven.com
info@balanceofseven.com

Cover Design by Rue Sparks
www.ruesparks.com

Developmental Editing by Charlene Templeman

Copy Editing, Formatting, and Proofreading by TNT Editing
www.theodorentinker.com

Publisher's Cataloging-in-Publication Data

Names: Wynne, Emily, 1983- . | Bruno, Emily Wynne, 1983- .
Title: Tales of Elsinore / Emily Wynne.
Description: Newport, VT : Balance of Seven, 2025. | Series: Princess of the pomegranate moon ; book 2. | Summary: After returning from Faerie to find that sixty years have passed, a trans priestess and sorceress travels the dying Earth she once called home in search of where she now belongs, guided by a book she cannot read and a hope she can't define.
Identifiers: LCCN 2025945617 | ISBN 9781947012509 (pbk.) | ISBN 9781947012516 (ebook)
Subjects: LCSH: Magic – Fiction. | Self-realization – Fiction. | Mythology – Fiction. | Goddesses – Fiction. | Environmental degradation – Fiction. | Transgender women – Fiction. | Women priests – Fiction. | BISAC: FICTION / Fantasy / General. | FICTION / LGBTQ+ / Transgender. | FICTION / Fairy Tales, Folk Tales, Legends & Mythology.
Classification: LCC PS3623.Y55 T35 2025 (print) | PS3623.Y55 (ebook) | DDC 813 W--dc23
LC record available at https://lccn.loc.gov/2025945617

29 28 27 26 25   1 2 3 4 5

To Vera always.
And to all my sisters,
the daughters of the Mother.

CONTENTS

PROLOGUE

The sun had long since set beneath the distant mountains that bordered the far side of the Great River Valley when the priestess roused from the depths of meditation. Rising and leaving her inner chamber shrouded by curtains, she stepped out into the night air and gazed up at the bejeweled lapis lazuli of the night sky.

She considered how different the light of the stars seemed to that of the little flames of the candles in her room—and how new.

Of course, that was silly, for the candle flames had been lit only tonight, while the stars had lasted for countless aeons, their light shining for millions of years before reaching this world.

Yet the matter that made up the candles—the beeswax and the plant fiber of the wick, now transformed into the energy of heat and light—was not new. Or rather, the paths the matter had taken, from energy to matter and back again, untold times before arriving in the priestess's hand as a candle she lit before meditating, and whose flame she passed from candle to candle to light her room—those paths were as old as the stars or older. This stream of matter and energy was from the stars and part of the stars—likely from stars far older than those that now appeared to shine in the sky tonight, stars long dead, now lying scattered across the cosmos within every being.

Or in tombs of iron.

The priestess shook her head beneath her hooded yellow scarf and smiled. She stood on an upper level of the great central temple within the city of Sanisa—the Temple of the Mother. From high in the terraced step pyramid, the priestess could see far across the valley—only not so far that she could see what she was looking for.

But she could feel it.

She had felt it in the back of her mind while she meditated tonight, pulling her as it approached, growing stronger as evening fell and the night grew long. A great sadness had surged from it as if from nowhere, only to be cut short by resignation and relief so strong that the priestess had awoken from her trance and followed it out of her chamber and into the night.

Someone is coming. Could it be . . . ?

The priestess feared she would lose the feeling pulling her in a direction she could neither identify nor follow, but it remained strong as she looked out over the valley and into the deep blue of the night between the shining stars. To the mountains she looked, far across the valley, though the one she sought was hidden in the far distance, beyond the curve of the earth. Leaning her hands on the stone wall around the terrace, she lost herself as she gazed, almost falling back into meditation, unable to distinguish one state from the other. Moments went by, or hours . . .

"Reverend Mother?"

The priestess turned toward the voice. Beside her on the terrace, a novice priestess bowed her head slightly, tugging uncertainly on the hem of her own short white dress. The flowers in the band holding back her straight black hair blew slightly in the breeze, which likewise stirred the hanging vines on the upper level of the temple. The older priestess pulled her yellow scarf down from her head, revealing brown hair tied back in a bun and bright soft eyes tinged with crow's feet that looked kindly upon her pupil.

"What is it, Nella?" the priestess asked.

"I'm sorry to disturb you if you were busy, Reverend Mother. Only, a couple of the senior Gallae wished to make sure you were well. You missed the evening meal, and you're usually so punctual . . ."

"I'm fine, Nella. I was only lost in thought."

"Thinking about what, Mother?"

The older priestess turned away and pointed to the horizon. "Look at the sky, Nella. Do you see those two planets? Within the next full turn of the moon, those two will come closer and closer, till they are in conjunction."

The novice sister looked at the shining planets. "I see them, Mother." She turned back to the priestess and inclined her head. "What do you mean by telling me this?"

"Only that things in this world come together. Then fall apart. Then come together again. And on and on."

"I'm not sure I understand."

"It's all right, little sister. Would you please go to the ones who asked about me and reassure them, then tell them I wish to speak with them? I think I should speak with all the senior Gallae and Pilli in the morning."

Nella nodded. With a concerned glance at the older priestess, she glided away gracefully in search of her sisters.

Dawn was approaching. As it rose pink and red in the distance, the sense of something coming nearer grew stronger in the priestess's heart.

She isn't just coming. She is here now. Somewhere in the world, at last.

The priestess drew her yellow scarf up over her head and began to walk around the terrace. She wished to look out to the east and greet the sun as it rose over the sparkling river. She wished to greet the sun and wait.

Starlight in the Ruins

"If I tell you what you want to know, you must give me something you carry in return."

The aged hag's voice was unnaturally high-pitched, a purposeful creak and crack that somehow communicated that she could, just as easily, speak with nearly any voice she wished. She spoke as she did on purpose, for effect; whether the intended effect was atmosphere or to annoy was unclear to Elsinore.

"What do I carry that would be of any use to you?" the young sorceress replied, her voice less high, less malleable.

While the hag seemed to have been taken aback at first by the sorceress's beauty—locks of teal-dyed hair spilled in blue waves from a black lace hood, and lively eyebrows arched over gray eyes—the hag now chuckled to herself. The young sorceress's smile faded to a more cynical grimace as she realized why. Though soft and lyrical, her voice betrayed an unplaceable quality that hinted at the depth of mystery with which the Goddess had made her body. It pained her, and sometimes merely turning her attention to her voice was too much for her to bear.

"I think you know what I want." The hag laughed. "What else would I want? You come to old Haudrin on the night of the conjunction. You ask the way to the ruined temple in the woods. You think I don't recognize the dress of a priestess of the Goddess? You think I don't know you a mage? What would a mage do at the temple during the conjunction, eh? What would she be taking with her to do it?" Haudrin cackled—honestly cackled—and Elsinore couldn't help but smile in turn.

"You know I could just look for the temple myself? I was only asking to save some time and to be polite as I passed by." But the young mage had already slung her thick canvas bag from her back and begun to root through it.

"And risk missing the conjunction? You should have arrived earlier if you meant to stumble through the woods with no direction." Haudrin leaned her hand against the weathered wooden frame of the cottage doorway.

The old hedge-witch hermit was right. The sunset was visible over the tops of the bent, scraggly pines that clustered around the edge of the clearing. Elsinore had reached the forest late due to her own dawdling and had little time to waste.

At last, Elsinore sighed and pulled from her bag a little parcel wrapped in cloth. As soon as it was out, the hag leaped from the door frame and snapped at it with long, bony fingers that spread widely from smoothly weathered palms. Stepping back with the graceful flourish of a trained dancer, Elsinore pulled the parcel out of reach of the old woman's grasp.

"Excuse me," the young mage said, "but I have very

little left, and I need enough for myself. Otherwise, I wouldn't even be here, would I?"

"Yes, yes!" the hag croaked. "Of course. I only meant to help you split it up."

Elsinore eyed her dubiously, but the old woman did not seem to notice. Her gaze never strayed from the package Elsinore held in her delicate, nimble fingers.

Walking away from the cottage, Elsinore found a tiny knoll by the nearest tree. She sat down, the skirt of her purple dress spreading around at her knees, and she gestured for her host to sit beside her. The hag followed quickly—she fairly glided—and sat on the little mound smoothly, directly, and purposefully. She had none of the young dancer's practiced grace, but she had no trouble moving, despite her age and the obvious weariness with which she had sighed when she had leaned against the doorframe.

Elsinore laid the parcel between them and untied the string, pulling back the cloth folds slowly. Within lay eight dried pieces of plant matter.

No, not plant matter. Mushroom.

The old woman's eyes widened as she gasped, and she muttered something Elsinore could not hear in a deep voice entirely unlike the croak she had affected earlier. Elsinore smirked. The hag obviously recognized the mushrooms. The once-red caps had faded to a dry old brown, but the stems and scattered spots were still white, despite yellowing deep in the wrinkles.

Recovering quickly, the old woman regained her unnatural croak. "These are from fairy rings. These are from the foot of the great Mount Koryb over the gate into Faerie. How could you possibly come by these?" The hag finally tore her gaze away from the mushrooms and stared in astonishment at the young wanderer. "You might have stolen them. Slayed a mystic who trod the hallowed stone of the foothills, one who dared ignore the warnings and slipped into the black-lit halls beneath the hills . . . but I rather think you came by these yourself, did you not? Ones such as you have a kinship with the place of death other mortals shy from."

Elsinore's clear eyes glittered from within the folds of her hood. "Either way, I'm really very resourceful."

There was a rustling low in the brush that cluttered around the roots of the trees at the woods' edge, and the old woman started. The noise grew closer, till a black cat pushed out of the leaves, eyes flashing green in the fading daylight. The cat padded softly to the women, curled their tail, and rubbed their fur against the young witch's leg as she scratched the little creature's head.

"Your familiar," the hag realized.

"I think of them more as a traveling companion of convenience. Isn't that right, Risky?" The cat settled in the crook of Elsinore's legs, folding their paws beneath their body, and looked at the old woman knowingly.

Indicating the mushrooms, Elsinore returned to the topic at hand. "Two pieces. I haven't got all night."

"Four," the old woman replied sternly.

Elsinore scoffed. "That's ridiculous. That's half my supply. I can't just get more of this. Two is more than reasonable."

"I thought you were resourceful," the old woman wheedled.

"Two," Elsinore repeated.

Unperturbed, the hag reached into the folds of her robe. Her clothes were well-kept; her dress was simple black, and the robe she wore over it was gray like the fur of a wolf, trimmed with a pattern in green thread. From a hidden pocket, she drew a small bent pipe that smelled pungently of cannabis. Pipe in hand, she searched the folds of her robe again, apparently for a match.

Elsinore's breath quickened, and she closed her eyes to hide her desire. As the search dragged on, though, she sighed, leaned forward, and snapped her fingers in front of the old woman. In the space between two fingertips flickered a little green flame that matched the cat's eyes. It was a simple fire cantrip, but it had many uses.

Using the green flame, the hag lit the cannabis and leaned back to smoke. The young woman shut her eyes again and steadied her breath, before turning back to her host.

"Three pieces, and you give me some of your weed." Muttering under her breath, she added, "It's been weeks since I've smoked."

"Four, and I'll give you all of it."

The old woman produced a pouch that Elsinore accepted without hesitation. From her belt, the young sorceress pulled a long, thin, straight pipe with a little metal bowl the size of her fingertip. She filled the bowl with loose shredded leaves from the pouch, lit it with another cast of her fire spell, inhaled, and exhaled a long, thin stream of smoke with a sigh.

Raising an eyebrow, Elsinore eyed the old woman. "Your plan is to get me high and then take as much as you want?" She took another drag.

"Only four," the hag repeated.

"Fine." Elsinore sighed. "Two stems and two caps." She pushed them toward the hag.

Showing no emotion, the old woman pulled a box from another pocket and handed it to Elsinore. The young witch sniffed it, confirming it was the same weed she was currently smoking. She slipped it into her bag, quickly folded her remaining four pieces of mushroom back into their cloth, and put the parcel away next to the weed. Then she held her palm out to the hag, arched an eyebrow again, and cleared her throat deliberately.

"What?" the hag asked.

"All of it?" Elsinore flicked her eyes at the wooden box.

The old woman clucked and sighed. "Yes, of course." Retrieving another pouch of cannabis from her robe, she gave it to the young sorceress.

Once she'd packed it away, Elsinore stood and shouldered her bag beside the back scabbard that bore the glittering sword she called Moonstar. She offered her free hand to help the old woman to her feet.

Once on her feet, the old witch nodded toward the woods. "The temple is an hour's walk if you keep a good pace, which I'm sure your pretty, young legs can do. That way, northeast. Follow the stream, and you'll come to an ancient, abandoned road; you'll know when you find it. You must follow it till you come to another clearing and the face of a long stone wall, too smooth to be natural. The temple is mostly sunken below the ground, lit by starlight from the open roof once you're deep enough inside. The conjunction should be apparent. The night will be clear. Good journey, young Galla." She bowed.

Elsinore folded her hands in a gesture of thanks, and Risky mewed. The two travelers took their leave of the hermit and set off into the woods in the direction they were given.

The height of the event wouldn't fall till some while after sunset, but it was best not to dawdle. The sun was setting early on this, the longest night of the year, when darkness loomed over the brief day before the sun's strength began to return. The deepest night of the Season of Shadows, before the earliest hint of the Season of Light.

Once Elsinore was past the brush, tangle, and vines at the edge of the forest, the ground was easy to traverse. Fallen brown needles carpeted the earth, dry by this time of year, and patches of wildflowers grew between the gnarled trees. The canopy was full, though it mattered not; once the sun set fully, little would be visible in the darkness of the empty black moon regardless. If the shadows fell too deep, Elsinore could cast her fire spell to spread enough light to see by, but for now, she trod on as darkness began to fall. The soft, almost imperceptible rustling through the thin dead leaves assured her that Risky traveled by her side.

At some point, Elsinore became aware that she was following a course of long-dead architecture, the bones of the forgotten road long since engulfed by the forest. Here, a low composite stone wall ran for a hundred yards; there, a rectangular structure squatted alone, its corner blasted out and its roof long since vanished and gone.

Mundane and poisonous mushrooms flourished in the husks of empty domes and tree stumps alike. From time to time, Elsinore idly felt in her bag to reassure herself that the mushrooms she'd brought were still there. Finding a fairy ring like the one where she'd found these was not an easy feat, but she could worry about that another time. She at least had more than enough for the ritual.

Damn that hedge witch's greed, Elsinore thought, but she comforted herself with a reminder of the weed she'd traded for. The hermit might have come out better for the bargain, but it was hard to imagine she could possibly have been more satisfied than Elsinore was with her replenished supply. Elsinore might get high too often, but that was something best dwelt on another time.

Elsinore quickened her pace as the ruined skeletons of old buildings loomed larger and stabler, and the trees fewer and farther between. At last, the trees cleared. Silhouetted against the dim starlight, she saw what the hag had described: a solid wall, several stories high, not of concrete but of pure cut stone. The wall curved away in either direction, a great ring with a circumference Elsinore could not guess, as its far points vanished in the dark of night that had fully fallen. She had come to the temple, still solid and proud yet more ancient than the other ruins in the woods.

Keeping a hand on the wall as the brush and terrain allowed, Elsinore began to circumnavigate the building. Surrounding the temple at a short distance were pillars—some fallen, some still standing, but all made of delicately carved marble that sparkled faintly in the light of the stars.

Elsinore was so enamored of their relative brightness in the dark of the early evening that she nearly collided with a tree. Stumbling to a halt, she took in the tall but drooping cherry tree, its leaves still green but barren of fruit. A curtain of its branches hung loosely against the wall.

On a hunch, Elsinore brushed the loose branches aside. Behind them, she at last found an opening in the smooth surface of the temple.

The young witch slipped inside. The narrow passage spiraled inward along the interior of the wall, and the soft soles of her boots tapped quietly across the smooth floor. The passage sloped downward, sinking into the earth as she spiraled into the temple, while far above, a narrow slip of sky could be seen, its darkness brilliant against the shadow of the high-reaching walls.

The darkness was immense. Elsinore cast her fire spell to see by, and yellow-green flame lit above her upturned palm, growing into a ball the size of her fist and casting an uneasy light all around her. As the passage widened, bas-reliefs curved along the wall, their shallow depths exaggerated by shadow and fear in the flickering light. The twisted bodies and distorted faces of gorgons and demons leered from the stone. Yet the subjects of the reliefs were vague and imprecise and might have interested Elsinore more in the daylight, perhaps, at a less urgent time.

She pressed on quickly but carefully, till she came to a wide-open space—the bulk of the temple. Before her stood a long-shuttered door set within an interior wall. Though perhaps the door had been recently opened; the space before it was clear of dust and cluttered stone. Perhaps the old hag came by now and again, to keep the place in better repair than the ruins outside it. Or perhaps the place was haunted.

Elsinore hoped it was haunted, or she'd be wasting her time.

The hinges creaked with rust when she pulled open the door; with her little strength, it took some effort, but not so much that she truly strained herself. On the other side sat a patio of stone, but beyond the steps, Elsinore found herself in a place of grass and clover, a garden bright and dewy and green, open to the heavens above. She dismissed her light spell; the stars seemed brighter here, their light clear and visible in the black sky.

The garden appeared well tended. Flowers hung from vines that traced stone trellises between columns of the same glowing white marble as those outside, the plant life and intricate stonework blending in the dark. Little trees grew in the corners, leaving open a field of soft, grassy earth the size of a town council hall. In the center of the field sat a low ring of stone, about knee high, interrupted only by steps going down into a sunken pit five feet deep. Within stood an altar and, around it, space for celebrants.

Risky mewed, reminding Elsinore of their presence.

"You stay up here and keep watch, okay?" The little creature pawed at her foot curiously, rubbed against the stone circle around the pit, and then sank into the grass. Elsinore smiled and descended the brief flight of steps.

At the foot of the altar, she removed her pack and sword and leaned them against the stone ring. She took off her boots and drew her hood back, slipping out of her black jacket, which she folded and laid aside. Rummaging around in her pack for a moment, she finally pulled out what she needed: the cloth package containing the mush-rooms and a book, marvelously preserved despite its ob-vious age. She took one piece of the mushroom from the cloth, then refolded the package and replaced it in her bag. With the mushroom piece and the book, the witch ap-proached the altar barefoot, clothed only in her short purple dress, and swung herself up on top of it.

Sitting down, Elsinore folded her legs and set the book on the altar before her. Then she looked up and located them in the sky: Fire Star, flashing red, flames licking about it as it twinkled in the night; and Shadow Star, slow and ineffable, dull as the deep sea and full of as many secrets. These two planets stood together, before the constellation of the Bower, the unlikely gods meeting in secret. The conjunction rose before her in the sky.

Elsinore laid the mushroom under her tongue, letting

her saliva soak it and draw out the concentrated essence that once flowed within. She could feel herself absorbing the substance of the dried cap. When she thought she had enough, she chewed the remaining solid mushroom and sat still upon the altar, hands at her sides and eyes closed.

After a moment, she opened them sharply, regarded the stars above, and looked down at the book.

The cover was decorated with a raised relief of a creature Elsinore did not recognize, yet it felt familiar on a deep, secret level. It was a turtle of some kind, wide and solid within its shell. Its neck and limbs were all extended, each long and coiled like a serpent and ending in a head with a wide-open mouth and eyes that glittered with inlaid crystals. The chief head, which sought out from between the true shoulders of the shell, was coiled backward and faced out from the cover, looking back at the reader.

Its eyes seemed to focus firmly on Elsinore's.

Above this image was text that presumably bore the title, though it was written in an ancient script Elsinore did not know. Straight lines connected circular nodes, or dots, at regular angles, a script she had begun to refer to as "nodiform." The witch was unable to read it, learned though she was in several languages and scripts, both practical and ritual.

The nearest guess she had come to after months of study was that the form of the characters was inspired by the constellations. What sounds or ideas they communicated, though, was entirely beyond her, and no other scholar or sorcerer she had met would admit to having ever before encountered such runes. The book had been taken out of a library in the depths of the Mountain of Faerie, a relic of some deep forgotten past when the Old Ones used winged flying machines and rapid, monstrous chariots of steel and light to encompass the whole Earth within their dominion. According to some dark whispers, they had even dared the blasphemy of launching upward on chariots of fire to lay claim to the Goddess of the moon.

Elsinore opened the book to a page she had marked with a ribbon, and studied a block of the strange, unreadable characters. As she studied, she took locks of her hair between her fingers and started to idly braid. The side of Elsinore's head around her left ear was shaved, and the rest of her hair fell past her shoulders in soft subtle curls upon her back and breast. The teal color recalled the blue-green leaves of the pines that gathered around the foot of the sacred Mountain of Faerie.

Finishing the braid, she tied off the end and flipped it over her shoulder.

Elsinore could not read the nodiform text. She had studied these pages continuously for months but could not make even a tentative start at their meaning. If, as she guessed, the text was based on the shapes of the stars, then some of the pictures and images on other pages seemed to support this. One page seemed to her to depict the Bower in the sky above, ideal trellises trailing from the key stars much as the worldly vines surrounded her in this garden. Lone, individual dots, unconnected to others in the text, seemed to travel across the page.

Meditating upon the image of traveling planets and the Bower—aided by her inquiries around the towns of the river valley regarding the best places to observe celestial events—Elsinore had come to believe the text might describe the approaching conjunction at the solstice, viewed from the temple where she now sat. Lack of true knowledge of the book notwithstanding, she suspected she was meant to be in this place tonight.

The text in the ancient tome was strange and unknowable, but if she performed the ritual correctly, an audience with an entity thus summoned might prove fruitful.

To summon a divine entity by reading the secret language of the stars during celestial events was a common enough practice for a mage, but to control it, benefit fully, and communicate usefully were another matter. One more rare and requiring great discipline.

If Elsinore lacked any grace, it was discipline.

A shiver ran along the base of the witch's spine and tingled along the back of her neck. Gradually, the red light of Fire Star and the deep purple blue of the sky spread around her, dancing on the white stone of the temple walls and the petals of the flowers. She lost herself in the pink and purple light sinking into the flesh of her pale hand, before realizing she looked not at her hand but at a flower petal fallen from the trellises that ran along the edge of the pit. It became harder, Elsinore reflected, to tell the difference between her body and the world around her. She was confident she could articulate it, if asked, but she could no longer intuit the division.

The mingled fire and dark light of the conjunction filled the sky with a pulsing, rotating light, shown to Elsinore by the mushroom essence that was coming into full effect in her body. She closed her eyes, but the light grew brighter still, pink through the veins of the flesh in her eyelids. The colors pulsed in a pattern, rotating and interplaying in a web, a tapestry of triangular configurations that carried the light from the stars inexorably to Elsinore's presence. A shimmer from Fire Star ran along the edges of the interlocking patterns, through and between them, coming closer, larger and at once better defined and indistinct—the sort of shape one could not hold in one's eye properly without becoming nauseated.

The shiver down the woman's spine became a tingle between her legs. Her vision swam, or rather the space in the garden swam before her, the pink flowers of the vines rising to mingle with the red light of Fire Star. The color around her took form, smiled a cocky grin, and raised an eyebrow.

The slim, strong physique of a beautiful man stepped toward the altar.

His hair was dark, his eyes black and piercing, and he wore a red vest, tight over his strong shoulders, and low-cut trousers that slid along the edges of his hips enticingly as he walked. Elsinore giggled; under the effect of the drug, she couldn't help herself, but nevertheless, she maintained enough presence of mind to set a boundary before the entity.

"Stop, spirit," she commanded, holding out her hand. On her finger, she wore a ring of silver filigree surrounding a tiny mirror. The light of Fire Star flashed in the reflective crystal, and the entity came to a halt. Elsinore felt a slight tinge of regret that he had obeyed, and her legs shivered again at the sight of his expression.

"I am Elsinore, Daughter of the Mountain, Woman of the Mounds, Priestess of the Pomegranate Moon. It is my wish to speak with you. Tell me your name. Speak. That is my first command."

The entity laughed. It was not a giggle tinted with hallucinatory revel like Elsinore's but a deeper, more knowing laugh. He held out his hand in welcome and spoke. His enunciation was clear, his voice sleek and sensual, with an accent the witch recognized from lovers she'd had in the past—dark-eyed women from a sunny land to the west by the edge of the sea.

"You are one of the Gallae," the entity said, avoiding her question. "One of the other-sexed priestesses of the androgyne ever-Goddess, of whose material spirit we all are part."

"You speak right," Elsinore replied. "But you speak not yet of yourself. I know what I am; what are you? Are you a manifestation of my will, my dream and desire? Or are you real, something come from above and within but nonetheless a true self-will? Answer me." She flashed the ring again before her face. "I charge you by my station and by the power of this place."

"I am both and neither," the entity replied, "as many things are." He eyed Elsinore knowingly. Her body tingled again in response, both to the sensual tone of his voice and to a shift in the air in the garden—a tangible rotation in visual space as the trees and balustrades and grass, clouds and stars and her own body on the altar flowed into and out of and through one another in the wheels and rings of the web. Was the entity before her a separate being from the air and the light? From herself?

"I am called Tybul," the entity said at last.

Elsinore lowered her hand with the mirrored ring. As she steadied herself on the surface of the altar, the entity called Tybul stepped closer.

"Stop," Elsinore commanded, lifting her head upright and holding out her hand with the ring. "My second command, Tybul."

The beautiful entity drew back and bowed his head in assent and anticipation.

"There are people whom I seek. Tell me where to find them."

"I cannot give you the answers you desire."

"Cannot or will not?" Elsinore demanded.

"It is not within my power," Tybul said.

"I have not yet told you the names of those I seek."

"Sister, from the shining throne on which I am seated, I see all that passes upon the Earth. I know whom you seek. But to tell you is not within my power, for the answers to your questions have been sealed from me, as they have been from other Powers of the same order. But I can lead you to the answer."

"Lead me, then. I command you."

"The answers you seek can be found in the book." Tybul nodded at the tome that sat before Elsinore. The young witch looked at the book doubtfully, and her head swam with the strange text on the page, magnified in its strangeness by the effects of the mushroom.

"Then teach me how to read the book," she said finally, pulling herself back.

"I cannot read the book, for I am in the book. But those who wrote the text can read it and teach others to read and write the words of it."

"What people wrote the book?" Elsinore asked. "Direct me to them."

"Sister, those who wrote with this text crossed the Great Circling Ocean long ages ago, beyond the edge of death and rebirth, and their memory has been forgotten, save only in the words they have written in stone and clay and in books such as this."

The being called Tybul took another step forward, and Elsinore's whole body shook with dizziness as she fell in a swoon, tumbling off the edge of the altar.

Heart racing, she braced herself for the hard stone step below, but instead, Tybul's strong arms embraced her, and the warmth of his deep pink light lifted her up onto the altar once more. Elsinore giggled involuntarily, then moaned in anticipation of pleasure as she felt the muscles of his shoulders and mapped the landscape of his chest beneath his vest. His hand lingered on her lower back, hers on his chest and around his neck. She traced her fingers from his neck up past his chin and played along his soft, smiling lips. His hand caressed her back, then lower, down her thigh, and she let him take the hem of her skirt and pull it up, dragging her dress over her head and leaving her arms in the air, her body freely shining in the starlight above.

In a single motion, he threw back his shoulders and pulled off his vest, casting it aside without breaking eye contact. Elsinore hastily folded her dress around the book for a makeshift pillow, then leaned forward, grabbed Tybul's head in both her hands, and kissed him till she grew dizzy again, pulling him down on top of her as she rested her head on the pillow. He slid out of his trousers, and Elsinore idly pushed them aside with her foot as he caressed her breasts, little but round and full and her own. He kissed her nipples, and she blushed and giggled—not, this time, from the effects of the mushrooms but with delight and pleasurable shame.

Real, honest shame broke through Elsinore's reverie when Tybul ran his hand along the side of her hip and inward to her penis. She rarely let her lovers engage that part of her in lovemaking, but he gently fingered it, so lightly, she gasped aloud in surprise at the pleasure she felt. She understood it to be more or less an enlarged clitoris, but even when she brought it into lovemaking, it was not the part of herself she took joy in—not that part, not then. But the tingling sensation shimmering across her whole body since the mushroom took effect—it was, she realized at last, centered there, in her genitalia. She felt herself guiding his hand with her own to finger it more tightly, till it actually became erect, for the first time she could remember.

It was certainly the first time since years before, in her adolescence, when she had begun taking the hormone potions her hedge-witch mother had taught her to brew. They had halted the alien masculinity that threatened to encroach on her body and brought to life the femininity born in her heart. Most definitely, she had never thought she would feel her clitoris do this again since she had been initiated at the temple of the Goddess. There, she had at last fulfilled her heart's desire with the castration ritual that had dedicated her fully to the Goddess's service—when she became Her Galla, a woman of transition, Her priestess and mage.

Yet she felt it—an erection so new and sudden and exultant that it caused her physical pain, an unasked-for eruption in a part of her body no longer suited for such things and so unprepared for that the pain was shocking. The rotating hallucinatory lights that composed the matter around her flashed and spun and throbbed with her pain. The sensation, she recognized in her delirium, was as much a part of the material of the world as it was of her body. It was as much a part of the plants of the garden, of her cries, of the light of the stars and the dark in between and the sound the wind made and the time it took for all of it to drift inexorably into the future. All of it was part of the body of the world; all of it part of the life of the Goddess.

The wheels that locked together to form the web of matter all around her rotated again as the beautiful entity called Tybul pushed Elsinore down against the altar and pulled her erect clitoris into his own—what? His penis? His vulva? Was there a difference in the celestial confluence of luminosity that composed his perfect body? Was there a difference at all?

The wild light of the planets in conjunction hummed purple and blue ever more deeply in the trance of Elsinore's vision as the girl's body pulsed all over, as Tybul took the lead and drew the girl ever further into paroxysms of ecstasy. She had never felt like this during lovemaking. Yet Tybul pulled her in deeper still, and she opened her mouth wide in a gasp that came out stifled and silent. Then she laughed and blushed and covered her face with her hands. But the rotating complexity of the web that underlay reality was visible even then, in her hands, in the dark interiors of her eyelids, in all parts of her body like the dark and the light, all part of the body of the Goddess.

Elsinore's mind flashed pink hot and white as at last she climaxed and saw, for the bare sweetest moment, the truth—the place where she belonged and the world she was inextricably part of. She saw it, and all she could think of to describe it was a metaphor she couldn't even remember. Then it happened again and again. She could hardly match Tybul, and she rapidly grew wearier despite being still in the manic thrall of the hallucinogenic mushroom.

At last, she held her hand to her lover's face and pushed him away, smiling and delirious and mad.

"I surprise myself," Elsinore said after resting a long time, catching her breath beside Tybul. "To endure such exhilaration with an entity of such tangible power. Though I suppose I did summon you for the purpose . . ."

"My dear sister, daughter of the galaxy," Tybul said with a playful mockery. "You did not summon me at all. I come here at the time of the conjunction, to this place made uniquely for it. True, your skill in the arts—and not a little your intoxication—allows you to see me, to feel and interact. But I am Tybul, the generation of love between the worlds of the conjunction. I am the manifestation of your sexual desire, the god of love. I am Sanguinus, the fruitful river. I am the Goddess's love for what grows in the earth, which is Her own body. I am what comes out of the underworld and what goes back in at the downturn of the season. I am the giver of generation, of life. I am what takes life away; I am death. I am the god of death, a devil—summoned indeed, but not by you. Summoned by Haudrin, the witch in the woods, to end your life and take the book. I am coming."

Sitting bolt upright, Elsinore spat a word of dismissal, a blessing and a curse at once, and flashed her mirror ring, which reflected the light of Fire Star. The light rays danced across the web of matter, and as if rolling into a scroll, Tybul was gone. But his words remained, echoing, drawn out slowly in Elsinore's auditory memory. Fighting back panic, she scrambled for the folded dress her head had rested on moments before, unfolded it, and gabbed the book. Its dense pages were heavy in her hands, and the embossed turtle on the cover regarded her as cryptically as ever.

"Thank the Goddess," the sorceress sighed. Pulling her purple dress on over her head, she scrambled down off the altar and found her bag, sword, hood, and boots. She finished dressing and, despite her haste, made sure to secure the book safely in her bag.

"What was I thinking?" Elsinore muttered. "'What else would I want?' she asked. She wanted the book! Her plan *was* to get me high and take what she wanted! Elsie, you absolute fool!"

"Maow." Risky scrambled up from their nap in the grass and pawed urgently at Elsinore's foot.

"You don't have to agree with me!"

Risky yowled again, growing more insistent. Finally, the cat looked up at the sky, arched their back terribly, and hissed, their fur standing all on end.

The stars fell dark, their light dimmed as if by clouds, though not a single wisp had been visible in the sky all night. At the same time, a fierce wind howled all around and down through the open roof of the temple. It grew until it sounded like a monstrous roar, the voice of some incredible force yawning deeply as it woke from its slumber somewhere in the underworld of the spirit. When the howl died down in strength, it gave way to a thin whistle that echoed and repeated off the walls and in Elsinore's mind.

Elsinore shouldered her bag and the sheathed Moonstar and dashed to the door leading into the spiral passage out of the temple, Risky hurrying close behind.

The dark frescoes and reliefs of the hall spun wildly in the shadows cast by the young witch's light spell, magnified by the effects of the mushroom that still lingered in her consciousness. Despite the dread inspired by the unearthly, thin piping tune that echoed through the hall, she tried to focus her attention on the way forward, but what little concentration she could muster was devoted to maintaining the magical flame hovering above her palm. At last, she let it go out so she could better follow the path leading to the egress with her hands, holding the walls in the dark so as not to stumble. At least with the one spiral path in and out, she could be certain she would not become lost.

In the darkness of the absent stars, the only way Elsinore knew she had finally left the temple and reached the open air was the disappearance of the wall from beneath her hands and the freshness of the air, less musty and ancient as she breathed deeply from her hurry and panic. She almost ran into the drooping cherry tree again, its branches brushing against her face as she passed through, and she leaned on it with both hands, pausing as she could to catch her breath.

Risky hissed again, their eyes—feline, at least, and perhaps even magical—able to see something approaching in the darkness that remained hidden from Elsinore's sight. Whether in response or as a natural reaction to the approaching danger, the cat's fur—usually black and glossy, reflective of the natural light around them—began to glow with a faint phosphorescence, a green light that once lit the sorceress's path into the Faerie hills below the earth. It was enough to indicate danger of unearthly origin, though too faint to illuminate the space around them.

Elsinore tried to cast her light spell once she had gathered herself, but the cantrip fumbled in her hand, her fingers fudging dully against each other, unable to produce the necessary snap. She waited a moment, then drew Moonstar. The silver-white blade did not even flash, the darkness was so thick, even with the light of Risky's glowing body. Elsinore stood totally still, her back against the tree, fear growing stronger.

Finally, after seconds that bled like hours in Elsinore's mind, something crawled around the edge of the temple wall. The thing was pale with a dim sickly light, a deathly glow like something out of another world—a ghost or a demon or a faded painful memory. The low light defined the shape of the temple in the shadows, and the blade in Elsinore's hand answered with a reflection as sharp as its keen edge, seeming to magnify the underworld light of the thing into the bright radiance of the stars.

With her breath and focus returned, Elsinore rose from the tree to meet the monster.

It was difficult to describe the thing with any real accuracy, and whenever she looked away, Elsinore found its precise features impossible to recall. It shifted subtly, as if moving behind distorted glass or beneath waves of clear water; it was at once one form, then another, then a third entirely unlike the others, the first shapes forgotten forever.

A head like a bird of prey, or a dragon, or a bull; teeth or fangs or tusks; horns swept up or forward, or else ears upright like a jackal. Its body was great and powerful, or else lanky and hunched to produce the illusion of size, or again a massive shell like a tortoise's with long, evenly tapered spikes. On taloned handlike growths, it stalked or slid or glided through the darkly shimmering air along the side of the temple toward the sorceress.

The light dancing off Moonstar trembled and scattered across the field, though Elsinore held the sword steady. She carried the blade out before her, pointed at the approaching thing, and she raised her other hand, the one bearing the ring, above her head.

"Halt, traveler!" Elsinore commanded, trying to commune as she had with Tybul. "It is my wish to speak with you peacefully. My name is Els—"

The thing turned, shifting through the air toward her. As the rows of knives on its shell cut through space with a painful shrieking whistle, it struck with a clawed amorphous arm.

The force of the sound and movement tossed Elsinore back, and Moonstar fell dully to the ground beside her. The light reflecting from its blade called out to her, and she drew it quickly from where it had fallen in the dirt as she rolled gracefully to her feet.

The world around her shifted again; the stars had returned, but now the thing moved as a shadow among shadows, indistinct as ever but perceptibly threatening. If Tybul had been the light of the stars together, this thing was the new moon, hidden, the hollow shape blotting a space in the night sky. It was ink smeared across a map in an ancient atlas, leaving the reader lost and afraid.

But as the thing rotated to strike again, Elsinore met its appendage with the edge of her blade, starlight sparkling off its tip. This time, the thing recoiled, pulling itself back from the sword strike, not retreating yet still retracting its body somehow from the blade. It called out again with its unearthly whistle; this time, Elsinore hoped, it signified fear.

As her opponent turned away, the girl flipped to its other side—so far as she could tell—and slashed with Moonstar once more. This time, the thing's reaction was one of pain: it shrieked and quivered, fields of stars waving across or inside its dark mass, though they might have only been reflections of the distant stars above. Moonstar could strike it and harm it; perhaps the thing was only material, flesh protean and distorted by the magic of the conjunction but earthly nonetheless. Or perhaps the sword, once used to fight through the dungeons of the underworld and blessed by the hand of the queen of the land below, bore a special property to wound such demons.

Whatever the case, Elsinore feared she had no better chance of repelling the creature with her sword than of slaying a sea serpent with a kitchen knife. Somersaulting out of reach, she dodged another strike from the monster's great talons, which materialized as if from out of a void. As she landed, she balanced with what little grace she could muster and held out her sword, struggling not to despair.

Risky darted out of a nearby bush, a black cat shining with the gleam of the stars. They arched their back and hissed. As the hiss deepened into a yowl, Risky dashed back into the woods in the direction from which the two of them had arrived, brushing Elsinore's leg as they passed. Sheathing Moonstar, Elsinore snapped her fingers to cast her firelight cantrip. With a theatrical motion, she struck the fireball with the open palm of her other hand.

The ball exploded in a sudden bright nova of light, illuminating the clearing of the temple—not like in daylight but with a burst like a lightning strike or a falling star. For half an instant, the entity before her turned away, whatever organs it used to see overwhelmed with the flash. Yet her understanding of the thing was made not a bit clearer by the illumination; still it was a shadow, its shape indistinct and mercurial, as unknowable to mortal sight in light as it was in darkness. Briefly blinded, at least it was distracted long enough for Elsinore to flee after Risky, back into the forest—back to the witch of the woods.

Elsinore could imagine no way to overcome this foe. If, as Tybul had said, it had been summoned by the witch, then the witch would know how to dispel it. Perhaps, as was the case in many summonings, it must continually flow from the font of the caster's will; if Elsinore could shut off the font, she could cut the entity off from its source.

She dashed through the wood, confident in the cat's guidance. The starlight shone only dimly, but now the ruined stone and fallen concrete of the ancient road bore a strange luminescence of purple and blue, like the light in the garden. Fallen columns and shattered fragments of once-massive walls lit the way through the forest, past empty shells of shrines and fanes to gods long forgotten, their images broken and lost ages ago.

These ruins fairly pulsed with forgotten energy, awake once more due to the power of the conjunction or perhaps the aura of the summoned demon or even the last traces of the hallucination from Elsinore's mushrooms. She wondered briefly as she fled how much of the demon was the product of her altered state, but she quickly dismissed it as irrelevant. The pleasure of her experience with Tybul had been real; so, too, was the danger she faced from the thing. Real or not, it was real enough—solid enough—to kill.

The broken road and glowing ruins thinned and fell away as Elsinore came closer to the witch's hut. Once near enough to approach but not be seen, she ducked behind a tree, leaned around the trunk, and tried to sneak forward to the next without alerting the hag. She kept a lookout, too, for any sound or light or singular lack of either that might indicate the creature.

Drawing Moonstar, she kept to the shadows as much as possible, the silver blade now dark as the new moon hidden among the stars. The hut was the same: secret, unlit, window shutters open but sunken in deep shadow like empty eye sockets.

A wave of nausea slammed Elsinore's body, like a troubled sea thrashing at the edge of a ship. Most likely, it was merely an aftereffect of coming down from the hallucinations, but it worried her, and she fought to keep herself upright as she moved forward. Pausing, she concentrated on letting herself drift over the waves until she found an equilibrium. Only then did she move on.

Arm at her side and sword pointed forward, she crept slowly toward the open door and the gaping darkness within. Looking around the clearing for any signs of trouble, she froze when something caught her eye—a still, silent shape in the field a few short yards from the hut. It was the spot by a near tree where the young witch had split the mushrooms with the crone earlier that evening. The spot had been empty then, only a low pleasant knoll in the sunlight; now, in the vanishing darkness of the night, something seemed to squat evilly beneath the tree or lie spread in the grass like a serpent, coiled to strike.

Turning to the knoll, Elsinore proceeded forward, though she was now out in the open, as brightly lit as anything could be in the wavering light of the stars. She silently cursed herself, wishing she had thought to prepare her spell of invisibility, which let her walk for a time between the folds of sight and air. But she hadn't expected to be fighting for her life tonight, afraid and sword drawn.

She hadn't expected any of this night to pass as it had.

Nausea washed over Elsinore again as she pressed on. It wasn't merely the drug; it was something about what she saw on the mound. As she drew closer, the darkness of the shade under the tree only grew deeper, the shape below less distinct. Elsinore was loath to cast her fire spell and draw attention to herself, but she had to see what it was. Besides, the sorceress reminded herself, in a pinch she could throw the fireball as a weapon. A simple one, perhaps, but a distraction nonetheless.

Drawing a deep breath, the young woman snapped her fingers. The fire burst alight in her hand, and she could finally see the menacing shape beneath the tree.

It was Haudrin. Her body was bent and ragged but stiff and entirely still, her face distorted in horror. The grass of the knoll was spread with her brown drying blood, glinting dully in the light of the fire spell. She could only have been dead a few hours, but the smell rising from the corpse was unearthly—surely the source of Elsinore's nausea.

"Gods," Elsinore muttered. "I hadn't wanted this to befall you, old one." It was quite clear the old witch had been slain by the demon she'd summoned.

The demon she summoned to take the book.

"How did she know?" the young sorceress wondered aloud. "But she knew I'd been to the gate of the Mountain of Faerie; if she knew I had the mushrooms, perhaps she knew I had something else from deeper in . . . ?"

Elsinore examined the body as best she could from a distance, reluctant to come too close due to the blood and smell. To have summoned an entity of such force . . . was it possible the hag had ingested all the mushrooms at once? Elsinore felt little desire to search through the corpse's robes, now tattered and spread in the congealing blood all around, but perhaps there was a chance, if only the slightest, that anything unused could be elsewhere . . .

Turning sharply at last from the grisly shape under the tree, Elsinore went back to the hut. It seemed less threatening now that she knew what lay beneath the tree. The ominous darkness of the doorway gave way to the yellow-green light of the spectral flame in her hand.

It was only a single room, small but cozily furnished and filled with odds and ends, scrolls and vials on tables and shelves. The place was undisturbed; apparently, the old woman had performed her ritual out under the stars, where she had then met her terrible fate. The interior had not been rendered a wreck by the demon, but it was still disorderly. It no doubt exhibited an order perfectly understandable to its former inhabitant, but with her now gone, its chaos was indecipherable to an outsider.

If the old woman hadn't taken all the mushrooms and had left any here, Elsinore had little chance of finding them. She cursed herself once again, both for the foolishness of letting the hag bring this phantom upon them and for unwittingly giving her the means to do so.

Elsinore looked here and there in the cluttered cottage for anything that stood out. Scrolls and tomes lay unrolled and open upon the tables and floor. As near as Elsinore could tell, they were all written in some personal shorthand, apparently as commentary to detailed watercolor diagrams of plants, herbs, flowers, and the distillation of each into tinctures and potions.

Elsinore flipped through one such codex on a desk. The charts were strange but detailed, and the mage was familiar enough with the drawings of herbs that, unreadable shorthand or not, she recognized the makings of several potions. Turning another page, she was startled a little by what she saw in the flickering light of her flame spell.

The illustration was not of a plant but of a horse—a mare giving birth to a foal. Women in dresses and robes stood around, each wearing soft caps with points or forward-bent apexes. On the next page, one of the women collected some flowing liquid—urine or menses—from the mare, and on the next, the women brought it to a table of bottles and vials, seemingly mixing it with other ingredients into potions. This page was accompanied by the greatest amount of commentary. Finally, the last image showed the women consuming the potion.

"It can't be," Elsinore muttered. "Surely this is only a potion that happens to be in a book the old woman acquired?" But the handwriting and illustration style seemed consistent across all the books and scrolls. It seemed likely to Elsinore that the hag had written or copied them all. This must have been a potion the old woman used, she realized. This must have been a drug she needed.

Elsinore searched through the bottles and vials on the

tables and dressers and stoves, casting empty or irrelevant vessels aside, but she found nothing she was looking for. Finally, she found a cabinet, old but clean of dust and clutter, and opened the little doors. Inside, on rows of shelves, she found them—tiny bottles containing a pale-red substance. The sorceress recognized it at once. She would test it later to be sure, but she knew already what she had found.

"No way," she said to herself. "You gave me just a bag of stupid weed, and meanwhile, you were holding out on me?"

This was the same drug Elsinore herself crafted and took—the medicine that had feminized her body and transformed it by the will of the Goddess from the boyish body she'd been born with to that of one of Her sacred daughters. It was a hormone potion, brewed from the urine and menstrual fluids of pregnant mares.

Studying the light glinting through the bottle as she turned in her fingers, Elsinore realized what this meant.

"She was like me," Elsinore said sadly. "She was . . ." She sighed. "The arrogant fool. Why did she do that to herself? She knew what I was and said as much. Why couldn't she have trusted me? Why was it worth trying to kill me for . . . ?" Elsinore looked back at the tome lying open on the desk and thought of the one buried in her bag, beside the weed and remaining mushrooms. "For this book?"

She considered her interpretation of the illustrations in Haudrin's journal and her inability to read the personal code the hag had devised for her notes and spells. She thought of the difficulty she had recognizing the work of a woman so much like herself and then thought again of the mysterious book she'd taken from the library of Faerie.

What did she really know of it? What could she really recognize?

Despite her arrogant assurance when she had begun the ritual, Elsinore knew quite well, deep down, that if she had interpreted the book and the spell correctly, she would know how to dispel this entity. That she could not do so proved she could not even begin to penetrate the surface of the text. And the overconfidence that had carried her into this night meant she was soon likely to come to an end, much like her sister who lay cold outside beneath the tree.

Elsinore sighed deeply and looked at the little bottles that filled the cabinet. There were many, but she thought she could manage to fit them all.

"It isn't as if she'll be needing them anymore, at least," Elsinore reasoned, lighting candles around the room to free both her hands. Then she brought out of her bag a cushioned carrying case, where she stored her own potions as she traveled. Her own bottles were almost empty; she had planned to brew more soon, but coming upon this cache meant she had much longer to go before she needed to work on it. The little bottles fit right in with her empty ones; she couldn't fit them all and wrapped a few more in cloths and rags. She stuffed them in the nooks of her bag along with the case, checking once more that she still had the book.

A piercing cry echoed through the cramped little house, and Elsinore screamed outright. Hearing something fall over in the far corner, she turned and jumped aside in a single fluid motion, hands out to cast a fire spell and throw it if necessary.

"Risky!" The cat looked up innocently from beside a scattered pile of pewter mugs and plates. Their fur was black and shining in the candlelight, no longer glowing as it had in the presence of the entity. Elsinore sighed. "Please don't scare Mama like that. You're a cat, or at least you look like one; can't you sidle up silently and rub your fur against my leg instead?"

Risky maowed again, tentatively.

"You're right, if you'd snuck up on me, I might have taken you for the demon and struck you. But that's ridiculous, of course. I have nowhere near the strength or magical skill to bring you harm, and you know it. If you ever turned on me, there'd be no competition. But you never would, would you? No, you wouldn't! Who's a good kitty? That's right! It's you!"

Elsinore crouched next to Risky and scratched the cat's cheek and beneath their chin as the little creature extended their neck and squinted their eyes in pleasure, the very picture of an ordinary house cat. They betrayed no indication of being an unpredictable witch's familiar.

"I wish I knew what you would do to defeat this entity, though. If you even could, after all. I suppose I can no longer hope to stop it by ending the witch's summoning spell."

Upon remembering the dead witch, Elsinore finished packing her bag and stood. She looked around the hut once more and quickly grabbed a sheet off the lumpy, disheveled bed. Folding it up to carry with her, she extinguished the candles and left the hut, Risky following behind.

The darkness in the yard surrounding the hut seemed less deep now, or else the stars pierced more brightly through the ageless sky. The conjunction still burned above, now elsewhere in the sky as the hours wore on, but still in effect. Elsinore looked up at the drifting planets, passing so desperately slowly across the backdrop of stars, and she realized what she had to do.

She had to wait.

Looking across the field to the knoll under the tree, Elsinore saw more clearly the body that lay under the branches. She approached it less hesitantly than before— instead evenly and with respect. She crept to the knoll, this time scarcely aware of the blood and the odor, and she flung the bed sheet out before her and over Haudrin's body. Kneeling at a respectful distance, Elsinore held her hands together on her chest.

"I hate to see any woman come to an end like this. Especially one like me. Goddess keep you, old sister." Closing her eyes, Elsinore sighed at the loss, at the misunderstanding, or simply at the world.

A rustle stirred the nearby grass, pulling Elsinore from her mourning ritual. Risky stood in the field, back to Elsinore, spine arched and hair on end, looking intently into the woods as they vibrated with a little growl. The familiar glowed once again with the faint unnatural luminescence of the underworld. But it was not just the cat who glowed; the whole clearing now bloomed with the unearthly fluorescent light. It glowed from flowers in the trees and wisps in the air, from the cavernous windows of the hut, and from beneath the edges of the shroud that lay upon the body.

A wind whistled down from the sky and through the branches, but the wind fell still as the whistle grew shrilly, till it was the entire night. The shriek rose and fell in time with the pulsing of light from above, from the mingled rays of Fire Star and Shadow Star. Climbing to her feet, Elsinore drew Moonstar and stood ready. The thing approached, and the mage silently prayed to the Goddess that she had the strength to repel it for as long as she had to.

"Visitor, I address you again!" she called, not waiting for the thing to appear. "I am Elsinore, Galla of the Great Goddess Tiranna, Kurgarra of the Sidhe, Priestess of the Pomegranate Moon!" Her voice was small against the whistle and the rustling leaves; it rang softly across the field, but the depth of voice the girl feared so much carried it along the edge of the wind.

The whistle died down, and the starlight on the trees at the far side of the field sank into darkness as the glow of hellish light from the earth shone stronger. Elsinore watched the trees intently for the shifting blank mass of the thing to step or shimmer or slide into view. She was sure it watched her, but she could not tell from where.

Turning to Elsinore, Risky hissed and spat and yowled incredibly, more in hatred than in fear. No, they didn't turn to Elsinore; they hissed past her.

Elsinore whirled on her heel. Haudrin's body was behind her. Tears welled in her eyes, scattering the dim light she could see by, when she thought of Haudrin's body being disturbed by the demon that pursued her. Whatever the old woman's intention had been, she didn't deserve to be treated this way.

But what Elsinore saw when she turned was far more terrible than the demon alone, and her heart cried out, though her voice caught in her throat.

The fluorescent light that glowed from beneath the shroud wavered as the sheet billowed in the wind. The shape of the old woman's corpse crouched low in the shadows, and to Elsinore's horror, it righted itself, dragging the sheet up. It—for Elsinore instinctually thought of it as Haudrin's body, not the woman herself—did not stand up like a living human but rather rose upward cleanly and directly, as if held by some outside force. Presently, it rose off the ground, the tatters of the sheet drifting in the air, before the whole shroud fell to the earth and revealed what had hidden beneath.

The hag, Haudrin, hovered magically above Elsinore's head. Her eyes were hollow, clouded white and vacant, but nonetheless focused only on the young witch standing alone in the field. Her skin was mottled with unnaturally rapid decay, her long, bony fingers frozen in greedy claws hanging low at her side. Her jaw was frozen wide in a silent scream. Blood, hours-dried, caked her mouth. She raised her head in a motion at once labored and quick, as if breaking rigor mortis and tossing itself into place, and it settled lolling to the side, eyes focused more strongly on Elsinore. Haudrin raised her sharp-nailed claws, the whole of the arms moving together in death, and they reached out to the young witch like the branches of an ancient, barren tree.

"Haudrin, what do you want?" Elsinore demanded. "Why do you rise? What has become of you?"

A low, guttural sound echoed forth across the field, filling the pit of Elsinore's heart with the black bile of fear and regret. The hag's voice was no longer high-pitched and cackling; now in death, it discarded all regard for appearances, all self-judgment and presentation, and carried only the deep moaning loss of the darkness of the grave. If a bear or demon or oracle called out with lament from a deep cave to the dark heart of the earth, it would sound in its agony and mourning like the voice that called out to

Elsinore now. The sound issued forth from the hanging jaw of the witch's corpse, and that alone would have been enough to overwhelm Elsinore with fear and sorrow.

Still, Elsinore replied steadily to the awful moan.

"I wish you no harm, sister. I wish only to know why you summoned the demon, why you pursue me, and why you return. I wish you peace, sister. I wish you rest." Elsinore held her hands out before her, Moonstar now sheathed, her face full of regret for Haudrin's fate.

The corpse of the old woman laughed, a deep guttural sound, the far-off lament of the grave. In the wavering light of luminescence, Elsinore saw a shape below the corpse, the air distorted like a mirage, the shape of the forest itself wavering in the air. The tendrils of the demon surrounded Haudrin and supported her.

The book . . .

The hag's voice was now not even a voice. She did not speak; rather, Elsinore felt her response as a rumbling vibration in the back of her head. Elsinore wavered, dizzy from the intrusion of the entity's intention into her mind and body. The hag's clouded white eyes shone now with hate and the luminescence of the field. So, too, did the eyes of creature she was now part of, which gazed upon Elsinore as if with a thousand eyes, each reflecting a different star, each focusing a ray of dark light upon the sorceress. Where the hag's body ended and the entity began was no longer clear; both were poised against Elsinore now, and the girl was too mournful and afraid to think.

"What have you done? Why are you trying to kill me?" Elsinore gasped. Though loath to use it, she drew Moonstar from her back and held it before her, ready to strike or repel the thing if it set upon her.

Give me . . . the book . . .

"I come by it rightfully. It was given to me by the Goddess, the Queen of Faerie, in the Heart of the Mountain." Elsinore's voice rose, imperious and indignant. "Why do you try to take it from me? Why shouldn't I possess the book?"

The entity shuddered, refusing to answer. It reached out arms or legs or appendages and dug claws into the earth as if bracing itself to move forward. Elsinore stood still, holding her ground.

"I command you!" she called. "In the name of the One who gave me this book, I command you to answer me!"

Haudrin recoiled and hid her face behind her arms as if shielding herself from a terrible fire. The creature supporting her shuddered, its shape wavered in pain, and its eyes flashed with the reflected light of the stars.

Summon . . . awaken . . .

"Awaken what?"

Awaken . . . Her . . . from the depth of the sea . . . in the carapace of the world . . .

"What does—"

The thing lashed out, holding itself back not a second longer. It attacked with Haudrin's arms, tipped with glittering claws like blades, while the body below tore gashes in the earth as it passed. Elsinore struck with Moonstar as she dodged to the side. She felt something push back and then give way beneath the blade.

The creature's momentum carried it forward to where Elsinore had stood a second before, and something—some shape that blotted out the shine of the dew on the grass—fell, slashed by the sword, and squirmed on the earth to one side. Haudrin's body was now grossly misshapen, and the thing on the ground resolved itself in Elsinore's vision into the hag's arm. Silently, the creature merely turned to face its prey.

The young woman and her opponents stood still for a long moment. Without warning, Elsinore sheathed her sword and broke into a dash back into the woods. The field left too little cover, and the fallen pillars and empty shrines on the broken road seemed a better setting to fight back against the monster's assault.

As she had hoped, the creature rolled inward on itself and, with its myriad appendages, launched itself after her, giving chase.

She hurried through the trees, pacing herself to pre-serve her strength for the fight, and she came at last to the ruins scattered along the path to the temple. As before, the fallen masonry glowed with an eerie luminescence, a phe-nomenon Elsinore now believed to be caused by the pres-ence of the entity. The color of the light shifted and faded and brightened, and the mage turned back to see that the variation of the light drifted in tandem with the movement of the creature in pursuit of her.

As it stopped before her, the walls and half-remaining masonry flashed brightly, illuminating the space around them.

Elsinore dashed forward as a claw whistled out from the mass of the terrible shape, and she met the protrusion with the edge of her sword. The blade sank deep into the material of the thing's arm as she ducked away from the still-rushing grasp of the rending hand. The thing whistled again in something like pain.

The noise cut through Elsinore's mind, a plaintive sound that left a melancholy tear in her memory. The vacuum of that space rushed to fill itself with a directionless regret. The loss she had suffered in her life nearly overwhelmed her. Not any specific loss, though she had no shortage to choose from. It was only a generic universalized sense, an ideal of the emotion that dominated her spirit and caused her vision to swim and her body to swoon.

She regained her composure barely in time to tumble to the side, away from a slash that rent a tree lengthwise down the trunk, sending each fragment falling in either direction.

The entity whistled again. The sound was indistinguishable from the accompanying keen of the hag, a call of rage and alienation, but this time, Elsinore let it energize and empower her. She followed the note, focused on it, and her sword rang out, slashing once more across the creature's chest from side to side and spilling a flashing light like blood from the gash, causing it visible pain.

Elsinore's aim was not to kill the creature; she never thought she could even if she tried, and she had no intention of trying. Nor, even still, could she bring herself to hurt the old woman, whatever form she now took. Elsinore knew what she had to do, and so far, she was holding on. She looked away, past the trees to the horizon in the east, and then back to the west, past the creature, to the setting constellation of the Bower and the fading light of Fire Star and Shadow Star.

The thing lashed out, and the sorceress leaped from its reach. Striking again and colliding with the stone of a broken wall, the thing somehow did the ruin no damage despite its grievous claws. Elsinore ducked under a fallen pillar held up at an angle by its own arch, and the creature's talon glanced harmlessly off the luminous stone. As she caught her breath, a revelation struck the young mage—some sense tied perceptibly but inexplicably to the well of loss in the back of her mind left in the wake of the entity's voice.

Under the brief cover of the pillar, Elsinore sheathed her sword to free her hands and dug into her bag. She drew forth the book. The jeweled eyes on the cover beckoned strangely, and the text within was, as always, unreadably ancient.

She climbed up on the pillar when the thing doubled back to compose its mass for another strike. She held the book aloft over her head, and the device on the cover glinted oddly in the light of the stars and the luminous ruins.

"Take the book, then!" the sorceress cried. Then she muttered sadly, "It's worth nothing. You won't even be able to read it." She tossed the tome roughly before her upon the flat surface of the fallen pillar's plinth. Quickly hopping back behind the pillar, she waited.

The creature roiled, its appendages extending and retracting. Haudrin rose to her full height above her unearthly mount, her clouded eyes suddenly clear with intense desire. With her remaining arm, she reached a greedy claw for the book.

Suddenly, hag and entity together stopped; the entity's eyes—if they were eyes—flashed, scattering a light as bright as the daylight, orange and pink and so sudden and strong that Elsinore had to turn away. As she did, she saw to the east what had caused the change: it was, indeed, the coming of morning.

The rose light of dawn crept through the gaps in the trunks and over the trees; the planets of the conjunction fell below the far horizon, obscured by the curve of the globe; and the rest of the stars faded from view as the sky turned blue with the new day. With the conjunction past and the stars invisible in the glare of the sun, the entity that had been borne upon the dark of the new moon gave its strange whistle one final time and dispersed like a mist in the growing daylight. Left still on the grass below was the unmoving corpse of Haudrin. Upon the stone before her, untouched, lay the book.

Elsinore laid her hand upon it. The book was heavy, even sitting there, and it took all the strength of her heart to lift it again, to regard it in both hands, with its incommunicable message. The gap in her spirit, the well of loss the entity had engendered in her when it spoke, remained. Even in the entity's absence—greater in its absence—the loss remained.

The sorceress retreated into the trees and, in a short time, had gathered enough branches, logs, and kindling twigs to set around Haudrin's body. When all was arranged, she cast her fire spell, held the little flame respectfully in her hands like a candle, and lit the kindling. Before long, the fire grew, engulfing the body, and consumed it.

Elsinore sat before the pyre, legs crossed, her mind in meditation. She never took her eyes from the pyre for as long as it burned.

When the fire had run its course and reduced all within it to ashes, Elsinore waved her hand in a circle before her, encompassing the funerary place in her vision. Then she laid a hand on the earth below and stretched the other out to the sky above. Reaching into her bag, she took out one of the loose vials she had tucked away in cloth and poured the drug out onto the ashes, watching as it soaked in. Perhaps she meant it as an offering to placate the old woman's spirit or as a show of respect or as a form of the libation due the deceased. Elsinore couldn't decide exactly why, precisely, only that it seemed the right thing to do.

The girl buried the book deep within her bag among her other supplies and the packed bottles. Shouldering the bag and her sword, she walked on for a while in the clean morning air, till she came out of the forest. She followed the stream that had passed through the wood and found a secluded cove cut into the rocks of a hill. In the quiet of this pool, Elsinore stripped out of her clothes and bathed, cleaning herself of the dirt and fear of the night before.

She ran her hands across her body, feeling her neck and shoulders and breasts and washing the sweat from her skin. Between her thighs, the little shape of her penis hung obscured in the water of the pool. She undid her braid, and her wet hair clung to her face and back, and she listened to the wind above the cove, the birds in the trees nearby, the chittering insects, the sounds of life and the earth.

When she was finished, Elsinore laid herself out on a smooth stone above the water to dry in the warm air—keeping to the shade, for she disliked the glare of the sun. Risky showed themself at last from a crevice in the rock, curling up on the stone beside their companion and letting her scratch them idly behind the ear.

As a warm breeze dried her, Elsinore realized the stone they lay upon was another fragment of a shattered wall. Had this cove been an architectural structure as well long ages before?

Elsinore's thoughts drifted with the wind. Could there be peace for her? Could the echo in the chasm in her spirit be quieted? Haudrin had found some peace, after a fashion, despite herself. Could there be peace for people like Elsinore? Even just for her alone?

At last, the sorceress dressed in her purple skirt and black hood and took up Moonstar and the bag that held her medicine and the book—that held her life.

She knew not where to go nor what to do. But with her familiar beside her, she set out away from the forest, away from the night, leaving the ruins of an ancient past that now glowed white, only granite and marble in the daylight. Moving only forward, she continued her journey.

THE BONES
IN THE WELL

The air was cold for the region.

Unnaturally cold, it seemed to Elsinore. She had been traveling for many days, bound for the city of Peshina, nestled in the far corner of a tributary glen of the Great River Valley the young wandering priestess called home. Until recently, the weather had been cool and bright; now, as she approached the glen, the wind cut across her skin like cold iron.

It was rare in the great valley for the air to freeze the streams and chill a traveler through to their heart, and Elsinore wore nothing to keep off the cold. She was dressed only in a short tunic skirt and a thin jacket with a wide hood that was more for show than for defense against the elements. Her feet shivered within the straps of her tall sandal boots, perfectly comfortable for walking great distances but not much use for keeping her warm. Even her familiar, Risky, had refused to follow her here and had fled the moment their cat paws touched the first hint of snow.

Elsinore clutched her body and her breasts tightly with trembling arms as snow drifted endlessly from the gray sky and the wind howled like a funeral cry.

In Peshina, the sorceress hoped to find audience with the priestesses of a temple to her Goddess. The temple at Peshina was smaller than the one where she had studied in her youth—not so long ago as Elsinore recalled it. But the priestesses in Peshina were renowned for their wisdom and skill in prophecy, and the young woman's mind rattled with many questions she longed to settle. The priestesses were Gallae, as Elsinore was—women thought to be boys at birth but whose true feminine spirit the Goddess made clear through dreams and special signs. The Gallae were women given leave by the Goddess to walk between the worlds of life and death, as Elsinore herself had done, though the priestesses of the temple had greater talents for insight and prophecy than the young woman could claim. She had been told the priestesses could read the fleeting letters written by the motion of serpents, a script ages older than any written by hand—secret writing through which the Goddess spoke of hidden things that had been and those that had yet to be.

She was very eager to reach her destination and speak with the priestesses of Peshina.

In her haste, Elsinore had picked what she remembered to be a shortcut through the glen rather than take the long way on the well-traveled trade route around the hills. But the unexpected cold made Elsinore question whether she could go on.

The wind moaned terribly as the day grew long, carrying snow from side to side, the world around the young woman veiled in gray and white and the distance to her destination unclear. She should have been able to see the city in the distance across the low valley, but the storm left little chance of that. She couldn't even be certain she hadn't been spun around and turned away from her goal by the snow shadows and the wind.

Elsinore knew a few spells that should have been helpful, magic she had learned from her mother and at the temple where she had studied sorcery as a priestess of the Goddess, but even they were of little avail. She snapped her fingers to cast a small fire she could carry in her hands to light her way, but the snow quickly smothered the magic flame, dispelling with it her only hope for warmth. She could focus a necklace bearing the star of her Goddess toward a particular destination like a compass, but the wind tossed the pendant about on its cord like a pendulum, making it useless as anything but a petty trinket.

By then, she could focus on no other magic, no other spell she had studied and prepared herself to cast; she hadn't nearly the concentration nor strength in this terrible storm even to call the words of power to her mind.

Elsinore trod on, shivering and afraid, growing ever angrier at herself for making the journey.

Once night fell, the storm subsided, but the sky was little different. The faint, faded sun had shone weakly through the solid gray clouds, which later diffused the light of the moon, so day and night both cast only a pale yellow-green glow upon the bone-white vale. But the light of moon and snow was enough to see by at least. Not far ahead rose the walls of the city at last, with its towers beyond, Peshina standing proud in the clear snow.

Elsinore's heart leaped, and the warmth of relief gave her the strength to quicken her pace. Yet as she came closer, the relief began to subside, and an uneasy premonition darkened the sorceress's hope. She slowed but did not stop, moving ever onward toward the city gate, but something was wrong.

The city was dark.

Like any other city of the Great River Valley, the towers and windows should have been alight with fire and activity, especially this early in the evening. Even as night deepened and the city slept, there would be lights in the lookout and the gate, as well as here and there in the windows as people rose for a time to read or meditate before returning to second sleep.

But the whole city was dark. No warm yellow light from fires brightened the cold gray of the diffused moonlight on the snow. A chill cut down Elsinore's back, this time not from the snow.

"I'm cold!"

Elsinore startled and stood still. The cry was the first voice she had heard in days. Looking down from the walls of the city, she saw a child standing in front of her. She couldn't tell where they had come from; she'd have sworn to her Goddess that she would have seen someone approach, but perhaps she had been too lost in wonder at the darkness of the city. She couldn't make out much about the child from this distance, only that they—she—had long scraggly brown hair covering part of her face and that she wore a long, tattered gray garment like a robe. Elsinore thought it might once have been white and grown dirty over time, but from where she stood, she could not tell.

"I'm cold," the child repeated, clutching her arms and shivering in the snow.

Elsinore's face softened with sympathy. "Do you come from the city?" She strove to sound strong to comfort the child, but a shiver crept into her voice. "I'm going there myself. You can come with me, and I'll get you someplace warm. To your family or a temple where you will be safe."

The child made no response but turned away and began to walk quickly toward the gate of Peshina.

"Wait!" Elsinore hurried to catch up. In her haste, she lost her footing and fell into the snow. She fell only to her knees, catching herself with her arms and keeping herself from falling prone, but when she regained her composure and looked up, the child was gone.

Standing, she brushed the snow from her arms and legs and continued at an even pace till she came to the gate. Still no light shone from the watchtower windows. Still the city loomed dark and silent, lit only by the even gray of the moonlight through the clouds. The gate stood tall, arched into the outer walls, and one leaf of the gate door was ajar. Though all was silent, Elsinore's mind grew dreadfully unquiet, roiling with questions. Laying a hand on the wooden door, she turned to look back at the vale behind her.

The snow stretched out far into the distance, to the hills at the edge of the glen. Her footprints remained as far as she could see—those she had left since nightfall at least, when the snow and wind had ceased their fury. She saw where she had fallen and her tracks leading to the gate where she stood. But there were no other prints beside them and no other sign in the fresh-fallen snow that anyone else had been in the field with Elsinore at all.

Elsinore slid through the open gate and into the city of Peshina.

All was dark. Here and there, snowdrifts piled against walls and dwellings, having been thinned off the lanes by the wind, though the way was still icy and white. A deep, unwelcoming hush crouched in the alleys and doorways. In a plaza not far from the gate was a marketplace; stalls stood empty, and lanterns hung unlit or lay cast about on the ground, displaced by the storm—or perhaps by storms long past. There was no hint that the place was inhabited, nor that it had been for a long time.

Doors into dwellings stood open, hung on their hinges, or had fallen entirely to the street. Each place was dark, empty, abandoned. There would be no answers here, not of the kind Elsinore had come seeking. There were no prophetesses to speak to her about what the future held or of the hidden secrets of the Goddess; the city was silent, empty even of its own past.

"I'm cold," a weak voice said.

Standing in the doorway of an abandoned room, Elsinore turned to look toward the street. The child stood before a little hill of snow and stared at Elsinore, eyes wide and featureless and white as the ice.

"I'm cold too, little one," Elsinore said, shivering herself. She had hoped to find shelter and warmth in the city, but though the storm had stopped and the walls broke the wind, the city was far colder than the fields, as if it gathered and enclosed the freezing air. "I'm—" A sudden gust interrupted her, taking her breath away. "I'm leaving this place, and I'm going somewhere warm. Out of this vale. I'll take you with me, and you'll be safe."

The child shook her head, greasy hair not moving, hanging in frozen icicles like gripping fingers.

"I'm cold," the child replied.

"I'll take you somewhere you can be warm." Elsinore darkly doubted she could make it out of the frozen vale but tried to keep the fear out of her voice.

The child only stared at the young woman, icy white eyes gleaming. When she next spoke, she intoned a poem that chilled Elsinore more than the air did:

The seed's not yet fallen from the stalk
That's to grow to the wood
That's to burn in the fire
That will warm me.

Turning, the child dashed down the city street, and Elsinore followed.

The cold had long since taken a toll on the young sorceress, and she struggled to keep up, even giving all her strength. She turned a corner after the child, but once again, the child was nowhere to be seen.

Elsinore now stood in a wide plaza before a great building, a palace or temple, raised above the road up a flight of stone steps. Pillars held aloft an ancient roof, sharply defined against the even gray light of the night sky. The sky made it clear that snow would fall once again very soon. Elsinore clutched herself tighter, feebly trying to ward off the cold.

This was the place she had sought—the temple of the Great Goddess where the priestesses dwelt, now frozen and dark as the rest of Peshina. Approaching the temple steps, Elsinore walked around an open well that stood in the center of the plaza. As she passed it, a wind seemed to blow from the well, icy air narrowly funneling along its cold stone walls, and she hurried past it as fast as she could to reach the steps and get out of the open.

She took care as she climbed not to slip, for though snow had been blown from the steps, the stone was icy and treacherous. When she came to the landing, the ancient doors of the temple stood solid and closed, unmoved by the wind and unbroken by time. Elsinore wanted to lean against the pillar by the door, to rest and catch her breath, but instead she pushed forward, leaned inward against the door, and pushed as hard as she could. Though she feared the way into the temple would be frozen shut, the doors slid open easily, as they were meant to, revealing the deep darkness within.

A blast of cold air rushed from the darkness. Elsinore nearly fell before it, but she braced her boot behind her, afraid she'd fall back down the icy stone steps. She moved on into the dark, the only light that of the gray snow-moon sky behind her.

Still Elsinore could not summon the will to cast her simplest spells. Even snapping her fingers to cast her fire spell took a focused effort she could not manage; she could not even feel her fingers, let alone move them well enough to cast her spell. But the temple should have been supplied with lanterns . . .

To her great relief, Elsinore found an oil lamp set on a ledge in the wall not far from the light of the door. In the box beside it was a fire striker and tinder; she fumbled with them in her numb hands but finally produced a light for the lamp. Warming her hands at the lamp's meager fire, she finally shivered not with cold but with delight, as the tiny flame gave her the first true warmth she had felt since entering the valley. It was so unnatural, this cold, so unlike the temperate climate of the hills and valleys Elsinore had passed through to arrive here, a city she had known so differently in travels with her mothers in her childhood.

At last, Elsinore felt not warm precisely—not from this little flame—but safe enough to stand and move on. Gripping the lamp tightly in fingers that were no longer numb, she turned to look deeper into the temple, casting the darkness back with her little light. Down the hall from the entrance would be the main chamber of the temple and the altar of the priestesses, or so Elsinore recalled.

In the dim light, she could not fully see the chamber, but there were shapes around the perimeter that made Elsinore uneasy. She found lamps still hanging by chains from the vault above and lit them, each light bringing clarity to the monstrous scene before her.

All around the chamber lay corpses, half decomposed, faces settled in solemn reservation or twisted in agony, all preserved in their terrible state by the ice. Despite the lack of any stench of decay, suppressed as it was by the freezing air, Elsinore turned back to the entrance and fought the urge to vomit into the hall.

Coming back to her senses, though still reeling, the priestess gazed in horror around the chamber. "What happened here?" she wondered aloud, her lips curling with disgust.

At that moment, a light—not natural, not from the flames—appeared at the far side of the chamber. Blue and cold, the light wavered but did not dim. As her eyes adjusted, Elsinore saw—it was the child! She stood beside a corpse that sat upon a throne—on the dais the sorceress had once known as the central altar of the temple!

What blasphemy against the Goddess of the Earth had led to a corpse being seated upon the once-sacred altar and to a horde of corpses littering the temple, Elsinore could not guess. But the ragged child stood in the darkness, radiating a cold blue-gray light, much like the snowy night sky that loomed low above the vale. The little warmth Elsinore had felt from the oil fire in the lamp failed in that light, and the cold returned more fiercely than ever. The child spoke again the cryptic rhyme:

> *The seed's not yet fallen from the stalk*
> *That's to grow to the wood*

That's to burn in the fire
That will warm me.

Elsinore slowly approached the throne on the altar. "What must I do?"

Unsurprising, the child—the specter—replied with the same plaintive complaint as always. "I'm cold."

Bracing herself against the growing cold, Elsinore climbed up on the dais. She once again considered the child's garb: the ragged robe; the greasy, unwashed hair; tired, hollow eyes, white as the snow; a strange sickly moisture of the skin. Not taking her uneasy gaze from the sorceress, the child raised a hand and pointed weakly at the corpse on the throne—at its chest and at what it wore.

The body was dressed in fine garments or had been once, before death and decay and freezing preservation wore the finery beyond recognition. From its neck hung a medallion, gold that glittered even through the thick frost, even in the dim firelight of the lamps. A golden circle with ornate rays emanating in a cross—the sigil of the sun god, the war god, the rival of the Great Goddess of the Earth of Elsinore's temple. The priestess's face darkened, and she reached out to touch the golden sun cross at the child's gesture.

As Elsinore laid her left hand upon the medallion, the child took her right. The child's hands were cold, colder than anything Elsinore had felt since entering this frozen valley, and the chill ran along her veins to her very core. In her heart, Elsinore saw—the child showed her—what had become of Peshina.

In Elsinore's childhood, the temple had been a haven, protecting the people of the vale, nurturing the city as the priestesses tended to the earth. But this little vale, a bountiful land of peace, was isolated from the rest of the Great River Valley and had drawn the jealous eye of raiders from the north across the Great River Gallas. Worshippers of the sun eager for conquest and dominance, a force of mercenary men seized Peshina.

Slaying those who fought against them, their captain claimed the awful title of lord. The bodies of the priestesses of the Goddess were abominations in the wicked eyes of the sun worshippers, and the warriors would have slain these women had the warnings the Goddess sent through Her serpents not protected them. The priestesses were forced to flee, unable to save the people of Peshina, though they tried in vain, and what became of them the child had not been told. But one of them turned back to the city at the last and cast a final spell. Speaking an occult word that all the city could hear, but which immediately upon its utterance not a single soul could recall, the priestess cast a prophecy upon the city. The Gallae would return, the child had been told, by secret means only the Goddess knew.

But that time had not yet come. The mercenaries slew and enslaved the men and took wives by force from the surviving women of the city, the captain taking she whom he deemed most beautiful. Soon after, she bore a child— the son the brutal man had prayed to his god for, to begin his would-be royal lineage by which he might establish a kingdom from which to conquer the Great River Valley for the sun god.

The child grew, and the self-styled lord waited till he was old enough to begin his tutelage. But the father was frustrated by the child's gentleness and meek, sullen sadness, which seemed beyond the boy's early years, as if deep in his heart he wanted some hidden, secret thing the father could neither tease nor beat out.

One evening, the lord returned early from a hunt and came to the palace he had made by desecrating the once-sacred temple of the Goddess. Not finding his son among the other boys nor at study, the man went to the women's rooms, where his wife and her sisters gossiped in their language of the valley, which he and his men had never bothered to learn. The conquerors had never accounted for the resentment the women bore their captors.

In their chambers, the women doted upon a girl the man had never seen. Adorned in a fine white dress the wives had given her and hair that had been gently coiffed, the girl laughed and sang in the language of the valley, happier than anyone in the city. The women watched indulgently as the girl played on the floor with snakes brought in from the gardens outside.

When she and the older women turned from their games to look at the intruder, the lord saw the girl's face, and he knew at last that she was his child—his "son"—whose heart's desire had been recognized and nurtured by her mother. The women remembered the peace they had enjoyed during their self-governance, as well as the spiritual guidance of the Gallae priestesses. They knew the signs, remembered the rituals and the truths of the Goddess, and had never allowed themselves to be led astray by the blasphemous dictates of their captors' jealous sun god. The final prophecy of the Gallae priestesses had come to pass, and the grand dynasty the petty lord had planned was snuffed out like a flame before it ever began.

In his fury, the lord trod upon the little snakes, then struck his daughter in the face and seized her arm, dragging her screaming from the chambers and from the temple. The women rushed to save her, but they were met by guards who held them back. They watched as the man dragged the girl into the plaza, then to the well, and hurled her into the darkness, where her screaming ceased.

At first, there was the fire of revolt. The women and other survivors of the conquest turned on their captors with knives and torches, burning their complacent oppressors as the mercenaries' blood spilled from their throats. The lord and his followers barricaded themselves within the temple.

Only then came the ice. From the well howled a fierce wind, like a mourning keen, and carried with it a freezing cold unlike any the dwellers of the vale had ever known. The temple was buffeted by blasts of wind, and the snows came as the sky darkened to gray.

The women at last fled, freed from their captors, to seek a new home in the Great River Valley. But the worshippers of the sun remained frozen in the temple, hidden even from the supposed grace of their god by the storm. They remained even now, starved and frozen, their corpses a warning that the Goddess would withdraw her warmth and fruitful abundance from those who desecrated what was sacred.

Opening her eyes, Elsinore found herself in darkness. The lamps had worn out, and the child had vanished as ever before. Only the weak light of the gray snowy sky remained, leaking through the chamber door to give faint glimmer to the medallion of the sun on the frozen corpse of the wretched captain that sat before her.

The priestess hurried from the temple, away from the awful chamber of death and regret. Outside in the gray night, the air was bitter, and the wind howled more than ever. A voice of mourning, of abandonment, followed in the wake of the wind, and the lamentation stirred memories of pain in the young woman's heart. She stared at the dim sky, longing for the hidden moon, but all she could see was snow.

Elsinore lowered her gaze at last to the plaza well, from which the mournful wind was borne out of the darkness to be carried across the entire vale. Carefully, she descended the temple steps and came before the stone wall and what lay beneath. There was no light in the darkness, no way of knowing the fate of she who rested below, save the effects of the terrible winter of sorrow that surrounded her.

Sitting on the ground before the well, Elsinore crossed her legs. Though the wind cried loudly across the city, the sorceress found silence in her mind, gazing through meditation into the pit of the well, beyond the source of the lamentations. In the soft earth beneath the water, before the ice had come, moss and seeds had grown, preserved in life by the cold as the corpses in the temple had been in death. Though she had not the strength to move much, the sorceress focused her mind on the form of a dance, on the movements that spoke of the mysteries of the Goddess, on the gestures of a spell . . .

At last, Elsinore's eyes flashed open, and she spoke aloud a single word. It was a word of power, a word that, once spoken, none who heard could remember—not even the sorceress herself, not till the spell was studied again.

From deep in the well came a rumble, a shaking of the earth, as something grew. The frozen soil beneath the stones of the plaza stirred, and the stones cracked and split, pushed aside by the life that twisted and thrust from deep in the earth. Shoots and vines grew, rapidly bursting from little things into wide branches green with leaves, and bright flowers opened all around like stars in a clear sky. From the well, also, the flowering life grew, rising up from the depths and the frozen groundwater, bringing to light at last what had been hidden in the dark.

The spell—Earth Maiden's Renewal—restored life and growth to the plants of the soil but bore with it this time a terrible revelation: Cradled in the branches that rose from the well, there rested a body, that of a young girl, bones clean of any flesh but still clothed in the tattered remnants of the once-white dress in which she had died. The scraggly hair, too, remained, mingled with the flowers that grew from the vines.

When the growth of the garden ceased, Elsinore saw new movement: From the flowers and vines and from the skull of the girl, many little serpents slithered away and crawled into the earth outside the well.

Rising, Elsinore stood gazing at the body. She stepped forward and cradled the poor little skull in the palm of her hand. Tears rose in her eyes, too hot from sorrow for the still-frigid air. She tried to blink them away, but still they came. The mournful song of the wind had stilled, and the city had grown silent at last, but now a cry rose up once more—this time from Elsinore. This child had deserved so much more.

The earth was still too frozen for burial, but the child's spirit needed to be brought to rest. Snapping her fingers, Elsinore brought her hands together, and in her cupped palms, there rose a little flame, a minor spell she at last had the strength and will to cast.

"Please rest, little sister," Elsinore said sadly. Bowing before the body, she set the flame within the branches at the base of the well. The twigs burst alight, and the fire spread quickly within the walls of the well, which acted as a firepit, keeping the flames from reaching the greenery around the plaza. The pyre warmed the night, and the smoke rose to the sky, spreading among the gray clouds that had long ceased to snow. Elsinore watched it all, never taking her eyes from the fire, never looking away from the body of the poor girl as the pyre consumed it.

She knew not how long she watched the pyre. Dawn approached as the fire grew smaller, the body at last reduced to ashes. Finally, some motion in the flames—maybe some moisture remaining in the plants—caused a sudden flare, startling Elsinore, who jumped back. The flames grew larger, only for a moment, and in the shape of the dancing fire, Elsinore saw—or thought she saw—the form of a girl vibrant with life, dancing, warm, a girl happy and clothed in a yellow gown of fire. The spectral girl laughed at Elsinore, and on some edge of the wind, the priestess could hear the laughter out loud, a cry at last of delight rather than mourning, a voice of thanks.

At last, the flare spent itself and trailed off into the sky, looking very much like a serpent of fire reaching for the stars, coiled in the shape of an arcane letter the sorceress could not read.

But perhaps Elsinore only imagined this, fatigued from her trials and from the cold.

The fire burned out as dawn came, and at long last, the gray sky cleared, and the morning sun shone down the alleys of the city and warmed the grove that remained in the plaza. Elsinore stood and spoke a prayer of stillness over the remains, commending the child to the care of the Goddess, in whatever form of rest She had to bestow. The child was now part of the earth, as she had ever been, as all people were.

Turning with sadness and resignation, Elsinore took flight from Peshina as the air at last grew warm, to seek answers to her troubles elsewhere.

MONMOTH
THE DOOMED SLAYER

Monmoth! The Slayer! His ax rang like a death knell against the armor of his enemies, who fell like mown wheat before his glorious strength!

"Beneath the banner of the Sun-King Rengis of Anj, the soldiers marched on, for the Sun-King's lust for conquest was insatiable. City after city had fallen to the Sun-King's army, no band of mercenary defenders a match for their spears and swords. But one man—this reaver . . . this hero—stood ready to defeat the soldiers at last. For Monmoth fought not for home and hearth nor for honor nor glory nor fear of loss.

"No. Monmoth the hero—Monmoth on whose head oracles in the far-off gloomy cities of the river had pronounced a doom none might anticipate nor forestall—Monmoth fought only for the exultant joy of battle. Like rags of sheep's cloth, the golden armor of the proud soldiers split beneath the ax of the mighty Slayer! Like sunshine, the armor glowed, and like lightning from a storm, Monmoth's ax cut through and darkened their failing day!

Only the felling of warriors beneath his iron brought him gladness; only fresh and running blood painted on the black iron of his ax brought laughter to his brooding lips.

"Only death brings Monmoth peace."

Seated in a far corner of the taberna, the black-hooded sorceress listened to this lurid tale with detached amusement. She smoked a long, thin, straight pipe with a metal bowl and mouthpiece, cannabis smoke trailing from her lips as she watched the man in silk act out each swing of his protagonist's ax. At the climax, he leaped up on the bar, revealing legs clothed in red trousers, and guzzled beer by the mugful to fuel his telling. The patrons thrilled to hear him tell the tale. Meanwhile, the sorceress kept her distance, little eager to join in their revels.

Only one other person sat similarly disinterested, more focused on his drink than on the storyteller: a sullen-eyed man with dirty black hair, muscled arms and bare chest noticeable beneath a simple, torn tunic, and a worn red cloak around his shoulders. No one else paid him any attention, but the sorceress could tell. She saw right away:

Monmoth the Slayer.

Still, while he might be the subject of the tale, he was less to blame for her disappointing evening than the garrulous man who hopped from table to table, collecting coins in his feathered hat for his tale and accepting offer after offer of drink.

Earlier at sunset, Elsinore had offered a different form of entertainment in the plaza outside the taberna, a more sophisticated kind in her estimation. She had danced, hips swaying hypnotically, fingers plucking at the air like invisible harp strings and drawing sorcerous notes from the aether that vibrated and hummed in the ears of her audience. She had cast irresistible eerie witch lights of strange shifting colors with a snap of her fingers, flames that danced around her as they whistled with unseen flutes. Finally, she had drummed upon her tympanum, beating a rhythm few could ignore—if indeed they could ignore any of her enticing performance.

When all was finished, she had held out the hollow of her hand drum for alms—alms for the Mother Goddess the priestess served, which allowed her to make her way from town to town, to procure food, ale, and a warm bed.

But the hollow of her drum had been sparser than usual this evening, and now she knew why. These locals had been saving what they had for this storyteller with his lurid tales of blood and death, and Elsinore had begun to feel like she'd come to the wrong town on the wrong night.

At least she'd had enough for bread, cheese, beer, and a decent bed in a private room.

Leaving her beer unfinished, she gathered her bag and headed to her room, which called to her for a long night. Once she'd stripped herself of her black hood, sandal boots, jewelry, and short bright-purple dress, the weariness brought on by the long day of travel and dance grew heavier. It had been too much to hope for a decent bath; this town was hardly a great city of the river. But the taberna at least had simple running water and a toilet, so she made do with washing just her face and privates.

Finishing her ablutions with a quick brush of her teal-dyed hair, she sighed. The room felt very empty without her familiar, Risky, who had taken a different path than Elsinore, as they sometimes did, when the sorceress had passed through the frozen valley surrounding Peshina some weeks before. No doubt the capricious cat would rendezvous with her soon enough, but for now, Elsinore felt anxious and alone. Sleep might dispel such feelings till the morning, at least.

No sooner had the dancer sat on the bed and gripped the rough sheets than someone knocked on her door. The bolt held fast, but she startled a little nonetheless.

Standing, Elsinore slipped her black jacket back over her shoulders and put up her hood. The jacket was short, but it covered enough of her body if she held it shut with one hand. Unbolting the door, she found herself in the shadow of a tall man standing head and shoulders above her, eyes still sullen and muscled arms crossed over his magnificent broad chest.

At a loss for how to react, Elsinore stared as blankly as if the hall were empty.

"Yes?" she managed to say after a long pause.

"I noticed you grow tired of the tale-telling, as did I. A tale well told, with a story worth following, is a marvelous thing. I apologize that my companion's was not so." He grinned humorlessly. "I'm used to it."

His voice was deep, tight and terse, but not unpleasant—like the bass string of a lute.

Relaxing, Elsinore leaned her head and left hand on the right side of the door frame and stared into his eyes. They were as deep as his voice—dark blue, like indigo dye.

The man gazed down at Elsinore with those blue eyes. "My companion is poor company tonight; he becomes full of his own pointless stories and surrounds himself with simple-minded folk who hang on his words and ply him with drink."

"And you thought to find more agreeable company?" Elsinore purred.

"Just so. And you seemed the most agreeable of all the women I've seen in this town." Raising his hand, he fingered Elsinore's chin. She shivered gladly.

Biting her lip, Elsinore opened the door fully for Monmoth to enter, then shut it quietly as he sat on the bed, knees spread and chin in his fist. Elsinore turned to him and lowered her hood but did not yet disrobe.

"What do you ask?" the man asked directly.

"What do you have?"

The man reached into a pouch on his belt and drew out a large coin that glinted in the candlelight. Standing, he took Elsinore's hand, pressed the coin into her palm, and closed her fingers around it, engulfing her hand in his. His hands were huge, calloused, but still strangely soft and gentle.

Elsinore smiled as he returned to the bed, and opened her hand. The coin looked like gold, and it bore the image of a solar disc with a stern face, surrounded by waves of heat or light. She fought to keep her eyes from widening in astonishment. This more than made up for her loss from the storyteller poaching her audience.

"I have sheepskins from the innkeeper," Monmoth offered.

Elsinore grinned. "You can save them for another girl."

Despite his impassive demeanor, the man raised an eyebrow in surprise—and perhaps with desire, Elsinore noticed with a slight grin.

"Don't get your hopes up. It's only that I won't be party to the death of a living creature, neither to eat its meat nor to use its flesh—not even its entrails. I have a supply of sheaths made of linen, smooth and thin and oiled with a special medicinal salve. They're more reliable than sheep-skins, nearly impossible to tear, and much more enjoy-able—for both of us."

The man smiled, more with his eyes than his mouth—Elsinore noticed he never smiled with his mouth—and he nodded definitively.

Elsinore approached him slowly, gracefully, and let her jacket fall from her shoulders to the floor, revealing her full breasts, belly, and dangling little penis. Rising from the bed slowly, Monmoth gently cradled her shoulders in his hands, ran his hands down her arms, and kissed her.

"My companion warned me not to go to you after we saw you dance in the plaza." He kissed her again.

"Oh?" Elsinore buried a kiss where Monmoth's cheek met his neck. "There are a few good reasons I can think of to warn against me," she said, smiling.

"He said you were clearly a priestess of Tiranna, and if I were wise, I would find some local girl to bed instead."

"That clearly didn't bother you," Elsinore hummed into the base of his throat.

"I knew it likely meant you would be better experi-enced in the arts of love than some provincial village woman. I knew it meant you were a traveler and less likely to stammer in awe of me after hearing those tedious stories. I knew about this." He slid his hand down her belly and softly fingered the young woman's penis.

"But most of all," he concluded, "a beautiful woman is a beautiful woman."

Unclasping his cloak, Monmoth tossed it aside, then pulled his tunic off over his head. Elsinore smiled subtly as she undid his loincloth, never looking away from his eyes.

At last, she pushed him down on the bed. She teased his cock with her lips till it grew long and firm, then unfurled a linen sheath over it and lubricated it further with oil from a glass bottle. Then Monmoth entered her from behind—softly, firmly, strongly—and they rocked in rhythm with each other in the dim candlelight on a simple, unfamiliar bed.

He stayed in her till she moaned, long but quietly, discreetly, and she reached back to dig her nails in his bottom. When she pushed him away gently, he withdrew.

Swiftly turning to face him, she took his face in her hands and kissed him. She wrapped her arms around his broad shoulders and her legs around his strong, muscled body above his hips, and he entered her again from the front. Standing, he lifted her into the air with ease, supporting her with his incredible strength as he thrust up into her.

Elsinore moaned loudly, unable to keep quiet as she had before, squeezing him as hard as she could. Only then did he finish, release, and slowly withdraw from her, laying her gently on the bed.

He remained silent the entire time.

Afterward, he lay back on a pillow as Elsinore sat up beside him, playing with his hair and smoking from her long, straight pipe of reed, the little metal bowl filled with cannabis. She offered it to him, but he refused.

"That's the affair of sorcerers and mystics," he said gruffly. "I'll have little to do with such things."

"Well, as you said, I am a priestess of the Goddess." Elsinore blew a long, thin stream of smoke into the air above them. "The practice comes more naturally to me, perhaps."

"I met another priestess of Tiranna not long ago," the man said. "To tell the truth, it was she who sent me here."

Elsinore furrowed her brow with curiosity and inhaled from her pipe again. "I wouldn't have taken you for one to make pilgrimages on behalf of holy women," she said thoughtfully.

"You'd be correct," the man replied. "It isn't a pilgrimage in the normal sense, nor am I interested in sacrifices and ritual cleansings. No, the story this evening, though florid and exaggerated, is true: I am an adventurer, and knowing me by reputation, the priestess hired me to do what I do."

"And what is it you do?" Elsinore asked. "Hew men's heads from their bodies?"

"If my mission calls for it. But I am a soldier of fortune, a fighting man—and a thief. And I was hired to steal a petty relic and bring it to the priestess who sought my service through her intermediary."

"Now I'm intrigued," Elsinore said playfully.

"It needn't concern you. I've troubled my lady enough with talk of business you have no interest in."

Elsinore did not reply but only looked at him. Once she'd finished smoking, she deftly twisted her hand in the air above her head and, with a simple spell, extinguished all the candles in the room. Smiling to herself in the dark, she nestled in the strongman's arm.

When the adventurer reunited with his garrulous companion in the morning, the sorceress accompanied him. The storyteller, whose name was Valustaf, smiled obsequiously at the strongman.

"A night well spent at rest in this pretty little town! A night well spent for us all on our several journeys." Turning, Valustaf gave Elsinore a brief, less pleasant smile. She grinned sarcastically in response. "But we must be getting on with our quest—on with our heroic task. And I'm sure she must have another lovely village to visit and so many important people to meet."

"Not so." Monmoth gave his companion his heavy traveling bag, leaving himself only the great ax on his back. "She will be accompanying us, Valustaf. Elsinore, I don't think you've met my friend."

Valustaf sputtered, though he clearly tried to hide it as he shouldered the weight of the bag.

Elsinore curtsied. "I've heard so much about you."

"Monmoth!" Valustaf gasped, but the adventurer had already pushed open the doors of the taberna, stepping out into the morning, and Elsinore followed.

"The glorious Tower of the Sun stands some few miles from the town at Rudern Hill. In ancient times, the tales tell, there was a hollow chamber beneath the hill, some barrow for a dead, forgotten god. A generation ago, on an abortive push into the Great River Valley, a band of mighty raiders, worshippers of the invincible sun, built an outpost on the hill. Though they were cut off soon enough from their kings, who pursued other conquests to the north of the valley, some remained here and dedicated it as a temple to the sun god, Rudash. And it is there that they kept a powerful image of their god—"

"That is what the priestess hired us to obtain," Monmoth concluded, plainly growing tired of the story.

The three had put good distance between themselves and the town—though they still had a long way to go—and hoped to come to the tower on the hill by nightfall. Night would be best for what they had to do. It would be best, Monmoth had growled earlier, for the sun not to see.

"So, it was a priestess of Tiranna—of the star goddess,

a priestess like me—who seeks this . . . this icon of the sun god? A priestess from the city of Sanisa?" Elsinore shook her head. "Why? What need could she have for that? What possible use?"

"We met far from Sanisa, closer to the lands we now pass through, in the city of Luteca, but she acted on behalf of some 'high priestess' in Sanisa who I do not know," Monmoth clarified.

"And the sorceress told me the reason for the need, though it makes little difference to me. Something to do with the icon 'impeding the flow' of one thing to another, 'preventing the thread from being strung through the pearls and sewn into the net' or some such magical nonsense. I don't much care the foolish doctrinal reasoning, and neither should you. I care only that I was hired to do this and gave my word, and I shall accomplish it."

Monmoth shifted the weight of the ax on his shoulders and pressed on, and Elsinore and Valustaf followed.

After midday, they stopped to rest and eat. Monmoth, ever uneasy, went on to scout ahead, while the sorceress sat hidden in the trees with the adventurer's companion.

"You two have been friends for a long time?" Elsinore asked, offering Valustaf water from her gourd. The man refused, taking red wine poured from a skin he carried.

"For the past year," he replied between gulps. "I aided Monmoth in a battle at Bulor. I provided safe passage in, sprung traps to clear the way—I promise you, even he would not have come out of it alive without my help."

"No? I'd taken you for childhood friends, together all your lives."

"Monmoth comes from a tribe in the steppes to the east. Only lately has his thirst for adventure brought him to the Great River Valley."

"And you?" Elsinore looked the man up and down, examining his bright-red trousers and coat, his feathered hat and belts and necklaces decorated with gold—styles unfamiliar to Elsinore in the lands she had been to, in the time she had been there. "Are you from the valley?"

"I am from . . . near here," Valustaf said hesitantly. "From the city of Luteca."

He grew quiet, perhaps tired of making conversation with the sorceress. His fondness for story and talk was so far clearly more general, and his obvious distaste for Elsinore would have been off-putting had she not shared the sentiment for him.

"I'm going to go refill my water from the stream," he said, though he had been drinking only wine all day.

When Monmoth returned, his face was dark, and he remained silent as he packed their supplies. By then, it was late after midday.

"How does it look?" Elsinore asked. "The way ahead?"

Monmoth looked grimly in the direction of the tower for a long time before responding.

"A patrol of guards traces a path in the woods approaching the hill. I have slain three of them. It should be simple to sneak to the foot of the tower under cover of darkness."

A sick feeling rose in Elsinore's stomach as she looked at the ax on Monmoth's back. It had been cleaned of any blood, but still its iron glinted with a dull red film in the late-day sun.

"Guards?" she muttered darkly. "I thought this was a monastery?"

"It's nothing of the kind," the adventurer replied. "It's an outpost. An isolated one, but it sits in wait for contact from emissaries of their lords. Their icon is sacred to them, but their faith is one of blood and conquest. I respect such a god, it is true, more than airy spirits of nature and mysticism, but my given task and the payment I have taken is a promise I would never shy from. The men of the steppe keep our word."

Elsinore said nothing in reply but nodded as she gathered her bag and followed Monmoth and Valustaf into the woods.

The three approached the Tower of the Sun as night fell. From the trees, the tower could be seen rising high on the hill even in the dark, black against the stars of the blue night sky. In time, two men armored in leather and gold approached from opposite directions around the tower, stopping as they crossed paths to confer. Or perhaps they stopped only to waste time and speak of trivialities and nothing, complacent from so long spent watching for attacks that never came.

Elsinore sighed, regretting that it was too late to abandon a pointless quest she had followed on a whim.

Monmoth gestured for her to wait, then he and Valustaf crept silently through the bushes and behind the guards, who now faced the tower. Without a sound, both men reached around the guards and slashed their throats with knives that glittered for only a second in the moonlight before being dulled by blood. Elsinore drew back, though she wasn't sure what else she had expected, and hesitated a moment when Monmoth gestured for her to follow.

The shadow of the tower stretched far down the hill, cast by the rising moon, which glowed in the sky in defiance of the falling sun. The three slunk quickly up the incline of the shallow mound, keeping to the shadow, and hid in the alcoves of the wall. By fortune, the shadow fell on the far side from the gate, unguarded by armored men.

"Well, sorceress?" Monmoth said. "Will your goddess aid you as we planned last night?"

Elsinore looked up at the tower, at the rough stonework and balconies, at the height that loomed far above. "The icon is in the chamber at the top of the tower?" she asked, not taking her eyes from the apex.

Monmoth nodded. "As I said."

"Wait for me." Elsinore tightened the straps of her bag and her sword on her back.

Just then, a cry went out among the guards, and the clatter of spears and swords unsheathing cut across the mound. Two guards ran toward their hiding spot, then four, then five, as the gatekeepers and the patrol joined together to meet the intruders without mercy. Valustaf drew two curved daggers, and Monmoth swung his ax from his back in a terrible motion, its double blades awful to behold.

The foremost guard fell first to the reaver, his spear little more than a twig to the ax, and he was cleaved from shoulder to chest. The knives of the companion slid into the second guard's neck, and the shadowy grass at the foot of the tower was stained with his blood. The other guards surrounded the intruders, keeping a distance but ready to strike.

"Go, sorceress!" Monmoth called over his shoulder, and Elsinore swallowed her reservations and acted.

With a hidden word of magic that immediately vanished from the minds of any who might have heard it amid the tension and clatter of steel, Elsinore cast a spell that drew a veil of mist around her. The white shadow mist shifted her out of the visible world and allowed her to walk unseen. Invisible to the guards, Elsinore began her ascent. Proceeding carefully, she found grips and footholds among the rough stonework, rested at each balcony, and soon enough, reached the highest one at the window to the upper chamber. No archers saw her climb within the folds of invisibility. No one called for help to stop her. No one even suspected she was there while Monmoth and his companion fought the guards with their bloody weapons at the foot of the tower below.

The window was wide and tall, perhaps to allow rituals in the light of the sun, and neither bars nor glass impeded Elsinore's entry, only black curtains. Steeling her nerve for what might lie in wait, she pushed the curtains aside and stepped into the room.

The chamber was sparse and strange, standing alone at the pinnacle of the tower. No statues or images decorated the sanctuary, and the stone walls were all bleached stark white. Four braziers burned around the room, evenly spaced between four black-curtained windows. Between one brazier and window, a short flight of steps led down to a door decorated in gold that was sunk into the floor.

In the center of the room, on an altar of wood and gold, rested the object she had come for.

Nestled on a bunched altar cloth the deep blue of the midday sky, the orb was perhaps twice the size of a human head. Its surface was smooth and undecorated, unmarked and clean. Elsinore couldn't be certain of its color—perhaps black, perhaps dark red, or perhaps that was only the tint of the fire. Color seemed to slip off its surface unnaturally, leaving only scant traces. But strangest of all was its composition. It appeared at once translucent and opaque, crystal in some way yet utterly incapable of letting the light from the fires pass through it. Elsinore stared at it for a long moment, unable to make her eyes focus on the object itself. It was difficult to fully grasp it in her sight, and her head began to throb from the effort.

A noise from the stairs jostled Elsinore from her wonder, and she acted quickly. Wrapping the cloth on the altar fully around the orb, she cradled it in her arms. It was lighter than it appeared, and she held it easily. Turning, she passed back through the curtains to the balcony.

Not giving herself a chance to feel dizzy from the height, the sorceress ran to the edge and leaped from the tower, still hidden in the invisible mist she had cast. As she leaped, Elsinore spoke the word to cast another spell, slowing her descent, and she drifted like a feather safely to the ground below. With all her concentration focused on the second spell, the mists of the first fell away, and she appeared, bodily and visible, on the grass of the hill in the shadow of the tower.

The fighting had rounded the base of the structure, and a trail of corpses, all guards, lay soaked in blood, the red horror dimmed not at all by the shadow or white moonlight.

The two adventurers fought with guards near the gate, their ax and knives flashing horribly as blood showered from the men who rushed to meet them. The sickening feeling rose once again in Elsinore's gut, but she swallowed it to shout to her companions. "It's done!"

When the next guard fell, Monmoth turned to the young woman and raised his ax triumphantly. He called to Valustaf, and the two ran swiftly down the hill to meet the sorceress who held their prize.

More guards emerged from the tower, hurrying in fast pursuit with swords drawn. Forcing the orb into Monmoth's hands, Elsinore ran back toward the hill.

"Stand back!" she shouted when her companions moved to follow. As the guards approached, Elsinore frowned and pressed her hands forward toward the curve of the hill.

Focusing the last of the magic she could call on for the moment, Elsinore closed her eyes and shouted a word of power—a word in a language long forgotten that hung in the air for an instant and vanished as quickly as it had been spoken.

The soft earth of the hill rolled beneath the sorceress's hands, rippling like a wave in the sea up and along the rise. The rocks beneath the soil rose up, high and ragged, and the guards had no time to react before they staggered and fell into earth that was no longer solid.

"Run!" Elsinore cried, and she and her companions fled into the trees while the pursuers struggled even to stand.

After an hour or so of running through the woods, turning at random, doubling back, and always making sure to cover their tracks, the party was sure they would not be followed or found. For some time, Elsinore feared they would become lost, but Monmoth was an outdoorsman and, among other talents, a tracker of great skill, trained by a nomadic life on the steppes.

At last, they came to rest by the edge of the wood, upon fallen pillars and broken walls of stone—some structure that had lain ruined for long ages but was still being reclaimed by the trees. Elsinore was sore and fatigued from the long day and grueling strain of the climb. She could tell Valustaf, too, was worn, sweating and panting and lying now against a mossy stone. Monmoth alone appeared fit and untroubled, and he scanned their surroundings for signs of danger.

"We can rest for a moment, but chase from your minds any thoughts of sleep," he cautioned. "We'll have to move on soon."

"Where will we go?" Elsinore asked. "The town where we met will be the first place they'll look for us."

"I mean to meet the priestess in Luteca within two days," the strongman said. "From there, she has promised us safe passage deeper into the Great River Valley, far from the reach of the worshippers of Rudash.

"And Elsinore," he continued, turning to the sorceress, "I suppose you may continue on with her to Sanisa. You will no doubt find fellow devotees to your goddess there."

Elsinore squirmed. "Perhaps I will." Feeling suddenly uncomfortable, she looked around awkwardly. She sighed when she spotted faint moonlight falling through the trees.

"I think I'll scout ahead to the tree line and see if I can find a safe path forward once we're out of cover. Monmoth will continue to keep watch behind us. Valustaf, you . . . you gather your strength."

The fancifully dressed man waved his assent, still visibly out of breath. He seemed to make a show of how worn he was.

Once past the trees, Elsinore stood in the bright light of a moon high in the sky. Blue-green grasses waved in the pale light over small hills and ridges, rolling on toward the mountains in the distance. Somewhere in a dell among those mountains stood the city of Luteca.

Perhaps it was time she met one of her temple sisters, those who lived in this day, who had grown and studied in the time Elsinore had been hidden from the world. Perhaps her fear was silly. Perhaps little had changed.

Perhaps.

Elsinore shut her eyes. She breathed deeply for a long while, smelling the grass and trees that surrounded her. Breathing life. Then, with some reluctance, she turned and made her way back to the broken stones where her companions waited.

It was quiet as she returned to the ruins. Monmoth would have little to say, but surely Valustaf would have caught his breath by now and be expounding at tedious length on some story or another. But she heard no speech in the woods, and no shuffling movement.

Then she saw.

Valustaf stood upon a broken pillar, leering at the young sorceress as she emerged from the trees. In his right hand, he held one of his curved daggers—dripping with blood. Cradled under the other arm, he held the orb of the sun, no longer covered by the altar cloth, its dark crystal allowing no light to pass through and reflecting no color. He grinned under his oiled mustache, barely containing laughter.

On the earth below him lay Monmoth—the body of Monmoth.

He lay face down, fallen in a pool of blood that was still fresh, only beginning to soak into the dirt. Falling to her knees beside him, Elsinore held his head in her hands.

So careful, so cautious, so observant, so strong—the adventurer, scourge of his enemies, had fallen to one he had never suspected, to one he had trusted with his life—

trusted in vain. He must not have even seen the other man creep up behind him, his throat slit before even his quick fighter's instincts could react.

Dropping his knife, Valustaf held the orb in both hands, thrust out before him. The awful thing seemed to pulse, to throb with some strange life that was not life. It appeared . . . not to glow but to dim. To dim itself and all the light around it.

Elsinore glared at the man in the strangely lurid darkness, bearing her teeth, unable to say a word. The terrible man broke out in laughter at last.

"Fool!" he cried. "You knew nothing of the designs of your fellow degenerate sorcerers of the river—knew not even the power the orb holds! They would have had it sealed away—even destroyed! They couldn't comprehend its use, its power, so tangled are they in the swamp reeds of their petty religion. They feared the sun orb's power to imprison the soul, the spirit—the direction, the momentum, the continuation of the life of the dead! With this power, I may seal the soul away, redirect it, prevent it from completing its recycling into the movement of the Earth, and use it instead to serve my will! *My* will, sorceress! I shall be able to slay the fools of the cities of the valley, the pagan worshippers of a goddess who soon will be forgotten, and I shall resurrect and redirect their bodies to serve the true Divine, God the Sun!

"As my father, who came to the valley with the faithful of Rudash, was driven off and slain by mercenaries of Monmoth's ilk—so now shall I clear the land of you pagan fools and claim that land for the true faithful! All to serve God the Sun, all to serve his faithful—and all to serve me!"

The wretched, bellowing man laughed again and

raised the orb above his head. The orb's aura blotted out the blue light of the night sky and stars beyond it, like a black sun that swallowed light instead of casting it.

Rising to her feet, Elsinore drew her sword, Moonstar, which sparkled in the starlight. The man laughed again.

"And you, detestable witch—you shall be the first to fall to my power. Behold! Monmoth, my undead slave—slay her!"

Elsinore gasped as the man in the dirt rose rigidly and stood before her once again, hunched, his arms limp, his black hair dangling over his face. His eyes, once cold and beautiful, were dark in the shadow, hidden from the moonlight.

No, not shadowed—

His eyes were simply black.

His throat gaped with a slash clean across, open to his windpipe, and blood stained his bare chest.

Elsinore fought the urge to vomit.

Raising his arms, the dead man stepped forward. Elsinore backed away, sword before her.

"Monmoth, don't," she whispered.

But the corpse's ears were as dead as its eyes. Unhearing, unseeing, uncaring, it was a grisly puppet strung only to the will of the miserable man who held the orb and laughed. The thing reached down, took up its ax, and swung with terrible force at the sorceress.

Elsinore leaped away, and the dead man swung again with a tremendous weight that cracked a tree in half as Elsinore dodged away. Over and over, the thing struck, tireless, lifeless, as Elsinore dashed away, still too horrified by the thing's resemblance to Monmoth in life to strike back. It was a grim thing—a parody of the man it had once been.

Finally, the thing swung and the ax stuck halfway into

a tree trunk. It would take only a second for it to wrench the ax out with its limitless strength, but that second was all it took for Elsinore to flip under it and kick upward. With a terrible crack, the thing's wrist was broken.

There was no reaction from the face of the corpse—it was without pain as much as it was without will or remorse—but the momentum forced it backward, away from the ax. At last, Elsinore had a chance. She struck fiercely with her short sword, slashing at the arms, the muscled chest. No blood oozed from the wounds—congealed in death, perhaps—and the thing was slowed not at all.

Regaining its balance, it thrust its muscled arms forward, unhindered by the broken wrist, and Elsinore's dancer dexterity was all that saved her from being caught and crushed. But the thing came again and again, unrelenting.

Elsinore cried out in despair. She had no more numinous potential to cast spells of force or weightlessness or invisibility—not till she rested and studied her spellbook. The thought of rest despaired her further; she was so tired, had gone so long without sleep, had strained so much all day and all night. All she had was the fear in her racing heart that kept her from the corpse's reach and a few simple cantrips that could do no real harm, little more than tricks.

But perhaps tricks were all she needed.

In one of the brief moments the thing's momentum carried it out of reach, Elsinore sheathed her sword before it could turn to grasp at her again. Snapping her fingers, she cast her fire lights in both hands, little orbs of glowing flame that hovered above her palms—a little spell that could scarcely cause harm. Dodging away from another lunge, she threw the fireballs, one after another, at the walking corpse's back—scorching the dead flesh, though not enough for the thing to notice.

Again she snapped her fingers, and again she danced away, waving the flames around her before hurling them at the thing's face, at the empty black eyes that could see nothing. Again and again, casting and dancing and dodging, merely singeing the unrelenting thing—establishing a pattern she was sure the loathsome man with the orb was watching.

When Valustaf laughed with derision, Elsinore smiled to herself—and struck. She cast the spell of flame in her hands, ducked out of reach of the warrior's corpse—and hurled both fireballs at Valustaf's face.

The arrogant man saw nothing till the fires struck him in the eyes. Then he shrieked.

"You bitch! You miserable—"

But it was too late. Instinctively, he raised his hands to his face, dropping the black sun orb from his high perch on the ruined pillar, and it struck a fallen fragment of stone and cracked with an awful sound like thunder. In his blindness, the crying man stumbled and tripped and followed the orb down, rolling on the ground in pain.

In an instant, the dead warrior stopped. It hung a moment where it stood, arms frozen before it, eyes black and unseeing. Then, in an act that chilled Elsinore's heart, it let out a wailing keen, a terrible sound, higher pitched than the man could have made in life. Turning, the thing dove straight at the fallen man, and before anyone could react, it plunged its arm straight through Valustaf's chest, impaling him as if on a sword, spilling blood in a frightful torrent upon the earth, and silencing the screams of the petty man forever.

So, too, did the dead man's keening cease. The body

fell limp upon its slain companion and at long last moved no more.

Elsinore stared at the grisly aftermath in wide-eyed horror.

She stood frozen for a few long moments, still as the corpses. At last, she pulled herself from her stupor and stepped forward—and found herself taking the orb from where it rested near the pool of blood.

It was a frightful thing still, even voided of its unholy magic. Its aura of shadow was gone; no longer was it swimming in darkness, difficult to see. It looked now only like a sad, broken bauble, a shell empty of what it had once held. It seemed hollow within—a shell, indeed—and at last, its crystal structure allowed light to pass through it, if only darkly.

Elsinore lifted it up, and with what weak force she could muster in her fatigue, she struck it upon the stone of the ruins before her. The orb shattered like brittle glass, pieces falling to the dirt. A few larger shards remained, and she took up a stone and hammered them till all that remained were bits and pieces, impossible to restore. Then, for good measure, she cast her fire spell again, lit the dry leaves and twigs aflame, and let them burn around the fragments. Only when she was satisfied did she extinguish it.

Turning, she looked at last at the bodies before her, at wretched Valustaf, at brave, beautiful Monmoth of the steppes. Monmoth the Slayer, who met his doom in a betrayal foreseen by none but the oracles who read the threads of fate—and the false friend who betrayed him.

She wondered briefly what to do with the bodies, then sighed. Reaching into her bag, she took the gold coin Monmoth had paid her and flipped it with her thumb onto the body. That was all she could do. She had put enough bodies to rest in recent times.

She thought of Luteca, several days' travel away, and the priestess who waited there—like Elsinore, a daughter of the Goddess. She thought of what she would say; it now fell on her to assure her sister that the task was complete—that the dark artifact of the sun cult was no more.

She felt so tired.

When Monmoth failed to rendezvous with her at the appointed time, perhaps the priestess would send another mercenary. They would make inquiries and discover that the mission had been successful but that Monmoth and his companion had not been seen since the fight at the tower. Soon enough, the bodies would be found in the forest, and maybe even some keen-eyed seeker would identify the ruins of the orb, its restoration impossible.

Elsinore thought of the priestess.

She decided she would not go to Luteca.

Elsinore turned away from the bodies and walked out of the woods toward the rising sun of morning. Her lingering adrenaline carried her as far as it could, till the fatigue caught her in a shaded hollow in the crest of a hill some ways distant. There, Elsinore sat beneath a tree to rest.

The Locket of the Lich

The clatter of swords rang out undimmed, echoing off the walls of the settlement hidden low in the valley, the sharp din ever louder in the fading light of the afternoon sun. The dull dying star colored all it fell upon the rust red of death, and the leering skulls of the undead soldiers marching beneath it grinned as taloned hands reached out to pull whatever they touched beneath the earth with the sunset. Villagers who should have scattered and fled stood fast before the dreadful wave, pushing back with pitchforks and wood axes in the hope of turning back the army of death. But death is inevitable, and though a few gruesome foes fell, the tide of living-dead soldiers rushed ever on, through the defenders and into the town.

With a glittering ring like the call of a bell, a silver blade flashed, cleaving one monster's skull from its shoulders, and its brittle bones collapsed in a heap. Again the blade flashed, and again a clear white light, like a moonbeam, shone coolly in the red heat of the setting sun. The eyes of the overwhelmed villagers were drawn to the light,

"""

and with every skull that fell and rib cage that broke apart, their hope grew. Those who looked to the light saw the sword was wielded by a young woman—a girl—in a spinning purple skirt and colorful scarves, blue-green hair whipping around her like pine branches in a storm.

Her skirts and scarves had flown in the town earlier that evening under better circumstances, when the girl had danced in the square at the foot of the temple. Then, her sword had been thrust in the earth before her, and she had only been a beautiful dancer who wandered the valley, collecting alms to support herself and honor her Goddess—the Great Mother of women and men and those otherwise and between. Now that the skeletons came, the girl fought more ably than any warrior and whirled more gracefully than any other dancer, and the beset folk of the town had hope.

But hope, like sunlight, is fleeting. From over the hill at the edge of town, a canopy rose. Upon a litter throne borne by four great skeletons, he appeared. His hands, clean ivory bones unnaturally supporting the barest tatters of flesh, were decorated with jeweled rings and bracelets of gold set with gemstones. The bangles clacked as he waved his arms in arcane motions before his face. Behind his head was set a rayed halo of flashing gold, like a sun disk, and he wore on his face a golden mask with the calm likeness of a man, eyes hidden deep in the shadows of its sockets.

The thought of what lay behind the mask brought a darkly familiar chill to the dancer's heart. Skilled in the magic arts herself, she read the sigils drawn with the motions of the necromancer's arms and could see with her subtle vision the swirls, ripples, and gashes carved in the aethereal aura surrounding him.

"Into the temple! All of you!" the woman cried, in a voice deeper and more commanding than many of the villagers expected. She had no need to repeat herself; the people fell back from the onslaught of skeleton soldiers, confident, if only for the moment, that the lovely stranger could command the situation.

Once all were within the walls of the temple, those at the doors fought off the encroaching enemies while the dancer leaped upon the altar. Holding her hand before her, she spun as if performing again in the square. A few of those nearby watched her incredulously, too shocked and afraid of their approaching doom to scoff. But when the dancer brought her finger to her lips, a silver ring on the finger flashed in the dim candlelight of the temple, and she whispered a word that few could hear. Those who could immediately realized they could no longer remember it, though their minds searched for its sound ever after in their quietest dreams.

The walls of the temple flashed blue—so briefly, it would have been missed in a blink—and the dancer—the sorceress—stood ready on the altar. The defenders at the doors were amazed. The skeletons, which they had barely kept from pouring into the temple moments before, were now stopped solidly at the threshold. A few slashed vainly at the door, unable to make their blades cross within, but most clawed with their bony hands, which fell away weakly, like fools playing silently before a crowd of children. The townsfolk at the doors stood back with smiles of wonder, though others kept their weapons at the ready, wary of what the skeletons might do.

From up on the altar, the sorceress could see far out the central door; out in the square, behind the horde of undead soldiers, the necromancer sat still in his chair. In a motion clearly visible to the young woman, even so far away, he held up his jeweled skeletal arms and turned his palms inward. At once, the undead in his command halted, straightened their clawing limbs, turned, and marched away, abandoning the temple and clearing the village.

The villagers began to cheer, and a few held their hands up to the altar in triumphant solidarity with the dancer whose spell had driven the monsters away. But her eyes remained fixed on the necromancer, who gazed back at her from the dark cavernous sockets of his golden mask. Only when the last of his soldiers had passed did he gesture for his attendants to follow, turning at last to disappear with the others behind the hills of the road out of town.

A few brave scouts from the village followed at a distance and, in short order, confirmed that the army of the undead had fully retreated and was now nowhere to be seen. Many of the most fearless defenders crowded to the sorceress, offering congratulations and words of astonishment. As the clamor died down, an old woman approached—a temple priestess, from the look of her robes—and she folded the dancer's smooth hand in hers, smiling.

"Thank you, kind traveler. Without your help, this could have been the day our oracles long feared. Your bravery and levelheadedness guided us to victory, if only for the day."

"For now." The dancer looked doubtfully out the doors of the temple. "My protection spell wouldn't have held for long, nor do I think it could have stood against a direct attack from a sorcerer skilled enough to command the dead. They were put off for now, at least, but I wouldn't hope it will stay that way for long. What did they want from you?"

Turning to two attendants, the old priestess looked

from one to the other, eyebrows raised in resignation. The attendants both nodded, and the priestess turned back to the young woman and sighed.

"I am Geru, keeper of the temple here in Daban. I can tell you are a mage of some skill. A traveling dancer with such potent magic and such strange dress, and—though your beauty has not gone unremarked by many of my people—it seems clear to me that you are a priestess yourself, are you not? What is your name, sister?"

The dancer laughed cynically, but her eyes softened right away, and she smiled gently at the inquisitive old woman.

"I am Elsinore Ningala. And I must admit, you're more observant than many. I am a Galla, a priestess of the Goddess at the great temple of Sanisa on the river. Since I left the temple, I wander for alms and seek those who are in need of the Goddess's blessing. Your town's need seems great; please tell me how I can help, and I'll do all I can."

"Ah, I know the Gallae of Sanisa, though you look not much like those I have known, who were sent by the Mother Battakes of the temple. But the mysteries of the Goddess are many and not mine to question. Please, come with me. Let me show you the relic of our shrine—what that frightful army no doubt came to take."

Geru led the way past the altar, the acolytes beside her, and Elsinore followed, curiosity brimming in her heart. She knew of no "Mother Battakes."

She hadn't long to consider, however. The high priestess drew an arcane sign upon a panel in the wall, and the panel slipped aside with a slow rumble, revealing a secret shrine within. Set solidly within the stone was a dull metal box, surely made of lead, with an ornate lock in its face.

With reverence, Geru drew from the folds of her robe

a key on a chain and unlocked the box. The process reminded Elsinore less of a holy ritual and more of precautions taken in vaults of rare treasure or artifacts of great danger in dungeons best not spoken of. Her curiosity had been replaced with apprehension, and she worried her eyes betrayed her fear.

"This is the thalamus," Geru said, "the inner chamber. This is what he wanted, the one who led the army. His return to claim it is something my people have long feared, since I was young." The old woman opened the unlocked lead door and drew from within an object whose beauty dazzled Elsinore, even in the darkness of the hidden room.

It was a pendant, perhaps the size of an open palm, hung from a glittering chain. Pendant and chain were both made of burnished gold, and intricate pictures were molded in the face, depicting scenes whose meaning Elsinore could not guess. It seemed, at least, that the delicate images all focused around the gem set in the very center of the pendant, a clear blue-white stone that caught the dim light and magnified it.

Then, to Elsinore's surprise, Geru snapped open the pendant—or rather, the locket—revealing the gem to be a window into the inner heart of the necklace. Elsinore stared at what lay within—first in confusion, then with dawning unease.

It was a toe, the bone visible, the flesh that still clung to it dry and rotted—a grisly relic of some saint Elsinore didn't care to know. She held her hand to her mouth and turned away.

"The necromancer wants to steal your village's . . . relic?" Elsinore asked, backing out of the inner chamber. Snapping the locket shut, Geru held it reverently in her hand.

"He wants to take it, yes," the old priestess said darkly. "Aurvandol he is called; the Archmage he styles himself. He fears the harm that could come to him if it is in the hands of another and wishes it returned to him. He swore a generation ago that he would come for it one day and destroy those who held it. It was his once. He sealed this locket himself, before my grandmother hid it away in the thalamus to keep it from him. It was his toe."

Elsinore's eyes grew wide, her mouth dropping open with a gasp. She looked at the locket with a mixture of fear and disgust, making no effort to hide her feelings. Looking at last at Geru, she struggled for words.

"So he isn't just a necromancer," the young mage said. "It's much worse; you're telling me he's a lich?" Geru nodded slowly, and her two acolytes turned their heads away in something like muted terror.

"What I now ask of you may be done by no one in our village, not even by me or my pupils. But you, Sister Elsinore, priestess of the Goddess Tiranna, mage of the temple on the holy river Gallas—I am certain you were sent to us by the Great Mother Herself in our time of need. Surely the sacred fortune of the Gallae who serve the Goddess can bear the reliquary and do what must be done to save us from Aurvandol."

Closing her eyes, Elsinore felt nervously for the little star pendant on her breast. She sighed with exasperation and, at last, resignation.

"I'm only a dancer and a mendicant and . . ." The young woman trailed off, thinking better of mentioning her sacred prostitution to the old woman and her young acolytes. "But the Goddess protects us all, and Her ways are a mystery, even to me. I'll do what I can to help you. I'll do what I must."

So Elsinore found herself back on the road sooner than she'd hoped. The townsfolk didn't have much food to spare and even less that suited her vegetarian vows, but they gave her good wine rather than water. It would have to do till she reached another settlement.

Her destination was the ancient town of Thrú, hidden in the hills some days' journey from Daban. Elsinore had never even heard of it, but truth be told, she'd heard little of Daban and had only stumbled on it because the road happened to take her there.

Geru had been quite clear that none of the folk of Daban could accompany her—a taboo Aurvandol had laid by sorcery upon the amulet made sure of that—and so the young mage moved on alone. She was to deliver the gruesome amulet to the thalamus in the temple at Thrú, where it had first been made, and destroy the relic there.

Why no one from Thrú made the journey to Daban to fetch the talisman was a mystery to Elsinore—probably another magical prohibition or taboo. She had little patience for the petty necromantic curses of such wizards; she was more comfortable with the protection, fae prophecy, and elemental magic of the Great Goddess. But Her ways were broad and mysterious, and Elsinore knew better than to turn resentful, even as she questioned her place in the world that is the body of the Goddess.

Elsinore walked all the following day. As night fell, she found an abandoned campsite by the side of the road, where she stopped to take some bread and a little wine. She started a fire to keep out the darkness of the night and sat smoking cannabis from a long, thin wooden pipe with a tiny metal bowl and mouthpiece.

As she smoked, the young witch became aware that she was not alone. A cat had slunk silently into the camp and sat patiently beside her. Their fur was sleek and black, better kept than one would expect of a stray, and their eyes shone yellow green in the fire.

"I was wondering where you'd gotten to, Risky." Elsinore tossed the cat a small hunk of butter from a paper wrapper. "I'm sorry I don't have any meat for you. You know how it is. I assume you make do out in the woods."

The cat—her familiar—meowed playfully and licked the butter with relish.

"You missed quite the tussle. I know how much you like it when I fight skeletons, so I'm sorry you weren't there. Don't worry, though! We'll probably run into them again by the time we make it to the next town. So that'll be fun!"

Risky made a sound like a hiss and a cough, clearly showing they were singularly unamused. Curling up, they laid down near the fire.

Elsinore laughed to herself and drew out the amulet she had promised to deliver to Thrú, wrapped in a linen pouch she carried alongside her traveler's bag and sheathed sword, Moonstar. When she unwrapped the locket, the clear blue gem glittered in the campfire as it danced in the faint night breeze. The amulet seemed like such a simple thing, but it was already putting her in quite a lot of trouble.

Elsinore startled as she realized someone else had approached the campfire, just visible in the dim light. Jumping to her feet, the young woman drew her sword with her free hand. Risky, too, leaped up and arched their back, letting out a threatening hiss.

It was only a girl.

She startled as well and drew back from the sorceress's and familiar's defensiveness, but she didn't run. She looked younger than Elsinore, tired and neglected, dirty, with torn clothes rumpled and ragged, and greasy, unwashed black hair. Her eyes were wide and fearful, looming over dark circles.

She looked, more than anything else, hungry.

"I'm so sorry, sister." Sheathing Moonstar, Elsinore held her hand out in welcome. "Do you need food? Please, sit by the fire and warm yourself. I won't harm you."

The girl looked into Elsinore's eyes, then quickly sat by the fire and began warming her hands. She moved sharply and suddenly, unconcerned with how she appeared. In a moment, Risky padded to her and curled up in her lap, and the girl scratched behind their ears as the cat purred.

"My name is Elsinore. I'm a servant of the Goddess. This is my companion, Risky. Do you have a name, sister? What are you doing out on the road at night?"

"I'm Rajel," the girl said sharply, hardly waiting for Elsinore to finish speaking. "I heard you talking to Geru, and I'm coming with you."

Elsinore's eyes darkened. "If you heard us talking, then you know it's very dangerous to travel with me now."

"I don't know anything about that. I just know you're going to Thrú, and I need to get there, and since no one from Daban travels to Thrú, you will take me with you."

"That's rather presumptuous, isn't it?"

"It isn't a presumption," Rajel said matter-of-factly. "I know it already."

"That's a presumption," Elsinore said, growing irritated. "And a mistaken one. I'm going to have to take you back to Daban. I can't have you tagging along. Have you got any parents back in town?"

"What makes you think I would have any parents?"

"You're a child," Elsinore said, growing more annoyed. She began packing her supplies back into her bag.

"I'm not a child!" the girl protested. "I'm almost seventeen!"

Elsinore glared humorlessly at the pouting girl. "That is a child."

"Anyway, I don't have any parents. They died a very long time ago. I was abandoned and left at the temple for the priestesses to look after."

"If they're to look after you, then they'll be searching for you." Elsinore sighed. "I'm taking you home before we waste any more time."

"They won't be. They know where I am," Rajel said quickly. "And that place isn't my home. I'm not even from Daban. Not really."

"And where are you really from?" Even as she asked, Elsinore felt a sinking sensation in her stomach. She suspected she already knew the answer.

"I'm from Thrú."

Elsinore sighed, her will to argue spent.

"What about you?" Rajel asked.

"What about me? I'm not from Thrú."

"I know that," Rajel said defensively. "I only meant, where are you from? Why are you on the road, anyway? Why not settle down somewhere?"

"I was away for a very long time, and my home changed. Now I suppose I'm trying to figure out where I belong."

"Are you looking for people like you?"

Elsinore sighed and closed her eyes. "Now and again,

yes. But there are people like me—Gallae—all around, and I don't really have to look hard to find them."

"Gallae?" Rajel asked. "Is that what you call it when you're a woman who looks like she has a dick hiding between her legs?"

Elsinore winced. "In a crude manner of speaking. Some of us have that problem resolved." Elsinore stopped speaking. She didn't want to have this discussion.

"Did you cut it off?" Rajel asked, wide-eyed.

"Rude," Elsinore snapped. "That's none of your business."

"I'm sorry," Rajel said. "I never knew people like you. There weren't any where I come from." She seemed suddenly sad and regretful. Perhaps she felt sorry for prying.

Elsinore's mood softened. "There probably were. Like I said, there are people like me wherever there are people at all. It's just in some places, we're harder to find than in others."

Rajel grew quiet, apparently done questioning Elsinore for the night. Before long, the girl was curled up by the fire, sleeping with Elsinore's blanket and Risky nuzzling beside her. With her bedclothes and cat occupied, Elsinore sat up for a while longer, alternately contemplating the fire and the blue-white gem of the amulet. She turned at last to Rajel, who slept silently next to a loudly purring Risky.

Watching Rajel sleep, Elsinore felt uneasy. It wasn't that she didn't trust this girl; rather, she felt there was something she couldn't see. Deciding she needed guidance, she drew from her bag a pouch containing a set of crystal dice etched with sigils drawn from the stars. Elsinore used the dice for telling fortunes in exchange for alms from those she met in her travels. Now, she decided to ask about the girl. Was it safe for her to accompany Elsinore on this path? Would she come to harm from the necromancer? Was it safe, indeed, for Elsinore to accept the company of this stranger, innocent though she appeared?

The witch grew more and more frustrated with each cast of the dice, until finally she dozed off late in the night, sitting up against a tree trunk. Try as she might, she could find no alternate reading; the answer she read in each cast focused directly and certainly on the one goal of Elsinore's mission:

The locket.

When morning came, Elsinore woke to find the fire had died out and the girl was nowhere to be seen. She scrambled to check her bag, rifling through till she found the linen wrapper. At last, she sighed with relief. The locket was where she had packed it away last night, safely hidden with her dice, spellbook, and potions, so the girl hadn't made off with it in the night.

What that meant, unfortunately, was that Rajel could be lost, alone, or in trouble. Elsinore packed her bag and grabbed her sword, and with Risky beside her, she set about searching the surrounding fields and woods. When she found no sign that a person had come through there, she backtracked till she came to a high point that let her see for several miles—not as far as Daban but far enough.

There was still no sign of Rajel.

If the girl had made haste, she possibly could have made it back to Daban before Elsinore woke and noticed she was gone. Deciding this was the most likely case, the witch turned back toward Thrú. She had wasted enough of the morning when she needed to find her way to Thrú as soon as possible. Rajel had evidently done well enough on her own to find Elsinore; most probably, she had come to her senses and found her way back home in the same way.

Unfortunately, the time Elsinore had wasted meant she had little chance of making it much farther than the next town before Thrú by nightfall. More importantly, sharing her food with Rajel—though the right thing to do—meant she had no more provisions and needed to restock.

This was a smaller settlement than Daban, hardly more than a little village, but people still gathered in the square to watch the lovely wanderer dance. Her eyes cast looks of mystery and longing that always seemed to set the hearts of the men and women racing as she tapped out a primal beat on her tympanum and cast twinkling magic lights with her witchcraft to brighten the dark evening. Delighted by the show, the people provisioned her well with food and lodging for the night, better than the campsite she'd found the night before.

After her dance, Elsinore gathered her belongings and made for her room at the little inn. She was only a little surprised by the voice that stopped her as she neared the door.

"So this is how you live? Dancing for coppers to buy moldy scraps of bread?"

Elsinore sighed, a habit she was beginning to grow tired of, and turned to face Rajel.

"There aren't a lot of other options on the road. I have other methods of making my way, but having you around—and I knew, deep down, that you'd be back—is kind of making that difficult for me, so it'll have to wait."

"What are you talking about?" Rajel gave Elsinore a sly look. "Are you a prostitute?"

"I'm a lot of things, and I have a lot of talents," Elsinore said deliberately, not denying anything. "For your information, I was talking about fortune-telling. But I think the aura from what I'm carrying may be interfering with my ability to read fates. I tried asking the dice about you last night, and they couldn't tell me anything at all. Where did you disappear to, anyway?"

"What are you so worried about?" Rajel asked. "I was following you. Maybe you didn't notice, but that isn't my fault. I don't think you're very observant."

"You're extremely irritating; do you know that?" Elsinore said through gritted teeth. "And anyway, on the topic of food, I had more rations, but when you tagged along last night, I gave them to you."

"Oh, I left those behind at the campsite for animals to eat," Rajel said. "I wasn't hungry, and I don't eat much."

Elsinore stared at Rajel, keeping her face perfectly expressionless as she tried not to lose her temper. She stuttered slightly, before giving up the battle entirely.

"You wasted . . ." She huffed and shook her head. "Goddess all around us! Next time, tell me that so I can take them with me!" Turning sharply, she kicked open the door to the inn, though she immediately thought better of her outburst as the innkeeper looked up at her in gruff surprise before returning to her work. Catching the door before it could slam shut, Elsinore held it open as she turned back to Rajel. "Well? Are you coming? We need to get some sleep before we set off for Thrú in the morning"

The innkeeper shot them a baffled look as Risky trailed behind Rajel, who sullenly followed the witch to the room at the end of the hall.

"I am sorry I'll be making you sleep on the ground a second night," Rajel said as they came to a stop, in a tone almost like real remorse.

Smiling at the girl, Elsinore opened the door. Two beds, neither very large, sat on either side of the little room. "I had a feeling you'd turn up."

Risky jumped up on one of the beds and curled up on the pillow. Joining her familiar, Elsinore scratched behind their ear and took off her boots.

Rajel took the other bed. As she lay down, Risky lifted their head, then jumped up, padded silently across the room, and curled up in the girl's lap. Rajel smirked.

Elsinore's jaw dropped in mock admonishment. "Traitor," she muttered with a little laugh.

Once the girl had turned over in bed, Elsinore reached into her bag. She drew out the linen and unwrapped it, revealing the reliquary. The clear stone sparkled in the candlelight, and the witch almost thought she could see through its clouded blue surface to the relic within.

"What is that?" Rajel asked, breaking Elsinore's reverie.

Elsinore hurriedly rewrapped the reliquary in the linen and put it beneath her pillow. "It's a locket."

"It's pretty. Does it contain a picture of your lover?"

Elsinore stared at the girl humorlessly. "It contains the severed toe of a lich," she said flatly, "so no, it does not contain a picture of my lover. That would have been nice, though. I would rather it had a picture of her instead. Thank you for the thought."

Rajel was silent for a moment.

"What's a lich?" she finally asked.

Elsinore inwardly groaned.

"It's an undead necromancer. An evil sorcerer. In life, its lofty goals exceeded the reach of its natural body, so it used sorcery and meditation to sequester all its human urges, wishes, hopes, fears—its own self—into one part of its body, which it then removed, freeing itself from the grip of death but also from all that made it human."

"The toe?" Rajel asked quietly.

"The toe," Elsinore agreed. "The lich can't be stopped until the relic is destroyed. And this reliquary can only be destroyed at the place it was made. In Thrú."

Lying back in bed, Elsinore stared at the ceiling, until she realized the girl was staring at her intently. Turning to look, Elsinore saw Rajel's eyes welling with tears.

"And you'll help me get there?" the girl asked. "To Thrú?"

Elsinore felt a sudden surge of sympathy. The girl looked as lost as she had when she appeared at the campfire. "Of course, sister," Elsinore said gently. "I'll do whatever it takes to keep you safe. You have my word." Then she doused the candles to sleep for the night.

When Elsinore woke in the morning, Rajel was gone again. This time, she was less afraid for the girl's safety, but she was still surprised. Rajel had seemed so eager for Elsinore's help; she'd probably just gone off to wash or eat.

Elsinore gathered her bag and sword. With Risky trailing behind her, she went to the innkeeper, who was cleaning the taberna from the night before.

"Excuse me. I'm sorry for striking your door last night." Elsinore bowed apologetically; she really was sorry she had lost her temper and kicked the door. "But can you please tell me—the girl I came in with then? Have you seen her this morning?"

"Girl?" The innkeeper furrowed her brow in surprise and confusion. "What girl? You mean other than yourself?"

"Yes." Elsinore sighed, suddenly annoyed. "Last

night, when I kicked open the door and started yelling at the girl I was with as she followed me in? I know you saw; you watched the whole thing."

"Miss," the innkeeper said, "I thought you were yelling at me at first. Then I thought you were mad and yelling at no one, until your cat followed you in and I took you for the kind of eccentric girl who talks to her animals. I didn't see any other girl last night besides you. I even wondered why you'd gotten a room with two beds—no one in there but your cat and yourself—but I'm not nosy."

Elsinore stared at the woman, unable to move, for a long moment.

"She was—" The young woman fumbled for words. "About my height? Dark hair?"

The innkeeper shook her head. "No one."

Elsinore nodded slowly. "Well, thank you for your hospitality! I must be going now! Come along, Risky!"

They took the smaller side road out of town. They walked all morning, crossing a significant distance. By early afternoon, they had come to a cliff, from which they looked down into a maze of complicated footpaths, cliff-side reaches, and hills that led to the hidden town of Thrú.

At no point along the road were they met by Rajel.

"You thought she was real, didn't you, Risky?" Elsinore asked defensively. The cat meowed brusquely without looking at her.

"Right? See, I don't know what that innkeeper was talking about. She must have been confused, or it was dark or something."

Elsinore had no time to finish speculating. The whistle of an arrow flying past her head broke her out of her thoughts, and it *thocked* sharply into the tree beside her. More arrows came at her, and she danced out of the way of each, her acrobatic skill making her more than capable of dodging their sting.

From over the rise of a hill behind her, the skeletons marched—soldiers of death, their eyes hollow and empty, their grins meaningless, their scant armor protecting only brittle bone animated by their master's fearsome will. Twenty or so approached; they put away their bows and drew their swords, cornering Elsinore at the cliff's edge.

She had nowhere to run.

Drawing Moonstar, the sorceress snapped her finger, and a green fireball appeared above her hand. As a habit, she waited for fear to give her opponents pause, before realizing the skeletal soldiers knew no reason to fear. Hurling the fireball into a pile of branches and grass before them, she started a blaze that burst suddenly, shattering one of her undead foes.

The others, however, were undeterred. They marched over the pieces of their fallen comrade and through the smoldering fire, directly toward Elsinore.

Just then, Aurvandol's litter crested the hill, and the lich showed himself, his golden mask shining in the afternoon sun. He raised his jeweled skeletal hands, and his army halted, swords and pikes trained on Elsinore. From behind the mask, Aurvandol spoke, his voice deep as a crypt, ancient and sepulchral.

"You have what is mine, eunuch. Return it to me willingly, and I shall merely allow you to die." The lich's voice filled Elsinore with such revulsion that her vision swam. She doubled over, nearly sick.

"And if I don't?" she coughed.

The lich rose in his seat and lifted his arms. Standing, Elsinore countered by raising Moonstar. The silver blade flashed white in the sun, and the lich halted. He remained still, but something intangible glowed deep in the hollow sockets of his mask.

As Aurvandol and his army waited, Elsinore sprang into action. She sheathed her sword, turned, and, as the lich cried out in dismay, she leaped off the edge of the cliff, into the trees covering the path to Thrú far below.

A few skeletons stupidly followed and were dashed to pieces, shattering on the branches and the side of the cliff. Elsinore performed a spell she had bent to this purpose before: Float, a minor cantrip mostly useful for lifting cups or curtains or juggling knives and jewels in her dances. It could in no way make her fly, but it could slow her fall enough to keep her from meeting the grievous demise of the unfortunate walking corpses that dove after her.

She fell swiftly but steadily and finally tumbled to the ground beneath the cover of trees on a wide, flat patch of grass near the end of the path down the cliffside. Rolling onto her back, she looked up the cliff. It would take hours to navigate the steep, twisting path down the cliff—particularly while carried on a litter—unless one plummeted as Elsinore had. The fate of the lich's soldiers made her doubt Aurvandol would follow her that way, and that at least bought her some time.

"Maow," Risky cried, pawing with irritation at Elsinore's face.

"Oh, I figured you'd find your way down here," Elsinore said. "You weren't much help in the fight, after all." Sitting up, she gathered her bag and sword, which had slipped off as she tumbled. As she did, though, she realized something had fallen from her bag. Her heart skipped a beat.

A few feet ahead, the locket lay on the ground, no longer wrapped in the linen pouch. The gem faced up, glittering in a sunbeam that fell through the branches, gloriously beautiful despite the awful relic it held. Just beyond it, looking down at Elsinore, stood Rajel.

Watching the girl curiously, Elsinore stood. "You went off ahead on your own again."

"No," Rajel said. "I was with you the whole time. You said you'd keep me safe."

Arching her eyebrows, Elsinore stepped slowly closer to her companion. "Even when I jumped off the cliff?"

"I . . . I must have been," Rajel said, sounding uncertain. "I think I fell a little further from the cliff than you, though?" The girl was starting to look confused and worried.

Elsinore held out her hands in a gesture of calm. "Please don't be afraid," the sorceress said. "I'm going to cast a spell; it's a healing spell and a spell of revelation that can disperse glamours and illusions. It can't hurt anyone. Will you let me?"

Rajel stared at Elsinore with fear in her eyes, but she nodded quickly.

Kneeling, Elsinore laid her hand on the amulet and spoke a word of power. The amulet flashed blue, as the walls of the temple had when she cast her spell of protection. But this light lingered. While the amulet faded to normal, light still shone through the crystal window, revealing that the toe glowed blue.

So, too, did Rajel.

As Elsinore picked up the locket, the light faded away from both relic and girl. Wrapping the reliquary in the linen, she stowed it away, then gently took Rajel's hand, her eyes soft.

"You are Aurvandol?" Elsinore asked quietly, without

accusation. She spoke in the same tone she would have used to ask if the girl were all right.

"No," Rajel said sadly. "He is me."

"Will you tell me what happened?" Elsinore asked.

"I'll show you," Rajel said. "I'll show you the way to Thrú."

Elsinore followed Rajel along the path through the trees. After a little time, they came to a wall, decades abandoned—overrun with vines and moss and, in places, half-buried in mud. Rajel led her to the gate, long fallen, leaving only a great broken opening in the wall of the town. Elsinore hesitated, then followed Rajel over the threshold of the abandoned city that lay beyond. Birds and animals scattered at their passing, too quick and hidden for Elsinore to identify. Risky kept close, their posture tense, but Rajel moved on, her destination clearly known to her.

She brought them at last to a structure of stone blocks built high and wide into the side of a cliff on the far side of town. The portal was dark and uninviting, but Rajel walked inside without hesitating. Elsinore conjured a fireball, which hovered over her palm, casting an eerie green light that allowed her to see into the structure. Wary of what they might find, she followed Rajel inside.

"Is this the temple?" Elsinore asked. "Is this . . . is this where the relic was made?"

"I think so," Rajel said. "There's something I'm not sure of. Something I can't quite remember. Something I've forgotten, from when I was very young . . ."

Her eyes flashed with fear in the dim light of Elsinore's spell as she stared in horror beyond the sorceress, and Elsinore turned. In the doorway, lit half by the setting sun and half by the witch light, was Aurvandol. The lich no longer rode on his litter but floated freely in the air before his prey, a hateful darkness spreading out from the eyes of his mask.

The wizard raised his hands palm up and brought them together in front of his face. The scraping of heavy stone echoed loudly in the wide temple space. Along the walls, huge stone lids slid off four coffins and fell to the ground with a crash, and skeletons rose from within, each raising a long, curved sword like a sickle. A distant red glow burned in the sockets of their skulls. Ignoring Rajel, who hid in the darkness at the far end of the temple, the skeletons set upon Elsinore, their blades whistling through the air as they flew.

Drawing Moonstar, Elsinore met the first skeletal champion's sword with a resounding clash. Her blade slid along the curve until it found the arm of the skeleton, severing it at the elbow. It was then quick work to behead it, and with a swift motion, she caught the skull and hurled it at the next onrushing opponent, breaking a rib and stunning it, halting its undead pursuit. This bought her enough time to slash it across the ribs, scattering it to pieces.

Two opponents remained.

Flanking Elsinore, they moved in, sickle swords before them. But the young woman was a dancer before she was a sorceress, and at the final swing of their blades, she backflipped away, and the two curved swords hooked together and flew from their wielders' hands. Bouncing to her feet with a handspring, Elsinore struck; with a quick slash and backswing, she took off the heads of the final two walking corpses. As the skulls rolled to the ground, the dull red light in their eye sockets faded to nothing.

Elsinore turned immediately to Aurvandol, but the lich had prepared his terrible magic for this moment. With a gesture, the sorcerer beckoned, and Elsinore was drawn forward irresistibly, floating across the floor and rising to meet the lich's eyes, hidden in the darkness of his stern golden mask. Elsinore struggled not to gag at the stench of decay that filled the air around the undead wizard.

"Hey, bony," Elsinore gasped defiantly. "You should have removed something else instead of your toe. Like two dangly things, actually! They're easy to grab and cut off! Then again, they've probably rotted off your skeletal ass by now anyway."

"The same things you've removed, no doubt, degenerate!" the lich rasped. The deep echo of his voice no longer frightened or sickened Elsinore. Instead, it felt somehow sad.

"Degenerate?" she scoffed. "Bitch, one of us is an animated skeleton, and it ain't me!"

"But you were *there*, weren't you?" the lich said. "The ritual of your ancient kin, the Gallae. You died and returned, crawled on your belly through the hidden crack into Hell and came back here, to the world of growing things. I can feel its fae magic in your aura and smell its fumes suffusing your body. The scent of death is all around you, stronger even than on me!"

While the lich pontificated, Elsinore readied herself to strike. With a tremendous force of will, she broke free of the lich's holding spell and swung Moonstar in an arc above, down into the lich's face mask. The soft gold of the helmet gave way to the sharp steel of the blade, and she cleaved the mask in two.

Elsinore withdrew the sword quickly as she tumbled to the ground, and the lich clutched his wounded head, wailing as the mask fell to the stone floor below. The golden solar halo behind his mask broke free, clattering to the ground with a noise like a cymbal.

The face underneath was almost unrecognizable as human, a corpse's face more terrible than those of his skeleton soldiers. The flesh remained taut on his skull, but rotted and dried, his eyes sunken lights in the dark empty flesh of his sockets. His lips were drawn back permanently from his sharp, rotten teeth, and the cartilage of his nose and ears had long rotted away. His gray hair hung in strands, like moss or webs from an ancient ruin, and was crawling with spiders.

The gash from Elsinore's sword was bloodless and practically billowed with dust, but the immortal necromancer was unstoppable. The wound closed up immediately with dark magic, and he rose to stand, hobbling on his self-crippled foot toward the girl before him.

"All you can smell is that I smoke weed, you noseless creep!" With a snap of her fingers, Elsinore cast a fireball at the desiccated walking corpse. He burst into flames but remained unharmed, his pursuit unhindered.

Elsinore turned and flew across the temple to Rajel and Risky, sheathing Moonstar and drawing out the reliquary in its linen pouch. "If you know where to do this, now's the time to tell me," she said quickly.

Rajel was looking around the temple, seemingly deep in thought. It didn't appear that she had paid attention at all to Elsinore's fight with the lich. Instead, something seemed wrong; she closed her eyes, as if drifting back into her memory, and her mouth moved slowly, silently, as if recalling words from long ago.

Suddenly, without a word to Elsinore, Rajel dashed out of the temple, away from her friend and past the slow pursuit of the implacable lich, whose hate was focused on the sorceress. Risky followed with the swift reflexes of a cat, and Elsinore, baffled and afraid, ran after them. Without the help of his servants or magic, the lich was hobbled by his crippled foot, but he would be unstoppable till the relic was dealt with. He would pursue, and Elsinore needed to finish the fight now.

She followed Rajel through the empty roads of the ancient city, down an alley hidden behind the branches of a pair of old trees. Following her through the darkness, she lost sight of her—till she noticed Risky slinking into a side door she almost couldn't see for the moss that surrounded it.

It was a little apartment, an abandoned dwelling, with a few rooms set around an entrance hall. In an inner room—the thalamus—Elsinore found her. An old stone tub was built into the wall, along with a sink and a toilet. Curled up in the tub, hugging her legs to her chest, was Rajel.

"This is really where it started," Rajel said, looking at nothing in particular except the images in her own memory. "I used to come here and cry. I used to wish I could take all of it—all my self-hate, all my discomfort with my body and what was happening to it as I grew up, all my fear—and put it . . . down there. I used to wish I could do that and then just . . . cut it off, and I'd be free and happy.

"But instead, I . . . grew up and became a man—became . . . him. And he buried himself in his studies to try to forget. He eventually fell under the influence of the cult of the sun god, Rudash, who claimed they could 'heal' him, that they could erase the wish—the need—to be me. He converted to the sun cult, and they taught him rituals to seal away part of himself in exchange for magic powers from god the sun. It wasn't the same. It wasn't what I had wanted. But he thought it would help him . . . forget. Forget me. Keep me from holding him back.

"So he isolated all his wishes, all his dreams, his gentleness and hope and the part of himself that was beautiful. He put it all in his toe, and he cut it off—cut me off—and all that was left was his lust and his power and his magic, and I was abandoned."

Rajel was crying, her cheeks wet, and her eyes were sore and red with tears as she turned to look at Elsinore. Elsinore sat on the edge of the tub beside her and put her arms around the girl, letting her cry. She sobbed into Elsinore's sleeve as the older girl held her. As Elsinore thought of the monstrous unfairness of the world.

"I wish more than anything," Rajel said at last, with a final sniffle, "I wish I'd had a big sister like you, who could have told me everything would be okay. Who could show me that it's okay to be like I am." Pulling back from Elsinore, she wiped her tears with her hand.

It was a moment too late before Elsinore realized Rajel had taken the locket.

"I'm sorry it had to be this way. But this is where it began—where I was born—and this is where I'll die."

Lifting the locket above her head before Elsinore could stop her, Rajel smashed it on the edge of the tub. The frame bent and broke, the crystal shattered, and the toe, so ancient and rotten and sad, crumbled away into dust.

Rajel vanished, leaving a hollow space in the air in her wake and the ruins of the amulet in the tub. Elsinore bowed her head in anguish as tears welled behind her eyes.

She could take no more—no more loss, no more mourning, no more death. Everywhere she went was surrounded by death; though she herself had escaped the hidden halls of the underworld beneath the Mountain, death itself was inescapable. It followed her everywhere, followed everyone she met, and she nearly lost herself in despair as she wept.

At last, Risky pawed at Elsinore's foot and meowed plaintively, before dashing off suddenly, out of the room and toward the alley.

"Wait!" Elsinore called as she followed them—only to find the cat stopped in a shadow at the door of the dwelling.

In the doorway to the alley, backlit by the risen moon, stood a young woman. She wore Aurvandol's golden robes, but they were ill-fitting—too loose. The way they hung made her look more childish than she would have otherwise. Her dark hair was clean and curly, and her eyes, though tired, smiled as wide as her mouth.

It was Rajel. She looked different, very slightly. No longer a neglected ghost, an ideal thrown away and forgotten, she now looked real, substantial. Her face showed tinges of the boyish puberty she dreaded, but she looked, for all those imperfections, alive and happy and whole.

A smile split Elsinore's face. "How . . . ?"

"I don't know," Rajel said. "I thought I was going to die. But I think, instead . . . I think he's gone. Aurvandol. The man I grew up into, the undead creature that took my place and lived in immortal misery. I'm back. Like I was before I gave up. Before I lost hope. I can't even remember what it was like being him. It's like it was a terrible dream."

Rajel rushed forward and embraced Elsinore and cried as she buried her face in the older girl's shoulder.

"Elsinore, you brought me back here, despite everything Aurvandol did to try to stop you. You showed me what it's like. You reminded me who I really am. Thank you. I can never repay you for this."

The two girls held each other in the moonlight for a long time, giving thanks.

"So, there's a few things you're going to want to do," Elsinore said as they made the slow ascent out of the valley of Thrú, back to civilization. Rajel had washed in the river, eaten some rations, and put on a gray dress Elsinore had carried in her bag that suited her better than torn rags or the sorcerer's golden robes.

"I'm a potion maker—I learned the craft from my mother—and there are estrogen potions I can brew for you," Elsinore said, talking excitedly. "I take them as well. They halt the testosterone your body produces and feminize you. You're young, so the potions will work well, but I've seen so many women who started far older—forty, fifty—who I couldn't tell from any other woman if I had to. And that's not even really important; what's important is how it makes you feel inside—"

"Sister Elsinore, I already feel gladder than I think I ever have. How far is this temple you're taking me to? Where women like us serve the Goddess?"

"Quite a long way from here, actually," Elsinore said. "But if we can make it to the great river, it might be easier going. There are Gallae, priestesses like me, but also Pilli, men who are like we are, who've had to find their way into masculinity as we did to womanhood. You can learn a lot from them too. They will be like the sisters and brothers you always needed."

Rajel smiled in the morning sun.

"Then I'll be fine. I'm glad I was able to start my family with a sister like you."

The Tillers of the Earth

The air was warm and clear, and the sun shone bright in a sky of deep blue, the only clouds thin white wisps on the horizon. The grass was dry and free of dew in the afternoon sun, and the scent of hyacinths drifted all around near the brook, a small shallow flow of water that emerged from a nearby spring and fed into the Great River Gallas.

While hyacinth was the strongest scent, other flowers and herbs also grew in abundance: Along the banks of the stream grew narcissus, and asphodel besides. In fields nearby grew tall herbs like fennel, with yellow flowers bright in the sun and seeds shaped like hearts, the name of which no one seemed to know. White-and-silver flowers grew too, with eight petals in the shape of a star and blue-green stems and leaves—the nissa flower, the priestess's favorite since childhood.

A grove of willows dangled their branches in the still air over the stream. In a patch of grass among the roots of one tree, the priestess sat in the shade, where the air felt cool coming off the stream. Her legs were crossed, and her hands rested on her knees, a neglected string of prayer beads wrapped around her wrist. Though her eyes were closed, she did not meditate. She instead let her thoughts and memories run free in the dark behind her eyes, for the warm air of spring and the scent of the season's flowers carried mourning and regret that she knew not how to tame.

The Season of Light bloomed all around, clearing away the clouds and mist of the rainy Season of Shadows, and soon enough, the sun would burn hot and strong and the earth would lay fallow. But now, at the threshold between seasons, the flowers bloomed, though so did the sense of foreboding in the priestess's mind.

She hated the heat and the summer and the sun.

The priestess, Elsinore of the village Nin, snapped her eyes open at last, dismissed the thoughts still clouding her mind, and stood. Brushing grass and dry dirt from her legs and short purple dress, she walked barefoot down the bank to the stream, where the smooth river rocks felt cool beneath her feet. The tall sandal boots she usually wore lay by the tree, along with her bag, her sheathed traveler's sword, and her hooded jacket. Her messy hair fell across her bare shoulders and the straps of her dress. Kneeling, she cupped her hands to drink from the clear water, then splashed her face to wash away her reverie.

Bent over the stream, Elsinore propped herself up with her hands in the water and gazed at her reflection. Gray eyes gazed back. Her hair hung over her shoulder, dipping into the water, and was dyed the teal blue of the distant mountain pines and shaved close around her ear on the left side as marks of her priesthood.

Or it had been at one time. She kept her hair dyed because she liked the color, and she kept the side shaved out of habit. But it had been a long time since anyone Elsinore encountered in her travels had recognized her as a priestess of the Goddess because of her hair. She was beginning to doubt there were many in the world who still could.

Once, Elsinore had processed from the temple of the Goddess in Sanisa and had stood with her temple siblings before the high burial mound on a rise of land above the banks of the Great River Gallas. Together, they had wailed in ritual mourning at the recitation of the story of the deity Galattis, who descends into the darkness below the earth at the turn of the seasons. And Elsinore had wailed, too, and wept in true mourning at the death of her lover—poor gentle Folia, a woman like Elsinore, who had endured such deep sadness in her short life and who had died so young.

That had been long ago—a year of Elsinore's time but decades, nearly a lifetime, in the natural world. For like Galattis, Elsinore had descended beneath the earth, to the heart of the Mountain that was Faerie, through the gate of the Ploutonion, seeking solace from the hidden nameless mourning that had stalked her for her whole life and had only grown deeper since Folia's death.

But she had found Folia again, radiantly beautiful in the court of the Goddess, the Queen of the Great Earth, in Her palace beneath the Mountain. And Folia had returned to the world, in some secret manner Elsinore did not know. Elsinore had followed, but separately, and she had not seen her lost lover since. She had some idea where to go, what to do, but . . .

Though she once had so great a need to seek the door to the Mountain, now she felt little urge to seek anything at all.

Elsinore had wandered the Great River Valley since

returning, performing her seductive dance in towns she encountered along her way. Now she found herself nearer the Gallas than she had been since her time at the temple.

Since the spring equinox—the Day of Blood—which once again came ever closer with the turn of the year, like the ebb and flow of the tide.

Elsinore found herself lost in thought and regret once more, gazing beyond the face of her reflection in the water to the stones of the riverbed, to the mound, to the Mountain . . .

To Folia.

Laughter and music rang out from nearby, from outside the willow grove in the field farther upstream, filling the air with the sounds of strings, drums, and flutes. Splashing the water with her hand, Elsinore dispelled her reverie, scattering her thoughts like the droplets of her reflection.

So much for quietly meditating on my own misery.

Something touched the back of Elsinore's shoulder as she stood, and she screamed shrilly, falling from the bank. Sitting sodden and embarrassed with her rear half-sunk in the shallow stream, she stared at the spot where she'd previously knelt.

On the bank stood a woman all in black. A loose black veil covered her long dark hair, and a tiered black dress left her arms bare beneath a mantle clasped at the shoulder with a pin bearing a lazuli gem. Her eyes were deeply shadowed with black like kohl, and her lips were painted the same color.

At first, her face was blank, but after a moment, her black lips broke into a cheerful grin.

"I didn't mean to startle you. Only, I don't like to speak if I don't have to. Will you join us, sister?" The young woman held her hand out to the priestess.

Elsinore took it and climbed out of the stream. Once she stood on the bank, her waterlogged dress weighed heavy against her skin, and she folded her arms indignantly. "You shouldn't sneak up on women in the wilderness like that. It . . ."

She faltered. Her first instinct had been to snap at her, but the woman's smile and soft expression quickly dispelled Elsinore's temper. She relaxed a little.

"But . . . it's all right. Join you where?"

"My friends are camped nearby, on the stream. My name is Juno, and we are priestesses of the Goddess."

Elsinore looked Juno up and down: her dress, her hair, a certain manner of her body that Elsinore recognized as familiar from those she knew at the temple. The stranger inclined her head quizzically.

"If you are a priestess," Elsinore said cautiously, "then we are sisters indeed." She thought a moment. "I am called Nisapa."

"Blue Leaf?" Juno asked. So she was at least familiar with the dialect of the city of the Goddess's temple. "Not an uncommon name among the Gallae, as I'm sure you know, but my sisters and I are hardly in a place to laugh about that. I knew a Nissa once, a senior priestess who taught me much."

Elsinore, too, had known a Nissa, a woman her own age, but that had been long ago, so she kept silent.

"Come with me, Sister Blue Leaf, dry yourself by our fire, and meet my companions."

Juno waited as Elsinore laced her boots, gathered her bag, donned her hood, and shouldered her sword, before leading her out of the trees and into the sunlight.

In a grassy field by the water outside the grove, a camp was set around a bonfire, newly lit and burning brightly, even as the afternoon wore down. Mules grazed nearby, and a covered cart with many bundles and bags stood by the side. In the camp, Juno's fellow priestesses danced and played music, delighting in the light, the air, and the heat of the fire. It was music in a style unlike any Elsinore had ever heard, unfamiliar but earthy and rhythmic.

There were four women: One, like Juno, wore black and drummed upon a large tympanum. Two wore white dresses with yellow scarves; one with bleached hair danced a little as she played a syrinx, and the other with curled brown hair sat on a log by the fire, playing a lute. The last wore a white dress with pink sashes, all decorated with flowers, including a crown of flowers woven from their stems.

This last woman danced around the fire gracefully and elegantly, her dress floating around her as if she were lifted by the heat of the flames and drifted along with the music. Her arms and legs moved as if she were a string puppet in the hands of a skilled puppeteer. She barely seemed to follow the drum; it was the strings and the flute that carried her.

Like the music, her dance was entirely unlike any Elsinore had ever seen. Her own dancing was focused on the fluid motion of her hips and belly, fingers delicately picking the air above her as she followed the beat of her own small tympanum and the glitter of lights cast by her fire spells. This woman's style was totally unfamiliar, as was the song her sisters played.

A strange feeling of loss shivered down Elsinore's spine.

Then she saw one other person, whom she hadn't noticed among the dancing and playing of the others. A girl sat in the grass by the fire, hiding her face with her curly dark hair but smiling and laughing, her hands alternately clapping along with the music and scratching the chin of a black cat who lay curled in her lap.

Rajel.

The music and dance stopped as Juno and Elsinore approached, and the woman in black with the drum leaped up, ran over to Juno, and threw her arms around her with a kiss. The dancer bowed to the others and to Rajel, who laughed and said something that Elsinore could not hear.

"So this is where you'd gone off to," Elsinore called to the girl sternly, though she half-smiled at her traveling companion of the past month.

The cat had been her companion and familiar for some while longer. But cats do as they please.

Rajel blushed a little and looked away. "Risky and I heard the wagon approach a little while ago. You seemed busy with your meditation, so I didn't want to disturb you. They found me and invited me to join them for dinner. Right, Risky?"

The cat did not respond, only rose and padded their way over to Elsinore's foot and licked her ankle.

"Anyway, I'm glad you're here! We were just about to eat!"

"Oh, Rajel, are you a priestess of the temple too?" Juno asked. "Your friend Nisapa was just beginning to tell me of her place in the temple . . ."

At the mention of the alias—which Elsinore had never mentioned to Rajel—the girl's brow furrowed. She glanced in confusion at Elsinore, who shot her a look that came just short of casting the evil eye.

"Right," Rajel said. "Yes, ah . . . Nisapa knows the temple in Sanisa well. I've never been there, though. El—Nisapa was taking me there. To show me."

"The paths laid by the Goddess meet in unexpected ways!" said the lute player. She was taller than Elsinore and more cheerful. "We make a return pilgrimage to Sanisa. Do you go there, as we do, for the Day of Blood?"

"Yes, of course," Elsinore said before Rajel could speak. "The season draws near. I can feel it in the air."

Elsinore smiled nervously, but if the cheerful woman noticed this manner, she gave no hint of it. Rajel raised an eyebrow in doubt, but Elsinore ignored her.

"Then please, make the journey with us, sister! My name is Lucia. Juno you've met."

The woman in black smiled and bowed her head to Elsinore, then took Rajel's hands and bowed to her as well.

"I'm Aemia," said the other woman wearing black. "Did you hear our song? Normally, I prefer to sing, but with Juno wandering around, someone needed to play her drum."

"Normally you wail and keen, you mean," said the dancer, casting the two women in black a snide glance. "Don't pay any attention to the funeral sisters. I'm who audiences come to see. I'm Fauna."

She took Elsinore's hand with a bow and kissed it. Elsinore admitted silently that Fauna was, indeed, very beautiful. Her long, golden hair was braided deftly with her flower crown, and her movements as she greeted Elsinore were as graceful as they had been during her dance. When the sneer cleared from Fauna's face, Elsinore couldn't help but notice a lively expression that made her resemble some unearthly beautiful fae creature.

"I thought her drumming was very lovely," Elsinore said, taking her hand back. Fauna huffed a little and went to the fire to tend to something brewing in a pot.

"I'm Sophia," said the woman with bleached hair, who

had played the syrinx. Lowering her voice, she added, "Fauna clashes with Juno often—and with Aemia, since she and Juno are lovers. It's tedious, but it's best to give them their space."

Elsinore nodded knowingly and spoke to clear the tension. "So . . . you were all sisters at the temple, then? And you travel together?"

"We are Gallae, as I gather you and Rajel are, Sister Blue Leaf," Aemia replied. "We travel the valley as metragyrtes—alms-gatherers for the Great Mother. We survive on what we are given for our performances, and what we have in excess we bring back to Sanisa, to distribute to our temple siblings."

Rajel looked at Elsinore with a question visible on her face. "Uh . . . Nisapa?" she said hesitantly. "You said the temple stores and evenly distributes the resources of the city? Does it need more from begging throughout the valley?"

"The temple economy of Sanisa cares for the needs of all the people of the city," Elsinore said. "Alms from the other cities and villages can help us travel the Great River Valley, teach of the Goddess, help people in need, and supplement the stores of the temple. And the temple stores aren't just for Sanisa. If other communities fall on hard times, they can come to Sanisa for aid.

"Or at least, so it was in my time," Elsinore clarified hastily. "There was once a famine in the region where I was born, when I was very young, and aid from Sanisa kept the people from falling to ruin and despair."

Elsinore paused, looked off into the distance, and sighed deeply and sadly. "Though not before many people suffered."

"Where were you born? There hasn't been any

famine of that kind in the Great River Valley for generations." Lucia peered at Elsinore. "When were you at the temple? You can't be much older than me, from the look of your beauty. Between twenty and thirty autumns, I'd guess? And I first went to the temple in my earliest adolescence. I don't remember you there."

"Nor I," Sophia said. Juno and Aemia shrugged and shook their heads, while Fauna eyed Elsinore curiously.

Elsinore blushed, first at the compliment to her beauty, then at the awkward position she found herself in.

"You're right, in part," she said with some hesitation. "But I suppose I'm . . . older than I appear. We weren't at the temple at the same time, most likely."

"But you know the Mother Battakes?" Fauna asked.

Elsinore stared at her blankly, before shifting her gaze from woman to woman. Rajel grimaced at Elsinore doubtfully from behind the others' backs and shrugged in confusion. Not yet even a novice, she knew less of the temple than any of them.

"The what?" Elsinore finally blurted out.

The other Gallae stared back at Elsinore in bemusement. Lucia looked her up and down as if in an attempt to assess her age. "If you were a priestess at Sanisa, surely you studied under the Mother Battakes."

"She . . . must have been after my time," Elsinore replied, though she doubted she sounded very convincing.

"She's been there our whole lives," Fauna said, "or nearly so."

"How old are you?" Aemia asked.

Elsinore cringed. *How old am I, after all? Twenty-three autumns? Eighty?*

"I'm as old as my bones, I suppose," the sorceress muttered. Then she laughed disarmingly.

"I'm sorry. I'm very tired. Rajel and I have been traveling for days, and I'm afraid I'm not making much sense. If I could rest a little, I'm sure I would be a little more clear-headed later."

"I've no doubt." Smiling softly, Juno placed a gentle hand on Elsinore's shoulder. "Will you eat with us? We haven't got meat, but we've made a vegetable stew—beans and leeks, flower peppers and onions and turnips, and I forget what else. And we have good bread."

"I made vows as a priestess never to eat flesh, so nothing sounds more lovely than that," Elsinore said.

"So have we!" Juno said, and the others seemed to relax a little.

Rajel rolled her eyes; it had been ages since she'd eaten meat, traveling with Elsinore. But she ate with as much relish as the others, and they all grew friendlier over the meal, laughing and sharing stories of traveling the valley. Risky curled up in the middle of Elsinore's crossed legs and begged for nothing; the cat caught secret prey in the tall grass when needed, and Elsinore never asked questions. Cats do as they please—most of all a familiar like Risky.

Once they'd eaten, Lucia took up the lute again and began to strum, slow meditative notes drifting into the night over the open field. Aemia hummed along softly, Juno kept a beat by drumming on her lap and knees, and Fauna swayed as Ragel joined in, giggling at her own awkwardness. Elsinore only looked out over the trees and the stream.

As the deep notes of the strings resonated in the instrument's drum and echoed in the hollow, Elsinore's eyes were drawn higher still to the clear night sky. Using her bedroll as a pillow, she laid back, unable to see anything but the stars and the night in between.

When Lucia stopped playing, most of the others seemed to be asleep. Certainly, no one said anything, and there was no shuffling for bedrolls and blankets. The fire had long since gone out, and Elsinore looked around without rising. As Lucia settled on a blanket, everyone else was silent and still. Allowing herself to feel safe, at least for now, Elsinore drifted off at last with Risky curled beside her.

When Elsinore and the others woke in the morning, four of the company went out in groups of two to gather herbs from the woodlands upstream. Lucia remained to clean up camp, and Rajel sat with Elsinore as the former ate breakfast and the latter took her potion bottles from her bag.

"You okay?" Rajel asked when Elsinore sighed irritably. Reaching into her pocket, she pulled out a handful of something. "Here, would you like some of these?"

Rajel opened her hand to reveal a clump of crushed berries. Her skirt was stained with reddish juice around the pocket.

Elsinore eyed the berries warily. "How long . . . have those been in there?"

Rajel shrugged and popped one in her mouth.

The sorceress groaned and turned back to her potions. "No thank you."

"You've almost run out," Rajel said, looking at the rows of little empty bottles in the case.

"Well, I only carry enough for myself. Taking you along wasn't something I planned for. At this point, I'd normally detour to a town to make more, but I think we're near enough to Sanisa now that it shouldn't be a problem. Besides, something tells me that if things get desperate, some of our new friends could help."

"Hey, Lucia!" Rajel yelled. "Can we borrow some estrogen potions if we have to?"

Elsinore cringed. "Not like that, child," she muttered.

Lucia laughed. "Of course, little sister. The others have gone to gather bunches of the ingredients to take with us to Sanisa, in fact. I see Sophia returns with some now." Looking beyond Rajel and Elsinore, Lucia waved at the other Galla, who carried on her back a great bundle of the tall fennel-like herb with yellow flowers. She set the lot on a blanket by the cart.

Elsinore kept quiet and tried to keep her face from showing how puzzled she was. Rajel just strolled over and took one of the herbs and twirled the thick stalk in her hand playfully.

"I never used to see these before," she said. "Not until . . ." Elsinore saw her face grow dark and sad, but only for an instant. Perhaps not even Rajel herself noticed.

"Well, not until traveling with Nisapa. What is it?"

"It's the main ingredient of our potions." Lucia looked at Elsinore and then the empty bottles, which Elsinore quickly wrapped up in their case. "Have you never made it yourself?" she asked, likely noticing Elsinore's doubtful expression. "Do you get yours from the temples? I can show you how to use the seeds for potions. It's quite simple."

"I brew it myself," Elsinore replied sharply. "My mother taught me. She was a midwife and a healer. It's the same potion she used to induce menstruation and abortion."

"Yes, exactly. So you know these techniques, at least," Lucia replied defensively, holding one of the yellow flowers. "That's what silphium is used for."

Rajel frowned at Elsinore. "You said you use mare's urine."

Lucia stared at Rajel in astonishment, which turned to a look of utter confusion as she turned her head toward Elsinore.

"Mare's . . . Sister Blue Leaf, what on earth are you teaching this girl? Why . . . why are you still using that? The Mother Battakes discovered the use of silphium before I was born. Are you a hundred years old?"

Elsinore's face burned, and Rajel flustered apologetically.

"I never used to see it until a few months ago," Rajel said. "Silphium?"

"It's found all over the valley," Sophia said, slipping in from washing at the stream. "It grows everywhere in great abundance. How have you never seen it before?"

"We're . . . not really from around the Great River Valley?" Rajel cringed a little as she spoke.

Lucia glanced at Elsinore. "That would explain why your manner of dress is so odd."

"But I thought she said she was a priestess in Sanisa," Sophia interjected.

Elsinore flushed even deeper, unable to meet the other women's eyes. "Well . . . I . . ." She couldn't think of anything more to say.

"Sisters! Sisters, help!" came a cry from the woods nearby.

Juno. She sounded breathless and afraid.

At once, Elsinore's embarrassment fled, forgotten amid the sudden adrenaline raised by a cry for help. She didn't bother to don her jacket, only shouldered her bag and grabbed her sword, buckling the belt of the sheath as she ran toward Juno's voice. Rajel and the other two followed close behind her.

Juno met Elsinore at the tree line and fell to her knees to catch her breath. Kneeling beside her, Elsinore put a hand on her back for comfort.

"Aemia and Fauna," Juno gasped, eyes red with tears. "They went into the stepwell to gather the silphium from the bottom. I heard Fauna . . . heard her crying . . . desperate . . . screaming in fear for help . . . please . . ."

Taking Juno into her arms, Sophia helped her to her feet.

After leaning on Sophia for a moment to regain her composure, Juno rushed back into the woods. "This way!"

As the others followed, Juno did her best to explain.

"We passed a deep stepwell some ways from the stream as we entered this vale a few nights ago. We almost didn't see it; it was ancient, abandoned, and overgrown with silphium. I think Fauna nearly fell in. Aemia was fascinated and begged us to return. When they went to gather the herbs this morning, Aemia must have talked Fauna into exploring."

At last, they emerged from the trees into a wide field. Huge stalks of the yellow herbs obscured fallen stones—broken walls of masonry mulched by long ages of neglect. A recent opening in the growth of the herbs cleared a path within; Elsinore supposed that must be where the girls had gathered their supply. Juno led them through, and Elsinore was taken aback by the structure they found within.

Huge and ancient, a great wide pit sank deep into the earth, with narrow, steep stairs descending in levels all around it, like a reversed step pyramid. Intricate, ancient, ruined carvings decorated the whole structure, all obscured by masses of the green-and-yellow silphium growing in the cracks of the masonry. Many stories deep the steps fell—as deep as the height of many towers Elsinore had seen in Sanisa. At the bottom, there seemed to be a wide patch of yellow-green grass.

No, not grass. A mossy pool of water.

"What is this?" Rajel asked.

"In times of drought and famine, stepwells such as these were a way to find the water table and ease the community's suffering," Elsinore explained. "But I suppose this one hasn't been needed for quite some time," she concluded, a little wryly.

She turned to Juno. "I don't see them. You're sure they're down in the well?"

"They went there, I know," Juno replied. "I heard Fauna and Aemia arguing. Fauna didn't want to go, but Aemia prevailed upon her at last. I didn't pay much attention; we're always bickering with Fauna about something. But later, I went back to check on them. Seeing they'd cleared a way through the plants, I followed and heard Fauna's cry from deep within. I never saw them, though."

"Why didn't Aemia go with you?" Elsinore asked.

"W-what?" Juno stuttered.

"You and Aemia are lovers, and Fauna can't stand either of you. I've known you less than a day, and that much is clear. Why didn't you gather with Aemia and leave Fauna with Sophia?"

Juno flushed, and her eyes welled with tears again. "She's always mocking and teasing us!" she cried. "She hates us. Aemia and I—we thought we could scare her. I said I needed to talk to Sophia and that Aemia should go with Fauna, and Aemia doubled around to mislead her into going to the stepwell. We just wanted to scare her with the height and make her think it was haunted by means of some simple spells we learned at the temple. We didn't think anyone would get hurt. Please help them! I'm sorry. Just please make sure they're safe."

Descending into tears, Juno said no more.

"Everyone stay here," Elsinore said. "You too, Rajel. We can see the bottom from here. If I need help, I'll call for it."

"Surely you'll need help, Sister Blue Leaf," Lucia said. "We'll all climb down together."

"No, we won't."

Elsinore snapped the fingers of her left hand, and a ball of flame sparked to life and floated above her open palm, held in place by the magic of the spell. With her other hand, Elsinore drew her short sword, Moonstar, its white leaf-shaped blade sparkling in the morning sun. Before the others could say anything, Elsinore stepped to the edge of the great pit and leaped.

Elsinore allowed herself to fall freely for just long enough to feel a moment's thrill, the rapid fall trailing her colorful scarves and hair behind her. Then, speaking a word of command—the memory of which fled her mind the moment it was uttered—she cast another spell, slowing her descent. She drifted down quickly but safely, her skirt and scarves flowing around her in the quieting wind. Her feet came to rest on one of a pair of ornate ledges just above the pool at the bottom of the stepwell.

No, not a pair. Now that she was in the pit, it was clear this had once been a single ledge, now broken and divided in the middle. Between the two sections of the ledge, rubble surrounded a cave that sank deep into the earth. The water of the pool flowed into the cave as far as the light showed.

The water was green with an unbroken cover of algae; nothing had fallen in and disturbed the algae as far as Elsinore could tell. She sheathed her sword and jumped down from the ledge with a splash. It was not at all deep, only coming halfway up her shins, and there was nothing in the pool but ancient fallen stones. She could now see, however, that the cover of algae was broken between the ledges, leading into the cave.

Elsinore didn't look up at the other women waiting at the top of the well. She preferred to imagine the looks of horror and surprise on their faces, relishing the stifled little gasp one of them made as she jumped.

Maybe one of them had fainted.

Elsinore smirked.

In the light of her magic flame, Elsinore could see that the water dried up only a short way into the tunnel, explaining why it was so stagnant and green. It gave way to mud, then to dry earth. The whole tunnel was earthen and rough, not hewn by the masons who had built the magnificent old stepwell; it looked as if it had been somehow naturally bored through the bedrock. Nothing grew here; once the water ended, the whole place was dry, and there was no light save at the entrance and from the flame Elsinore had cast. The silphium stalks stopped growing at the edge of the cave, coming no further in than the pool. The place was dismal and uninviting.

But Aemia and Fauna must have come here if they were in the stepwell at all.

While Elsinore puzzled over the situation, something splashed in the water behind her.

Of course it was Rajel.

"Elsinore!" she called into the tunnel, very clearly out of breath from climbing. "I mean . . . Nisapa! Wait! I'm coming!"

Rajel found her friend standing still, tapping her foot impatiently and glaring at her.

"Why is it no one I tell to stay away ever actually listens?" Elsinore muttered as she proceeded further into the tunnel.

"Well," Rajel said, still catching her breath, "why is it you tell people to stay away from you?"

Elsinore stopped and turned back to glare at Rajel again.

"Oh." Regret filled Rajel's eyes. "Oh gods, Elsinore, I didn't . . ."

Elsinore sighed. "No, I'm sorry. I've been in a bad mood this morning."

"You've been in a bad mood since we met these women," Rajel said gently.

Elsinore stayed silent for a long moment, unsure what to say.

"They're annoying and dramatic and childish," she said at last.

"That doesn't mean anything," Rajel said. "You say the same thing about me."

"That's because you are annoying and dramatic and childish," Elsinore teased, and they both laughed.

"I just . . ." Elsinore trailed off in frustration. She couldn't order the stray thoughts in her head: Rajel, these new Gallae, the newly sprouted herbs, the season and the air and the light . . .

And . . .

"I don't know what I'm doing! Where I'm going. If

anything is right. I don't know what to do. I spent so long trying to find my way that I lost it, worse than ever before."

"You're worried there isn't a place for you now," Rajel concluded.

"Aren't you?"

"No." Rajel put a hand on Elsinore's back. "I feel like I have a second chance. You gave me a second chance, Elsie. And I know you have one too, even if you haven't realized it yet."

Closing her eyes for a moment, Elsinore fought to keep her focus. It wouldn't do to dwell on these doubts here when people needed her. She smiled softly at Rajel and resumed her push into the tunnel.

"Let's make sure these girls are all right and then head to Sanisa."

She had walked some ways before she realized Rajel hadn't followed. The younger girl stood still, watching Elsinore with a curious smile.

"Are you coming?" Elsinore asked.

Rajel grinned brightly. "You got it, sis."

As they walked, the tunnel curved, and the daylight from the well disappeared behind them. There were no carvings, as there had been in the well, no branching paths, no evidence of design of any kind.

After walking for some time, Elsinore halted. Rajel began to speak, but Elsinore held out her free hand to silence her and waited.

Very faintly, such that Elsinore could not at first tell if it was imaginary, a slow, quiet moan floated through the tunnel from ahead. Elsinore dismissed her fire spell, casting them into darkness once again, but as her eyes adjusted, she could make out a very dim blue light emanating from around the next curve of the earth.

"Do you remember how to cast the fire cantrip?" Elsinore asked quietly.

"It's the only spell you've been willing to teach me!" Rajel hissed. "It's all I've had to study for weeks; of course I know it."

Elsinore snapped her fingers again, casting the ball of fire above her palm, and Rajel did the same. Her fingers fumbled a little, less practiced than Elsinore's, but the ball of glowing flame appeared above her palm and stayed there, hovering. Elsinore noticed Rajel's eyes light up with excitement in the glow of the magic flame.

Even with the echo of the tunnel, the moan seemed low and muffled. The slightest sound—even footsteps upon the soft earth—obscured it. But Elsinore moved quickly now. Had the women been hurt climbing down the step-well? But if so, why had they gone so deep into this tunnel, into the dark?

When she cleared the next curve of the tunnel, Elsinore halted, and Rajel nearly collided with her.

By the wall of the tunnel hunched a glistening mass, glowing with faint blue light. At first, it seemed to shiver and pulsate, before it became clear: smaller masses, like pods, crawled across the surface of the larger mass, leaving trails of glistening slime in their wake.

This was the source of the muffled moaning.

Elsinore held out a palm, motioning for Rajel to keep back, then drew Moonstar. She inched closer to the mass until she saw the horrible truth.

It was Aemia—moaning, incapacitated.

The glowing, crawling masses were huge worms, each the size and shape of a cucumber, encasing Aemia in layers of ooze, through which the pleading moans from her closed mouth could be heard only faintly.

Elsinore knew Rajel had realized the same thing when the girl began to scream.

"Rajel," Elsinore said, keeping her voice even, though she struggled not to let it tremble. "I need you to be calm. I need you to hold your light as steady as you can. Can you do that for me?"

Rajel nodded sharply, holding her mouth tightly closed to stifle a horrified whimper. She held the magic flame out in her right hand, which she steadied with her left. It was clear she was trying desperately not to panic more.

Dismissing her flame, Elsinore gripped her short sword with both hands and crept toward the incapacitated woman. She wasn't sure she wouldn't attract the worms' attention, but she was sure she had no choice. Delicately but swiftly, and careful not to strike Aemia's body, Elsinore slashed with her blade and struck one of the crawling things, at once slicing into it and flinging it off Aemia so it hit the ground some feet away. As Elsinore watched, the thing began to crawl off, away from Aemia.

Now that she could tell this would work, Elsinore did the same to the other worms. A few times she missed, her sword swiping at the air, held back by her fear of cutting Aemia. There were a dozen of the huge terrible things all over her body, but each flew away with the cut of the blade, one after the other.

Another fear stayed the force of Elsinore's swings: If one of the worms were to be bisected entirely, both halves might live and crawl and return, as other worms do. She was careful to hit them only enough to fling them from their place on Aemia. But none returned; each of the glowing things crawled off with the others, deeper into the tunnel, away from the women and the light Rajel held.

Once she had cleared the last, Elsinore examined Aemia carefully. Still incapacitated, her low moan still reverberated through the layer of slime encasing her. Her eyes and mouth were closed, but she seemed—Elsinore prayed—to tremble slightly.

Untying a bright yellow scarf from her waist, Elsinore turned at last to Rajel. "Do you still have a waterskin? I didn't refill my gourd before this mess started."

Keeping her flame steady in one hand, Rajel quickly grabbed the skin from her bag with the other and handed it to Elsinore. The sorceress poured some of the water over Aemia's head and used more to wet the scarf. Then, stifling a gag, she began to wipe Aemia off, unsure she would do any good.

It took time and more water from the skin, but at last, the thickest layers came off the poor woman.

She began to tremble more forcefully, moaning louder, but still she remained insensate.

"Wait a moment." Rajel awkwardly dug around in her bag again with one hand and removed a gray jacket. She gave it to Elsinore, who draped it over Aemia, and the trembling quieted a little.

For a few moments, there was no other change. But finally, Aemia began to cough heavily. Then she spit and retched and, at last, opened her eyes.

Elsinore gave her the last of the water to drink, and Aemia sat shaking for a long time before she spoke.

"Oh, Goddess. Thank . . . oh gods . . ."

"I'm sorry, sister. I'm so sorry." Elsinore held her shoulders in comfort, disregarding the lingering slime that seeped through the jacket. "Can you walk? We need to get you to the surface right away."

"I . . . I think so. Fauna . . ."

"It's all right. I'm going for Fauna next. What happened to her? Is she in the same state as you?"

"Fauna . . . she . . . oh, Goddess . . ." Aemia groaned.

Elsinore's face darkened. "Is she . . . ?" She trailed off, not speaking her fear aloud.

"No!" Aemia yelled, suddenly animated. "No! She's in there! She . . . stay away! Please get me out! Get me—"

She descended into a convulsion of coughing and retching.

"Rajel, are you strong enough to help her outside and up the steps?" Elsinore asked.

"I think so." With Elsinore's help, Rajel pulled Aemia's arm around her own shoulders to better support her.

"When you come out, call to the others for help," Elsinore said, "and come back with water, rags, and medicine if you can. I'm going for Fauna."

"Be careful, sister," Rajel said. Each woman smiled a goodbye, and Rajel set off slowly, taking care not to rush or hurt the injured Aemia.

Casting and following her flame, Elsinore pressed deeper into the tunnel. Eventually, she came to a wide chamber—a cavern cut by time into the rock itself, with hollows and age-old natural pillars, vaster than her little magic flame could light. Holding her barely cleaned sword ready at her side, she peered into the darkness, unable to hear anything beyond her racing heart, though moments ago her footsteps had echoed in the cavern. Carefully exploring the edges of the chamber, she found that the far side fell away into a vast chasm, though how deep she could not tell with her little flame.

Turning from the pit, Elsinore dismissed her flame and waited in the dark.

Finally, the sword she held before her reflected and magnified a dim glow moving in the distance of the deep hall. From pillar to pillar along the edge of the cavern, casting the same subterranean blue fluorescence as the worms, it approached slowly but ceaselessly, till at last Elsinore could see its ominous source.

It was a human form shuffling across the rough stone, glowing like the worms.

And it was approaching Elsinore, even in total darkness.

Elsinore cast her flame spell once more and nearly fainted when she finally saw the body clearly.

It was Fauna, standing tall and proud, her face half obscured but for a wide senseless grin, arms up and out like a figure of a goddess receiving offerings, her long white dress torn and stained and trailing behind her.

Tightly twisted around her body was a massive glowing worm the size of a terrible python.

From her foot, it twisted up one leg, up the front of her pelvis and around her torso, over her shoulder, tight around her throat, and up the back of her head like a helmet's crest. Its face—or so Elsinore assumed, for both ends looked alike—stretched down Fauna's brow, covering her eyes. Another worm coiled around each of her arms, ending at her hands.

Grinning ever wider, Fauna finally spoke, a croaking parody of her own voice.

"The whispers of the earth! The pulsing of its flesh, the beating of its heart! Oh, do you hear it? Now we see and hear all! The body that sees with its body, the body that is two and one and All! Do you see it, sister? The eternal bodies of the Tillers of the Earth!"

"Fauna?" Elsinore said slowly, her eyes wide in

horror. "Can you hear me? It's Nisapa. Do you know me? Do you remember your sisters? Remember Aemia? Your sisters fear for you. I want to help you, Fauna. To go back to the sunlight . . ."

"To wither in the sun!" Fauna croaked. "To shrivel and die, to waste away far from the embrace of the great earth! Fool! Hatred! To make us suffer! Fool who would take us away, so we cannot till the great earth! Oh, to till the earth! The flowers grow, the grass lush and green! The corpses rot into food, flesh broken down, once more to be part of the earth! Birth and death and life! Such that a great high sage may progress through the guts of the *worm*!"

Holding both arms out toward Elsinore, palms open, Fauna lunged with a terrible force. The sorceress dashed aside, but Fauna turned, her motions sudden and sharp. The worms on her arms writhed hungrily, reaching out from her body for their new victim. Elsinore slashed with her sword, but unwilling to harm Fauna, she couldn't cut closely enough to only strike the worms. She fought to drive her away—this poor terrible creature, possessed more horribly than any might be by a demon.

But the worm was relentless, uncowed. When Elsinore ducked behind Fauna for cover, the poor woman's arms bent back, and she scrambled backward, able to move and see just as well with the body of the worm. Wretched, jerking and shuffling, the creature pursued, unstoppable, unreachable, all-seeing, and mad.

All-seeing, Elsinore realized.

The whole body of the worm was its eye, sensing light and heat, which drove it forward and back through the dark mass of the earth.

Elsinore dismissed her flame spell, casting all into darkness but the terrible sepulchral glow of the worm.

The creature wailed in frustration with Fauna's voice, a sharp piercing cry that echoed off the walls of the cavern. Too long it lasted, far longer than Fauna's natural breath should have carried on.

Finally, the wail grew softer, till it sank into a hum, sinking and rising and sinking again. The hum grew deeper, till it seemed to shake the whole cavern in the dark, and with it, Elsinore's fear grew deeper as well.

A blue light became visible from the edge of the cave, a light like that of the worms but wider, stronger, growing slowly and rising like some unnatural underworld dawn.

To Elsinore's sickening horror, the source of the light emerged from the pit.

Wider than a person—wider even than an ancient tree trunk—a titanic worm raised its front end over the edge.

It was as wide, Elsinore realized, as the tunnel through which she had entered the cavern.

"Mother of all the gods!" Elsinore cried. As the twin horrors of the incredible worm and the possessed woman advanced from either side, the sorceress found the strength and presence of mind to act. Calling to her lips the secret word of a spell, she cast a veil of aether around herself, hiding her from all sight as she moved invisibly through the mists between matter and memory, between sight and intuition.

Invisible, she ran.

The worms on Fauna cast around blindly with the woman's body, sharply, furiously, feebly. The woman's ever-grinning mouth ceased its humming and began to voice a new sound, one strange and unfamiliar. At first an awkward, unnatural cry, it broke and resumed, again and again, till Elsinore realized it was an imitation of laughter.

"From the earth, we shall rise!" the worm croaked

through the voice of the woman. "The god shall rise! We shall rise under this body's direction, and we shall digest the surface as we digest the dead beneath the earth! The god shall devour the cities as a corpse, shall fertilize the soil with the bodies of the living! All shall fall, shall fertilize, shall rise again in a new spring! *The Tiller of the Earth* shall rise and bring new life! All hail the Tiller of the Earth! Ay, ay, the Tiller of the Earth!"

Elsinore hid away, half behind a column of rock, and steadied herself enough to remove another scarf from her waist. Then she waited.

Only when the flailing things controlling Fauna had put more distance between themselves and the massive creature of the pit and slowed did Elsinore move to action.

Hand wrapped in the cloth of her scarf, Elsinore grabbed the body of the worm from around Fauna's throat, lifted it up, and with her sword, sliced it in two. Wrestling the terrible oozing thing from Fauna's head, Elsinore hurled the severed end at the giant, and it disappeared before it into the pit.

The grin melted from Fauna's face, and from her emerged another terrible wail. Elsinore wasn't sure yet if this was the wail of the worm or the wail of the woman, but it was clearly a cry of pain.

Elsinore refused to stop. With one unseen hand, she grabbed parts of the worm, and with the sword in the other, she sliced it apart, throwing them into the pit, beyond the reach of their prey. The woman flailed and convulsed, such that Elsinore feared hurting her with the blade, but Elsinore wrestled her down as best she could, until finally the last of the frightful parasite was gone.

At last, Fauna lay still, breathing shallow, but still living. Elsinore stood in front of Fauna as if to shield her body and turned to face the hideous god from the pit, the Tiller of the Earth. Its head remained level, steady, fixed on the spot where Elsinore stood, invisible though she was.

Could it see her, hiding in the mists between planes, as no other eyes could? Could it see at all?

As Elsinore stared through the shifting mists, an image came unbidden into her mind, as if transferred into it by the uncanny mind of the great worm: an image of all that was and that had been—gone. Broken down and devoured, cities fallen and forests rotted, mountains crumbled and riverbeds filled with soil—

Then new mountains pushed up from the surface, and new rivers were burrowed through the valleys, water flowing from the new highlands to the sea. Over long ages, trees regrew, not like those of old but shapely and purple and strange. Creatures flew through the air with many wings like the petals of lotus blossoms, and others crawled across the earth with spherical bodies clear like crystal. New cities were built in the valleys and riverbanks, shaped to house new people, not like those who now toiled and died and were born but who walked on bent legs like birds, with conical cranial protuberances on the crowns of their heads and hair that rose and floated like flame. They sang with voices like the wind, and their eyes saw things that were and that were not, things between and within each other; they saw more clearly than those who see now and could see colors beyond those we know.

Then it all vanished—all these fantasies, these dreams—and all was a beautiful, soft light, like a blue dawn.

I am sorry you are so angry.
I am sorry you are so alone.
I am sorry you are so afraid.

I am sorry so much has changed.
But everything will change and change again.
All will pass away, and all will continue in what it
will become.
And you will pass away, and you will continue.
Again and again and again.
You are not here, yet you will always be
everywhere.
Do not be afraid.
You are part of each other.

For a long time, the Tiller of the Earth stared at Elsinore—if its action could be called such. At last, the great worm pulled back, straightening itself again, and began a slow retreat into the pit once more. The light grew dimmer and dimmer. Elsinore remained facing it, gazing into the pit, until all was dark once more.

All she had seen vanished, like a dream upon waking.

For a long time, Elsinore remained in the dark, kneeling on the ground. The only sound was a shallow, rhythmic breathing, though whether her own or Fauna's was unclear to Elsinore in her state.

In time, the sound of footsteps approached, and voices, all reverberating off the walls of the tunnel.

"She went deeper looking for Fauna! Hurry!"

Rajel.

Fauna groaned as the others burst into the chamber, gasping and directing each other. Some tended Fauna, helping to carry her back out, while the others called for Elsinore.

Realizing she was still invisible, Elsinore dismissed the spell. The mists of invisibility parted, revealing her kneeling still, back to the others, peering into the chasm.

"Nisapa!" Rajel called with relief, rushing to her friend's side. "Elsinore," she said quietly so the others couldn't hear, "are you all right?"

At first, Elsinore did not answer, only slowly turning to Rajel. Pulling herself out of the dream state felt difficult, like rising from a troubled and restless sleep. But at last, she focused on Rajel's face, saw the flickering flame of her fire spell, and smiled softly.

"Yes. I'm fine."

Elsinore used her scarf to clean her sword of the last of the slime, before sheathing the sword and dropping the scarf into the pit. It dropped quickly, heavy with so much residue, and soon vanished, a spot of turquoise swallowed up by a sea of impenetrable black.

Rajel helped her to her feet, and together they followed the others out of the cavern, out of the tunnel, and into the light of day.

Once back in the stepwell, Elsinore waited at the mouth of the tunnel as the others carefully took Fauna up each level of narrow steps, surrounded on all sides by stalks and bunches of silphium. She told Rajel to go up with them and that she would follow shortly. Once all were safely free of the well, Elsinore turned back to the cave and gazed deeply into the tunnel. The sun was now past midday, and light fell very shallowly into the opening. The darkness yawned deep, as wide as the pit in the far chasm. Elsinore stared for a long time, tried to remember . . .

She shook her head, dragging her mind back to herself. She could cast one more spell before needing to rest and study, and she knew what she had to do. Pressing her palm solidly against the wall of the tunnel, she looked deep within herself to focus the magic and spoke one final word of power—a word that cast the spell and then fled from her mind as totally as the now-forgotten dreams and images that had filled her mind in the cavern. The spell was called Push.

The walls of the earth shook, the tunnel trembled and bent, and Elsinore ran, fleeing from the opening as fast as she could, back out into the mossy pond. The spell caused a quake in the walls, and in moments, the tunnel was filled in with earth and debris and was sealed.

Once back at the camp, Sophia tended to Aemia and Fauna. They still needed care from healers, but they lived and woke, though they were very weak and fatigued. Neither remembered much of what they had experienced, and Elsinore was reluctant to share much detail—only that they had come into danger together but were safe and needed to look after each other, as all the sisters needed to do. She would tell the healers more if it was needed to treat them, but for now, she shared no more. For now, Fauna embraced Aemia and Juno, and they all reconciled and laughed at their own foolishness.

They all washed in the stream using soaps and perfumes carried in the cart, and it was a very long time before any of them felt truly clean. They stripped and washed their clothes as well, and since it would take time for them to dry, Fauna lent Elsinore something from her wardrobe. It was a long white dress, sleeveless and clasped at the shoulders, of a style unfamiliar to Elsinore, which at first made her uncomfortable. But Fauna said it suited her, and even Rajel laughingly agreed. Elsinore felt more herself when she added her short black traveler's jacket, leaving the hood down while her hair dried, and she was thankful she hadn't worn that at least into the cavern.

Once ready, they set out for Sanisa. A few of them rode in the cart, which was hitched to a few of the mules, and the rest rode alongside; they would reach the city in a day or two.

"Your sword is very beautiful," Lucia said, riding up slowly beside Elsinore. "But it's a very old style. Where did you get a tool like that?"

"My mother made it for me," Elsinore replied, smiling sadly.

"The same mother who taught you the use of mare urine for your feminizing potions?"

Elsinore laughed. "No, actually. My other mother."

"I'm curious why your mothers used ancient potion techniques and antique swords," Lucia said, "but I'm sorry for pressing you so." There was a sincerity in her voice that put Elsinore at ease.

"I'll share more sometime," Elsinore said. "Perhaps once we arrive at Sanisa. For my part, I'm curious to know more about your Mother Battakes. We had no high priestess when I practiced at the temple. I'm still not sure how to feel about the idea."

"She's less a high priestess—not a ruler at all, at least, if that eases your mind. She's more of a guide. She's very wise and has seen places most of us can't imagine, so her words and suggestions are given great value. But no one of us is bound to obey her will any more than one's own. She is highly respected for what she knows—things about life and death that give the rest of us hope. I think you will enjoy meeting her."

"Does she have a name? This Battakes?" Elsinore asked.

"Of course she did, once. I don't know it; most of us know her only as the Mother Battakes."

Lucia turned to look back at the cart, to be sure the others were all right, and smiled.

"Thank you, Nisapa, for everything you've done for us."

"I'm glad to have met all of you," Elsinore replied. "I have much to learn, I suppose."

She was silent for a long moment, considering the world she was in now.

Wondering.

"And I look forward to meeting the Mother Battakes."

ELSINORE
AND THE BATTAKES

ARRIVAL

The great city of Sanisa sparkled as brightly as the river upon whose banks it was founded. The polished marble, colorfully painted statues, and murals of the buildings glittered with sunlight as brilliantly as the flowing water did, and at night, the windows and floating lanterns cast light of all colors about the streets and onto the river. From a distance in the highlands, the city resembled a nebula glowing at the edge of the galaxy, mirrored on the surface of the Earth.

People from many lands, throughout the Great River Valley and far beyond, traveled to Sanisa from season to season—to stay, to visit, to experience the cosmopolitan majesty of the whole world in a single city. So, too, came the pilgrims—those who worshipped the Great Goddess of the city, as well as those who had belonged to the community of Her temple and had since wandered the world, teaching of Her love, performing rituals, and using Her magic to heal and tend to the sick and suffering.

Among those pilgrims came Elsinore of Nin.

She arrived in the early evening as the sun settled beyond the river. She came with her companions: Rajel, the young woman awed to silence by the grandeur of the city, much as Elsinore had once been; the five Gallae sisters who called themselves metragyrtes, gatherers for the Mother, who dispersed to make preparations for their stay; and of course, Elsinore's familiar, Risky, who leaped from the wagon and chased a tiny shadow into an alley in a way that would have worried Elsinore had they been an ordinary cat.

Crossing her arms, Elsinore looked up at the temple of the Goddess Tiranna, a massive, decorated ziggurat complex that loomed above the towers and walkways of the city.

"You're sure you'll be all right going with Lucia?" Elsinore asked, turning to Rajel. Lucia, one of the metragyrtes, had offered to introduce Rajel to the temple, for the girl wished to study and undergo initiation into the sisterhood of Gallae, priestesses of the Goddess.

Rajel smiled. "I will be. Thank you, Elsinore. For everything. For bringing me here. For saving me."

She paused a moment, then hugged Elsinore, squeezing her tightly.

"Thank you for being my sister." Rajel said, with a catch in her voice as if she was holding back tears.

Elsinore grinned. "Get going! There's lots to see, and you'll have all the time you need to see it and learn. You can always come find me if you need me."

The two women parted at last, leaving Elsinore alone for the first time in weeks. Alone, yet standing in a plaza of a city teeming with people. She closed her eyes, inhaled deeply, and sighed.

Home.

Or as close to such a thing as Elsinore might still have.

She wandered the streets for a few hours, hood up over her eyes, reacquainting herself with the life of the city. She knew she would go to the temple, that it was drawing her in like a vortex, but she would delay it as much as she could.

That was what she'd been doing for so long already.

Very little had changed in the stage of the city itself, though the players were different. The districts, the market stalls, the homes, and the shape of the alleys were all the same as ever, beautifully maintained or fallen to disrepair in roughly the same proportions as she remembered. It had been only a year or two of her life since she had last been in Sanisa, but it had been sixty years in the life of the city and the world.

After buying falafel from a cart in the market, Elsinore sat on the edge of a fountain to eat.

"Goddess all around us," she muttered to herself as she took a bite. "It *feels* like sixty years since I last ate falafel this good."

"Maybe the cooks have gotten that much better since last you were here," said someone she hadn't seen standing nearby. Surprised, Elsinore turned to see a young woman in a long black dress, with purple shawls tied around her waist and hooded over her dark hair.

Elsinore swallowed her mouthful. "I suppose you'll tell me the man with the street cart has been selling falafel right there for his entire life, and everyone here already knows him well, and he's a city institution?"

"No," the woman replied, laughing a little. "He's been

in the city for a few months. I'd say he's well on his way to becoming a city institution, though; his food is delicious."

"Oh," Elsinore said. "Finally, something that's new to everyone and not just to me."

The woman inclined her head, smiling. "What's that?"

"Nothing. My own preoccupations," Elsinore replied. "Have a seat. My name—" Catching herself before she could give her real name, she feigned choking on a bit of falafel to hide her hesitation. "My name is Nisapa."

"Blue Leaf? Your hair is lovely," the woman said, at once translating the name Elsinore had given and remarking on the teal dye of Elsinore's hair hidden beneath her black hood. Elsinore let her hood down and shook her hair free from the tail that was coming loose anyway. The hair around her left ear was shaved, a mark of her role as a priestess in her time, but she pushed the locks on the right behind her ear to keep it out of the way as she finished eating.

"I'm Giana," the woman said.

"That's a lovely name." Elsinore kept to herself the observation that she was appropriately dressed for having a name that meant "nighttime."

"You're going to the temple, I assume?" Giana asked.

"Isn't everyone who's come to the city going there?" Elsinore deflected.

"I suppose they are," Giana said. "I'm a priestess there. I have been for quite some time. And I have a knack for telling who's come as a tourist and who truly needs something from the Goddess or Her attendants. You have the look of a woman who may be one of Her priestesses herself, don't you?" Giana met Elsinore's eyes, but Elsinore looked away.

"I may have been," Elsinore replied cautiously. "Elsewhere in the valley. I . . . I doubt we would have been in the same places at the same time."

"Really?" Giana replied curiously. "Because you dress much like Gallae priestesses here at Tiranna's temple did only a generation or two ago. You didn't practice here?" She casually fingered the edge of one of the bright turquoise scarves tied around Elsinore's waist, which fastened her purple dress underneath her black jacket.

Raising an eyebrow, Elsinore flicked the tassels of Giana's own purple scarves and black dress.

Giana laughed. "I like old fashions. Like you do. Like your sword—it's in remarkably good condition for such an old style."

Elsinore fingered the grip of the sheathed sword she'd set beside her. Its crescent-moon handguard gleamed in the sunlight, and the little crystal star on the pommel glittered.

"Actually, my mother made it for me. She . . . was a blacksmith," Elsinore said distantly.

"She had excellent skill, and a fine eye for technique, then." Returning to the subject at hand, Giana added, "If you're going to the temple, you can come with me when you're ready. There are rooms for former priestesses making a return pilgrimage for the festival. Whether you practiced here or . . . elsewhere in the valley, as you said, I'm sure it would be all right for you to stay there."

"Thank you, sister," Elsinore said. "I'd like that. I'm ready to go whenever you are."

Giana smiled, stood, and took Elsinore's hand.

It wasn't until they approached the temple, the ziggurat's levels rising high above the broad avenue and the ceremonial walls and surrounding buildings, that Elsinore ventured to ask what had been on her mind.

"The . . . the Mother Battakes? How difficult would it be for me to arrange a meeting with her?"

"The Mother Battakes is very generous with her time and her wisdom. It wouldn't be very difficult at all for a traveler to meet with her. But for you . . ." Giana stopped and turned, looking Elsinore in the eye. "For you, it would be very easy indeed, considering she's expecting you."

Elsinore let go of Giana's hand and took several steps back. "What?"

Giana smiled. "The Reverend Mother has many gifts and deep insight into the flow of time. She's expected you to arrive for some time now and thought you would be arriving at the coming of the equinox—at the Day of Blood. She told me and a few other senior Gallae to look for you: a young woman dressed in the manner of a priestess of the temple of our mothers' time, or our grandmothers', with beautiful blue-green hair shaved on the side, carrying a sparkling sword and answering to the name Blue Leaf."

Elsinore's jaw dropped as she stared at Giana in amazement.

"She told us some other things too, but I think that covers it for now, doesn't it, Sister Blue Leaf?"

"Every time I hear of this Mother Battakes," Elsinore said darkly, "I find more questions to demand an answer for."

Giana laughed lightly. "That's always the way with her, sister." She put a hand on Elsinore's arm and smiled, gentle and encouraging. "Don't worry. She's a very kind and compassionate person, and I've never heard of anyone who doesn't like her the moment they meet her.

"And by the way," Giana added as she headed for the

temple again, "you're pronouncing it wrong. It's *bodh-a-kess.*"

"*Bodhakes,*" Elsinore repeated. "Meaning . . . ?"

"Not every name has to have a meaning, does it, Sister Blue Leaf?"

Elsinore settled into a room on a lower level of the temple. It was much the same as the room she had lived in during the time she had practiced here; most were laid out the same, in a dormitory quarter housing the priestesses and priests of the temple.

She laid in bed for a long time. She was tired from her journey to the city but unable to sleep with so many thoughts crowding her mind. Her sword rested against the bedpost, and her bag sat beside her on the sheets. Reaching inside, she drew out what she was looking for right away.

It was her rooster doll, a soft little thing of yellow cloth with a rainbow ribbon feathered tail. She held it to her breast as she lay on the pillow, thinking.

It was here in this temple that it had been given to her.

She gave it to me, Elsinore thought. *Could she . . . ?*

Elsinore couldn't finish the thought. She didn't even, exactly, know how she meant to finish it.

Sitting up, she kissed the doll and stuffed it back in her bag, shouldering it as she stood and left the room.

Elsinore found a girl, clearly a novice Galla of the temple, passing in the garden nearby. The girl smiled timidly. She wore a short white dress and flowers in her straight black hair.

Elsinore held up her hands, both in greeting and as a gesture of calm. "Excuse me, sister. I'm . . . I'm a visitor here. For the equinox. I'm sorry to bother you, but could you tell me where I can find the Mother Bodhakes?"

The girl looked Elsinore up and down, at her apparently strange dress and hood, and stared a moment at her teal-colored hair.

"Are you Blue Leaf?" the girl asked.

Elsinore smiled a little cynically. "I am. Am I expected?"

"Of course." The girl seemed a little relieved. "I'll take you to her chambers."

THE BODHAKES

Elsinore pushed open heavy double doors. Sunlight shaded at intervals by the colonnade behind her spilled into a dark chamber lit by numerous candles set on shelves in the walls or on the floor. Though a little larger, it was otherwise like the other dormitory rooms.

As she crossed the threshold, the doors slammed shut due to their own weight. The high windows were blocked by heavy curtains, and it took a long moment for the young woman's eyes to adjust to the dimness of the candlelight.

At the far end of the room, short steps led up to a shrine of tables covered with tapestries, on which sat many statues of divinities dressed with tassels and ribbons. The gold and bronze of the statues glittered in the candlelight, and shadows danced fitfully in the crevices of those made of painted stone. All seemed to be goddesses, some in poses of meditation and others dancing.

On a pillow before the altar, a woman sat cross-legged, facing Elsinore, hands folded in her lap, one hand in the palm of the other, thumbs meeting above. Her robes were bright yellow and saffron, decorated in fringes of a blue-green ivy pattern. The robes were twisted around her on the floor and pillow, as if she had just turned; Elsinore suspected she had faced the goddesses before being alerted of a visitor's presence and had turned to greet her. Her head hung, her face hidden by a yellow scarf hooded over her head.

Elsinore could not see her face, but there was some aura about her, something familiar. Or was that only hope? Was this woman at last . . . ?

The woman slowly, almost ritually, raised her hands to the edge of her scarf and drew it slowly back as she raised her head. Though darkly lit, her face was clear.

Elsinore did not recognize her at all.

The woman smiled very sadly. Her smile was beautiful, lighting the room more brightly than the candles, but there was a tinge of grief in her eyes. Some part of her suffered, some deep part that Elsinore could not see. She gestured for Elsinore to sit before her, on a pillow matching her own, and Elsinore did so in the same cross-legged position.

"Sister Blue Leaf, welcome home."

The woman's voice was soft and high, and though Elsinore supposed she must be a Galla, very little about her voice and body gave that impression. She showed no sign of a birth not meant for her, of the long work with potions and medicine-craft that aligned the body with the heart. Her face was soft and unmarked but for little wrinkles at the corners of her eyes that the shadows cast by the candles exaggerated, which betrayed an age perhaps slightly greater than Elsinore's—her only features that did so. She had a shallow brow, narrow shoulders she kept close to her body, and subtle breasts curving beneath her yellow robe. Her brown hair was pulled back in a bun at the base of her head. Although she was seated, she appeared taller than Elsinore.

Yet so, too, was there little of Elsinore to indicate her origins, having spoken of her heart to her mothers at so young an age.

"This was my home once, very long ago," Elsinore said at last. "How do you know of that? Who are you, and why do the people of the temple treat you as they do?"

Beside the woman, on one side of the pillow, sat a hand drum, a tympanum like the one Elsinore carried, with its hollow side up. On the other sat a shallow bowl, almost like a cymbal. The drum was filled with pieces of bread, and the bowl with a dark liquid, deep red in the candlelight. Instead of answering the question, the woman took the drum and, from it, a piece of bread. She ate the bread, then passed the drum to Elsinore, who cautiously held it, not yet taking the bread.

"This isn't Faerie," the woman said gently. "You may eat without fear, sister."

Elsinore ate a piece of the bread, not taking her eyes from the woman who sat cross-legged before her. The woman then took the bowl and drank from it, then passed it to Elsinore. It was filled with a deep pomegranate wine. The two sat and stared at each other for a long moment, before the woman nodded and held out her hand, gesturing for Elsinore to continue the ritual.

"I have eaten from the drum. I have drunk from the cymbal. I have read the letters in the stars, and I have stolen into the inner chamber. I . . ." Elsinore paused in her rote recitation of the litany and stared at the woman, more doubtful than ever. "I am your sister."

The woman repeated the litany, speaking more emotionally, more lyrically, than Elsinore had. Then she set the drum and cymbal aside and reached out to take Elsinore's hand. The sorceress gave it reluctantly.

"You are safe, Sister Blue Leaf. You are home. And I know you. I know your name. You are Elsinore of Nin, and you have returned here at last from the twilight space beneath the Mountain, in a manner few others have done."

Elsinore raised an eyebrow in suspicion. "You know my real name?"

"I do. I know your name well. And what is more, I know your true name. High Priestess of the Pomegranate Moon—EN.SIN.NU.UR.MA." The woman enunciated softly, her lips and tongue shaping each syllable perfectly, and each struck Elsinore in the heart like a blow. Recoiling, she stood from the floor, her eyes on the priestess in yellow sitting on the meditation pillow, whose lips still smiled sadly.

"How on earth and hell do you know that name? No one knows that name!" Elsinore tried to draw her sword before she remembered she had left it in her bedroom.

"I know much about you, Elsinore of Nin. How you were born and abandoned in the woods, seemingly a boy left to die during famine. How you were found and raised by women who recognized you for the girl you were. How you came here to the temple of Tiranna, the Star, She who leads the lost on the broken path of light across the ever-turning ocean. How you lost what you love most and were led by your mourning to the gate under the Mountain. And I know your name."

Breathing heavily, Elsinore shut her eyes tightly to hold back tears of anger and fear. She shook, shivering all over. No spell in her mind could save her from this fear;

she did not even know what she feared. This woman, who knew things no one on earth should know? Or did Elsinore fear her own past? Did she fear herself still?

Elsinore opened her eyes and regained control of her breath. The Bodhakes sat still upon the floor, looking at Elsinore with eyes that welled with sympathy.

Elsinore's fear left her then as she looked into those eyes, and she sighed.

"You know my name. What is yours?"

The woman smiled softly in reply. "My name when I came to the temple some twenty years ago was Nana," she said. "But that is not my true name."

"Then what is your name?"

"To tell you that, I will start at the beginning. When you hear my story, perhaps you will understand."

THE STORY OF THE BODHAKES

I was born in a small village at the bend of the river Gallas, in Nin—a place you knew well, Elsinore Ningala. My father died before I was born, when his fishing boat capsized and he drowned. I never knew him. The village midwife tended to my mother till she gave birth to me, and when my father died, she took the both of us in to live with her and her lover, the blacksmith, as we had no other family. Those two women had lost their daughter nearly twenty autumns before, and caring for my mother and me helped salve a wound that, nevertheless, never really healed. So the midwife, Milanda, and the woman she loved, Glamis, carried a sadness with them always that I could see even as a child, which was perhaps one of the earliest signs of my gifts.

But they cared for my young mother as their own

daughter, even if she could not replace the one they had lost. And oh, how they loved me, their grandchild who played in the reeds by the edge of town, singing with birds and listening to their beautiful voices. I told my grandmothers that the birds sang secrets to me; that the magpies were funny and playful and wished to be women so they could dance with the young men of the cities; that the ravens were haughty and proud, and though they told me I should love them and fear them, I thought they were only silly and sad, but I still loved them for that.

The birds told me other things too; they reminded me of things I already knew but had briefly forgotten at my birth. They told me that the magpies really had been women once and would be again. They told me that I had been too, and I sang and was so glad, because though I seemed to be a young boy, I thought I could remember being a woman once, and if my friends the birds told me so, then I knew it was true.

One morning, I brought a message to my grandmothers from the birds. They were preparing to go on one of their yearly journeys, where Milanda the midwife visited cities and towns throughout the Great River Valley to find people to help and heal. I always thought there was something they were looking for on those journeys, but every time, they returned without having found it, and it made me sad that they were sad, though they never said they were.

I walked up to Milanda as she packed the cart, and I took a white-and-silver flower from my hair that a bird had given me, and I handed it to her. The flower's petals were shaped like a star. I told her what the birds had told me: your daughter will come home someday, though you may not see her for a long time or how you expect to.

Glamis had been occupying herself making sure the cart was sturdy and ready for the journey, but she turned to us and said, "Your mother is back at home, little one. Not to worry; we'll see her and you when we come back in a few months, like always."

"I was not talking about my mother," I replied.

Milanda looked again at the flower I had given her, its eight white-and-silver petals like a star, its stem and leaves a deep blue green. Then she began to weep. Her lover leaped down from the cart to take her in her strong arms, and they held each other for a long time.

I hated to see my grandmother cry, and I asked if I had said something wrong. I was only delivering the message the birds had given me. Milanda could not reply through her tears, but Glamis stroked my head and told me not to worry. She told me that they loved me as their own daughter and thanked me for telling them what I had. She then gently led both of us, her partner and me, back home to my mother, and they did not go on a journey that year. They stayed and took care of the folk in Nin, and I played with my grandmothers in the fields and with the other girls in the village, and I talked little with my friends the birds. I no longer told my grandmothers what the birds said to me when I did listen to them. I didn't want to see them cry.

As the years went by and the other children in Nin began to grow into young women and men, I thought much about what the birds had told me, that I was once a woman, and I thought of how much I wanted to be one again. But one day, when my mother remarked what a fine young man I would become, I began to cry and told her I would not be a man; I would be a woman, like her and my grandmothers. Milanda consoled me, and she and my mother sewed me a beautiful dress for the spring festival, which I wore with a crown of starflowers in my hair when I danced with the boys as the magpies wished to do.

Soon after that, Milanda asked if I would rather grow to be a woman or a man. I did not tell her about the birds, but I told her that I could not imagine ever wanting to be a man. I told her I had been a woman once, long ago in some time I had forgotten, and that I wished more than anything to be one again and to remember. She looked at me strangely but took me in her arms and stroked my hair. She told me about her daughter, whom she had lost years ago, and how she was like me and how beautiful she was. She told me of the last night she had seen her daughter, of how she had left to discover what haunted her, and something about that struck me as so familiar that I began to cry. I told her once again that I knew her daughter was safe, only very far away, and she would return someday, but my grandmother only smiled.

Soon after, she gave me potions she had brewed in her apothecary; potions that brought my body in harmony with the calling I heard in my heart since listening to the songs of the birds. With them, I became a woman as I grew older, as the other girls in the village did.

As I came of age, I thought to follow my grandmother's path as a midwife, and I soon accompanied her and her partner on their journeys to nearby cities of the valley. One year, we came here to Sanisa, the Jewel of the River, where I met all kinds of people from the far reaches of the Great River Valley and beyond. And I met women like me—Gallae—and men likewise, who were called Pilli, and others, those who studied at the temple of the Goddess Tiranna. Milanda was close friends with a well-respected figure here at the temple, who had known

Milanda's daughter years before. I spoke with them at great length and soon decided to stay and learn of the worship of the Goddess and the history of people like me.

I devoted myself to my studies and to the Goddess and learned spells of great power to alter the world around me and techniques for calming and clearing my mind. As I meditated, I felt I could hear more than only the voices of the birds; everything spoke to me: animals and flowers, trees and the river and the wind. They spoke to me of things I had forgotten but soon learned to remember—things I should not have been able to know, for my birth had been not so very long ago in a village far from the city.

When I entered certain rooms and looked into certain mirrors in the temple, dizziness would wash over me like the rushing tide, and I would remember things that I no longer remembered once the dizziness had passed. Ardena, the senior Galla and friend of my grandmother, kept close watch over me, fearing for my well-being. They had been at the temple when other Gallae and Pilli had died of sickness before, and they felt the loss as heavily as my grandmothers felt the loss of their daughter. I noticed that now and again I would say things to Ardena that made them turn their head and look at me strangely, as if I had said something they remembered but that I could not have discussed with them before.

In the spring, as the equinox in the Season of Light approached, the Gallae and Pilli of the temple prepared to celebrate the ritual for the Day of Blood, as many now gather to do in the coming days. When nightfall came, we processed from the top level of the temple to the Place of the Mound, the burial site outside the city at the edge of the cliff overlooking the river. I could not even approach;

some terrible force, some memory, threatened to pull me in under the mound, and I knew if I went, I would never return. I cried and screamed, and while the rest of the acolytes performed their rite, Ardena brought me back to the temple and tended me as I slept.

They asked me to rest for a few days while they sent for others, a priest and a priestess, who had studied once at the temple and now lived in far corners of the Great River Valley. They said these students knew much of the history of the temple and the ways of the Goddess and would be able to help ease what was plaguing my mind.

The two came with unnatural swiftness, aided by the magic of the Goddess: a Galla priestess named Nissa, and a Pillus priest named Uras. The two conferred with Ardena. One day, they asked me to Ardena's chamber as the sun shone brightly through the windows. Uras and Nissa were there, and Ardena welcomed me into their room. Hung all around the walls and on shelves were Ardena's ritual tools and clothes and figures of gods. We sat around the wide table in the center of the room, and Ardena asked me something very strange.

"Nana, if you will, I would like you to look around the room and tell me if you have memory of any of these things. Can you remember if any of them belong to you?"

It took me a moment to understand what they meant. But I stood to look around the room more closely. As I pushed some things aside to see others, something strange caught my eye.

"None of them belong to me," I asserted.

Uras's and Nissa's faces curled with confusion, but Ardena just looked at me over the fist they held pensively to their mouth. Looking at them, I felt assured at last of the truth. I took something gently into my hands: the doll of a rooster, made of soft yellow cloth with a tail of ribbons in many colors.

"This. I remember this," I said. "But it does not belong to me. I made it as a gift, and I gave it to someone whose thread is woven with mine."

Ardena fell back onto a pillow then, and Uras and Nissa looked at each other with eyes of fear and wonder. Ardena began to cry and asked to be left alone for the rest of the day.

Uras and Nissa took me out to the terraces of the temple to breathe the fresh air in the sun. We looked out from a high level of the temple, out over the fields of the valley beyond the city, the bend of the river Gallas to the northwest. I remembered this view—not from my time there as Nana but from before. I remembered looking out from this terrace with Uras and Nissa. And with you.

"Do you really remember?" Nissa asked me finally.

"I remember everything now." I looked out at the river as it wound its way out of sight, beyond the horizon to the sea. "I remember falling ill, and I remember you and Uras staying with me while I was sick. And I remember her. I remember Elsinore by my side, always. I had been sewing that rooster doll that is now in Ardena's chamber, and I gave it to Elsinore just before leaving her. I remember her lying in bed with me, holding me, till I fell asleep."

I turned at last from the vista far away and looked at Nissa and Uras, who had tears in their eyes.

"And that's the last I remember of her. Of Folia," I said. "Then came death."

And I told them more. I told them that Folia's was not the most recent life I remembered. I remembered another life, that of Delidua, who danced in the Ganzir. Who met you, Elsinore, and who was the first to remember being Folia.

Nissa and Uras spoke to each other in hushed tones and whispered arguments then, and they took their leave of me once they were sure I was safe. They saw that I was looked after, and I did not see them again till Ardena had arisen late the following day.

I fell under Ardena's tutelage right away, though they told me often—it embarrasses me to say—that they learned as much from me as I from them. I credit this precocious learning to my friends the birds and to the wisdom of Milanda and Glamis. But there still were things I knew, things I remembered, that I credit to no special wisdom of my own but to the chance experience of my past and the providence of the Goddess.

Ardena sent for my grandmothers, and after some months at the temple, I left with Milanda and Glamis when they set out to travel the valley as they still did, season to season, even now as they had grown so old. As I said—as you well know—Milanda's skill as a healer and a clairvoyant was welcome wherever she traveled. But this time, I did not merely accompany them as I had when I was a child; this time, skills flooded my mind, secrets of healing and care, things I knew not from my life as Folia but from other lives, lives before, which I knew but somehow had never known. I treated the sick, tended to their wounds and illness, and the skill with which I led the people of the towns back to health astonished even Milanda, brilliant and learned as she was. Everywhere I went, everyone I tended, begged for the secrets of my talent, and I knew no answer to offer but the grace of the Great Mother. My example encouraged many to honor Her, not by any coercion but by their own curiosity and eagerness to give thanks for Her blessing. In this way, the religion of the Goddess spread through the valley, and many learned to follow Her way.

For three years, I accompanied Milanda and Glamis in this way, before finally we parted, our eyes stinging with tears. I would not have left them, but they decided at last to follow a path they had long desired to, one they hoped would lead them to answers for why they had lost you and what had become of you, their first and beloved daughter. I bestowed upon them what blessings I could as they passed out of the valley and into the wider world, seeking its mysteries. They went elsewhere, following rumors of secrets of the Old Ones, looking for places where their records might be kept, where news of you might be found, and I have not seen them since.

For a year or so after this, I wandered the valley alone, tending and healing whoever I could, and a wondrous thing followed in my wake. When the rain fell and the sun shone bright in the fields, I found my footsteps left blooming flowers and herbs—a sign, I thought, of the holy skill I had learned from the Goddess in the depth of the Mountain. I recognized the herbs from my life as Delidua: green stalks with yellow flowers, a species of fennel, new on the Earth of my time, but with a history and lineage that reached back ages past, vanished from the world during the time of the Old Ones due to their greed and mistreatment of the Earth, which led at last to their fall and annihilation.

This herb is silphium, a gift from the Goddess, a gift from the earth, and an herb I knew from my reading in the library in the Kur and the palace of the Ganzir. Seeds clung to me, not physically but spiritually, invisible seeds taken out of the Ganzir when my mindstream led me back to a life in this world. As my spiritual power grew, they scattered in my path, sprouted, and lived, and now the valley is blessed with the holy herbs, the ecosystem adapting as if they had always been part of it. I think they had always been meant to be.

My wandering soon led me back to the temple, where my skill and wisdom was revered, much to my embarrassment. But in all my memories of past lives, there was much to offer my siblings and many secrets of the Goddess long forgotten.

But most importantly, most brightly, I remembered being Folia, remembered in full, and what's more, I remember what came after. I remember the space I was borne to after her death, awakening in a field of glowing gold in a place between lives, between births. I remember being led by smiling figures, folk who resembled birds, to the golden city of thrumming song and marvelous creatures of light. I was not a life, not a person there. For a time, I was not a bead strung on the cord that threads between lives but only the thread itself, and my name then was a secret. My name then was true.

I was not yet Nana, no longer Folia, no longer the names of countless other lives, countless other beads strung upon the thread. Not recognizing you in my liminal blindness, I told you the name of the veil that covers my deep name—Delidua—and that is who I was in that place in between lives.

And then it was you, Elsinore—your defense of me to the emanation of the Goddess who ruled in that place, your insistence upon the truth, your negation of the ban on return from the deep intermediate place of the Kur. I have spent many years meditating on your actions and on mine and on the nature of that place and of the path of the threads of all living things. And I believe it was because of you that I was granted the insight of memory, the refusal to forget past lives and the liminal place, as all forget upon birth. It was because of you I remember, and I owe you not only my present life and my time with your mothers, who became like my own. I owe you my salvation—not from death, not from the intermediate place, but from the cycling tides of the ocean of rebirth itself. Sometimes, I can see dimly—but, I feel, increasingly clearly—what is to come, and I wonder if there can be a release from the suffering that suffuses the natural order of birth and rebirth.

And as I grew, as these last twenty years have gone by since that day in Ardena's room, I have grown to know my siblings in the temple well. The Gallae and Pilli, the Enbi otherwise and in-between—we each have a small piece of this insight, even if we cannot remember all of it. I have come to think this is why we are as we are, why we are drawn so strongly and directly toward that which is beyond the body we were born to. It is not desire—not in the base sense of desire, which is the root of all life's suffering. Part of us remembers what we were, remembers other births, other lives, other beads on the threads that are sewn into the great web knitted by the Goddess with Her celestial needle. Each is but one step on the road of light that leads beyond the web, beyond the ocean of matter and phenomena that is this world of suffering. And remembering, synthesizing, becoming one not only with our own past but with all life—this is the way we will find release and salvation.

The others of the temple called me wise, though I never called myself wise. They looked to me for guidance, and I offer what I can, though I refuse to lead as a lady or a queen. We are all one here, as we all have been at the temple since you and I were here in our youth, caressing each other beneath the bowers and whispering our secrets to each other. Perhaps I have become a successor to Ardena, who passed some years ago, who was respected for their experience and wisdom.

The name Nana no longer meant much to me, so dizzy I became from my knowledge of the past, and I adopted the title "Bodhakes," a name I found in the archives of the Kur when I was in between. The name of one who was chief among the predecessors of the Gallae very long ago, even in the age of the Old Ones. The name of one who seeks to awaken and to aid others to awaken. It suits me, I think, as the role of Galattis, the Goddess who descended and returned, suits you, my dear Elsinore.

I remember you, Elsinore. I remember everything. I remember this life as Nana, with her mother and her surrogate grandmothers, Milanda and Glamis. I remember being Folia, her little life, with the pain of her mother's sickness, of her own sickness, and how happy she—I—was with you then. I remember lives before. And I remember the space in between: the intermediate period after death and before birth. I remember the fluttering thread of the mindstream unweighted by the bead of a life, the thread dancing endlessly at the Ganzir in the wind between lives, the thread that is called DILI.DU.É.DUḪ.A—"Walking Alone in the Halls of Waste." I remember that time in between before you found me—you, Elsinore, the bead of life strung on the mindstream thread called EN.SIN.NU.-UR.MA, "High Priestess of the Pomegranate Moon." With that sparkling bead that you are, you spun around me and bound up with me once more, allowing the Goddess, with Her black star-iron needle, to sew me once again into the fabric of life. And I remember what you did for me; I remember, Elsinore. I remember you.

And I love you. I love you still. More than I can ever express.

<h1 style="text-align:center">AFTERWARD</h1>

Elsinore sat cross-legged on the pillow before the Mother Bodhakes for a long time, her eyes closed, looking not at the other woman but inward. She wanted to cry, to weep, to wail senselessly and take the woman before her in her arms and hold onto her, never letting go.

But no tears came to her eyes.

She sat still.

"Elsinore?" the Bodhakes said, "Please talk to me."

Opening her eyes, Elsinore glared at the Bodhakes. "What of the doll?"

"What of it?"

Elsinore reached roughly into her bag, which sat beside her, pulled out the rooster doll, and hurled it at the woman's chest. She caught it nimbly and cradled it in both hands, before setting it on her lap.

"Why do I have this? If you and Ardena had it then, how did it come to me? It was left for me by . . . it had to have been left for me by her."

The Bodhakes looked at the rooster doll for a long time before raising her face back to Elsinore's, whose eyes were red, not with tears but with anger.

"Your mothers returned to the Valley of the Mounds before the Mountain many times in the early years you were gone. Before I was born as Nana. When finally they stopped coming—never, I urge you to remember, giving up hope—others came. Most especially your friend and your mother's: Ardena. They explored far into the Valley of the Mounds, dared to reach the foot of the Mountain itself—

whether through a bolder nature than Milanda or by strength of their status as a Galla, I cannot say for sure. But they never found whatever it was you found; they never found the way *in*.

"But they saw many strange things among the mounds, in the shadows of those ominous pillars, built tall and terrible as if to drive explorers away. And Ardena told me—all this I know from what they shared with me—that one night, they found a doorway ringed with stone, not in the Mountain but in one of the great mounds near the shadows of the pillars. Beneath this mound was a passage and a circular hovel like a tomb. On an altar in the center, Ardena found this."

The Bodhakes held up the rooster doll.

"I can only guess that when it was taken out of the Ganzir with Delidua, who was Folia and was reborn as Nana, the rooster doll was taken physically—perhaps by one of the chimerical guardians of the Kur—and secreted away to be found later.

"But I do know that Ardena took it then and kept it, before giving it to me when I recognized it—when I was recognized as who I had been.

"I kept it with me here in the temple for some time before making a pilgrimage to the foot of the Mountain myself. I took the rooster with me, and tracing your steps to the library, as Milanda and Glamis had told me, I left it with someone who knew you, hoping you would find it when you returned.

"And you did," the Bodhakes concluded, and she gently handed the rooster doll back to Elsinore.

Elsinore stared at the doll for a long time before she finally felt the tears come to her eyes.

"You say you love me still," Elsinore said, her voice

cracking as she tasted the salt of her tears. "But did you ever really love me? Ever really know me? You? Nana? Mother Bodhakes? Folia knew me, and you remember her, remember being her. But how can you really be her? Your face is familiar but strange, a shade of a memory growing so distant . . .

"What you've told me . . . it is incredible, a miracle I have never known. Please, tell me . . . tell me what you remember. How you remember. I . . ."

The woman in yellow took Elsinore's hand in her own and looked deep into her eyes. Her own eyes, those of Nana—the Bodhakes—were so familiar. So beautiful. So young. Eyes Elsinore knew so well in an older face she had never seen. They caught the light of the candles and flashed brightly, as if they were in the midday sun.

Finally, Elsinore turned away. She could not make herself meet those eyes any longer, so familiar, so distant . . .

"When I was young, before coming to the temple," the Bodhakes said softly, "there were many boys I knew in Nin. Lovely, gentle—boys I had grown up with, who had known me as I flowered into womanhood as they did into manhood. I loved many of them, felt their hands on my breasts in the tall grass beyond the border of the village, their lips on mine, their . . .

"Well," she demurred, blushing in a way that surprised Elsinore even after all she had heard. "Of course, we did what young women and men do.

"When I came here to the temple, before Ardena recognized me—before I recognized myself—I grew close to other Gallae, to the Pilli. I learned much more of the marvelous varieties of love that the Goddess has granted us.

"But none of the love I shared with those boys in Nin,

nor even with the Gallae and Pilli like me—none of it was any deeper than a shallow pool left in a field by the rain. Something was missing, something I had forgotten, though my life had barely begun. As if I knew in my heart that I had experienced real love once but lost it, and could no longer remember when or how . . .

"I looked for it for a very long time. For something like what I had forgotten. Until finally, the memories of my past lives brought with them the memory of you, my Elsinore. I was looking for you; I was always looking for you. No love I found could compare to the memory of the days and nights we spent together long ago—of those nights beneath the bower of the trees under the stars, of the secrets I shared of my dreams, of my place and yours, woman but otherwise and between the nature of women and men. Nor could anything compare, nothing at all, to the memory of you holding me in your arms that final night.

"Now that I am the high priestess of this temple, I love all the sisters and brothers here, but never in the manner I loved boys in my youth or my peers when I began my studies. I love them as a mother loves her children, for I am their mother in this place, and I am responsible for them, though I do not command them. But they look up to me as children to their mother, and I have been alone, for all the community that surrounds me. It has been so long since you . . ."

Elsinore raised a hand gently to cover Folia's lips.

"That's all," Elsinore said. "I understand now. Folia—Nana—I . . . I need you. Your touch. Your smell. Your eyes. I . . ."

Folia cut her off at last with a kiss, deep and eager, and they clasped each other's hands tightly. They fell together to the floor, Elsinore pushing Folia down, till her head lay on the pillow that moments before had served her for meditation. Elsinore pressed down on her lover, remembering how she had felt in another life. For all that had changed, for all that was different, this at last was the same.

Elsinore raised her head, though only slightly, and whispered sweetly to the woman below her. "I don't care who you are now. I know you. I've found you. I love you. I'll never let you go."

Elsinore woke from first sleep during the deepest hour of the night, still in Folia's simple bedroom. Propping herself up on her elbow, she looked at the woman sleeping beside her. With the curtains of the window now open to the night air, a moonbeam fell across her body, painting bare flesh and tangled sheets in its light. Elsinore gently stroked strands of Folia's hair that had fallen loose from the bun as they made love, and smiled.

Before long, Folia stirred and smiled as well.

"I'm a light sleeper," she muttered.

"I know," Elsinore replied. "You always were."

"Elsinore," Folia said quietly, lingering on her lover's name, saying it at last—no longer in distant memory but in her very presence—as she gazed into her gray eyes.

"Hm?" Elsinore responded languidly.

"I need you," Folia said. "I mean . . ."

Still half asleep, Folia roused herself enough to express the thoughts that crowded her mind in her low ecstasy.

"I need you here," she said. "Here with me. You're the only one who can understand. The only one who's seen what I have and returned with the memory still living in your mind. The Mountain. The city in the heart of the earth. The Goddess. That place in between death and new life."

"I'm here, Folia." Elsinore stroked her lover's cheek. "Whatever you need me to do. Whatever name you want me to call you. I'm here, for as long as you need me."

The two women held each other silently for a long time, there in the silver light of the moon. They both fell to sleep again, untroubled at last, sure of each other's presence.

Safe.

THE BOOK

The ritual of the Day of Blood came and passed. Months went by, and life at the temple fell into an easy rhythm, guided by the seasons. Rajel mixed readily with her sister Gallae and saw Elsinore regularly, updating her with unbridled excitement about what she had been learning.

Life finally seemed simple to Elsinore. Peaceful. For the first time in as long as she could remember.

Elsinore had left the book with Folia—the book given to her by the Goddess Herself, taken from a high shelf in an inner library of the palace of the Ganzir. Written as it was in a strange script Elsinore could not read, she supposed Folia, with the insight she carried, might have a better understanding of its contents. The script was entirely unknown in the lands of the Great River Valley, even by sages of great learning. It consisted of dots or circles connected by lines, like nodes or pictures of knots in cords, and so Elsinore had taken to calling the script nodiform. Folia laughed at this name and adopted it herself. But even with the knowledge she had gained during her intermediate time in the Kur, with all she had read and studied—even with the knowledge of lives long before—she knew nothing of this script or what language it had been used to write.

There were images in the book too, strange symbolic pictures that had baffled Elsinore, and meant nothing to her when she studied them. But of these, Folia had begun to form theories after much study.

She was certain there were images, repeating over and over, that depicted, though somewhat obscurely, a mountain, and the mountain was a goddess, and the peak was like Her face but broken off. The peak was sometimes a pointed stone like a needle and sometimes fixed by a setting into a statue in place of a head.

And there was, Folia believed, a map.

One day, Folia came to Elsinore as the latter sat on a wall in a garden on a high level of the temple, looking out at the sunset in silence. Folia took Elsinore's hand and kissed her cheek, and the two women pressed their foreheads together for a long time.

"Elsinore," Folia said at last, "I need you."

"I know, my love," Elsinore whispered.

"I need to ask you to do something."

Elsinore pulled away and laughed. "Oh, that wasn't flirting?"

"Not this time, love," Folia said, smiling.

"I never want to let you go again," she continued. "But I know now that you will always return to me. And I know that your skill, your resilience, your talent—I know that you are the one who can do this thing. I know that you're meant to."

"I'll do anything for you, Folia," Elsinore said, though she grew uneasy. "What do you need me to do?"

"I need you to travel somewhere. I need you to deliver

a message. I need you to find something—two things, things that were lost very long ago—and I need you to bring them back here to the temple.

"I think the Goddess is telling me . . . I think that when this is done, when these things are brought back here and reunited . . ."

Folia took Elsinore's hand and squeezed it tightly.

"I think I will be able to read the language in the book."

THROUGH THE GATE OF THE WIND

The wind cut across the narrow passages of the canyon, and sand rippled through like billowing curtains trailing tassels of glass. If any person could have survived long enough to inhabit this mournful place, they might have seen the figure of a traveler trudging through the storm, an uncertain shadow moving steadily through the folds of the wind. They would have likely dismissed the figure as one of the many ghosts that howled up out of the cracks torn in space by the harrowing currents, their true bodies wandering through any number of lost hells.

And perhaps, in this case, they would have been close to guessing the truth. For the traveler, though living, was a sorceress, a Gallae priestess of the Goddess of love and death, and a changeling late of Her Majesty's court in the halls of the hollow mountain of Faerie. But now, she was lost in the surging sands of the canyon, and she was giving up hope.

Elsinore, the sorceress, thought back to the guide she had met at the small settlement near the entrance to the

Gate of the Wind, a twisting mountain pass that was one of the only places of ingress through the long mountain range in the north. The man had seemed surprised to see a traveler such as her and had gaped awkwardly. Whether this was due to her queer attire—a short purple dress and a black hood that covered locks of teal-dyed hair—or to her presence so near the Gate when the winds threatened to strip the uncovered flesh from a mortal's bones, Elsinore had not been able to tell.

"You'll forgive me, young woman," the trader said, "but a pilgrim without a mount is a worrisome sight in this part of the world. If you rode a horse, I would make your chances of passing through safely as better than even. On foot . . ."

Elsinore frowned beneath the lace of her hood, mostly at his doubt in her capability. She had traded a couple of copper pieces for some fruit and crusts of bread from his cart to last her a few days. When the man had encouraged her to take dry cured meat as well, even without payment, Elsinore refused.

"I'm a capable woman, and I'll be fine as I am and with what I've taken." The sorceress's voice was husky—especially so from traveling in the dry climate, perhaps, but nevertheless, it made her self-conscious. "I've heard the Gate of the Wind is a maze, and to become lost there means a fate from which no animal flesh or mount would save me. I don't need to risk the life of another creature to make my way easier. All I wish is for you to tell me the right way through to the country of Tabitia on the far side."

Looking down at the dirt and sparse grass by the traveler's tall, well-worn boots, the trader cleared his throat. "I suppose this animal accompanies you of its own accord, then?"

Elsinore followed his eyes to her familiar, a cat black furred and sleek, clean of the drifting dust that seemed to float forever like a fog in this land. She smiled.

"Risky is more likely to come safely out of that canyon than I am." Bending, she stroked the cat's head. When she looked back at the trader, her eyes were visible for the first time under her hood. They were piercing gray, and the man stared into them for a long moment.

Sighing, the guide motioned her to come to the cart and unrolled a beaten cloth map he pulled from the seat. "Keep to the southeast path," he cautioned. "And keep your wits about you. I doubt that little short sword you carry will do you much good against the shades that scream in the wind—nor even if you merely take a wrong turn and stumble across a griffin's nest!"

Elsinore had, of course, taken a wrong turn; she was quite sure of that by now. Though the blinding sands carried on the wind made it impossible to see more than a few yards around her, she knew the walls of the chasm surrounded her because of the angle of the dim sunlight above. For days, she'd trekked through this dismal maze, living on the rations she'd bought from the guide while her water ran perilously low. She had not come to any waypoint marker, and now she fought to keep dread from rising in her heart. She had long ago come to doubt how much further she could go on. Risky had survived in their own mysterious way, silently hunting small animals Elsinore could never see.

At last, for no reason the girl could tell, the cat yowled and spat and dashed off into the sand-strewn wind alone.

"Risky! Wait!" Elsinore called, hurrying after them.

The wind died down at last, at least for the moment, and the traveler saw her familiar a short sprint ahead, warily pacing around a pile of strange round stones in a corner of the pass. Looking around, Elsinore saw that she was, indeed, in the wrong place. This path ended fifty yards or so ahead by the stone pile in a box canyon, and she would have to retrace her steps to find any way forward. She cursed the pass and the sand and covered her face with her hands to hide her panic from herself.

Sighing, she dropped her hands and turned back to Risky. "What have you found? Is it a suitable place for me to lie to await my death?"

She started to follow the cat and nearly tripped over an exposed black stone. Something about its shape made the sorceress uneasy. Two more lay ahead, and Elsinore drew back with a gasp when she realized the black stones were shaped like recumbent human skeletons, half-buried in the sand and the earth, mouths open to the sky, eye sockets hollow and unseeing. Perhaps they were fallen statues or parts of decorated pillars, carved in this frightful shape to scare travelers, though why this would be necessary in a place so naturally forbidding was beyond Elsinore. There was something terribly lifelike about them.

Growing warier, Elsinore moved around these grisly stones to find the cat hissing at the pile ahead of them. These were the same dark-gray stone as the skeletons and had the appearance of perfectly smooth orbs, slightly elongated like ovals.

Eggs?

She approached the pile and saw beside it another stone exposed entirely. It was another skeleton—this one not human in the least. It had a long body with four legs, like a lion, perhaps, but several times larger than the woman. It had a tapering tail like a snake's, and its head was strange and fantastical. The skull bore wide, staring sockets, each beneath a long forward-facing horn, and its mouth was a beak, like an eagle's or that of some other incredible bird of prey. But strangely, the creature's mouth was full of flat, gnashing teeth, not at all like a bird's. In a ring behind its skull was a bony crest, like a crown or a halo.

Elsinore was sure this must be a griffin, the pinnacle of all beasts of earth and sky. Reaching out with a tentative hand, she felt the beak beneath her fingers, and the smooth black stone felt hot, warmed by the sun and the rough desert air.

A glint of light ahead caught Elsinore's eye as she stood.

On the wall of the dead-end canyon, a deep alcove was lit by the slant of the sun. Within, a statue was carved from the living rock—a figure, perhaps three times life size, of a woman or goddess seated cross-legged. On the woman's head sat a cylindrical crown or hairdo, but most strangely, she had no face. It was not broken or worn away; rather, it looked as if the head had been carved with a deep pit that had once held a separate piece as or in place of a face. Whatever had once been there was now gone, leaving only an enigmatic hollow.

The hands of the statue were folded one on top of the other in her lap, and in the flat of the upturned palms rested an object that glittered in the sun, dimly veiled though it was by the sand that still drifted in the air. From what Elsinore could tell, the object appeared to be silver and circular.

She approached, intending to climb upon the statue's knees to look closer, when she was startled by a flash from the object. Perhaps the air had cleared of sand for a moment, leaving a sharp beam of sunlight to flash off the metal, tarnished though it was. The light momentarily blinded Elsinore.

Risky's hissing grew more hostile and so loud, it was not even drowned out by the rising wind that picked up around the chasm once more. The sand whirled quickly in the tight space, and Elsinore's vision was rapidly obscured. She braced herself to keep from being knocked over by the tumultuous currents of air, as it picked up greater speed than ever before.

Mercifully, the storm was short lived this time. As the wind died down and the curtains of sand fell away, the world resolved once again around Elsinore, and she caught her breath at what she saw.

The pass was gone. The mountains themselves appeared to have melted away, and with them, the figure of the goddess. All around was a softly rolling marshland, obscured not by stones but by the massive fronds of monstrous plants. The air was thick and humid, heavy with the damp waters of the marsh, utterly unlike the dry, sandy desert of the mountain pass.

Despite the mysteriously altered scenery, the pile of stones remained. Only, they were clearly no longer stones; the smooth black oval boulders were now white oversized eggs. Elsinore stood frozen in confusion.

A dreadful animal call, like the sounding of a wide horn, echoed across the landscape, and Elsinore broke from her trance and immediately spun around, instinctively drawing her sword.

Two horrible realizations fell upon her in quick succession. The first was that the skeletal statues she'd tripped over, though hard to see, were now the gored, blood-soaked bodies of newly dead travelers, half sunk in the marsh, faces staring sightlessly at the setting sun. The second was that the cause of their death stood before her: Still some space away, though not nearly far enough, was a behemoth, the griffin itself restored to life. Its body was covered in leathery scales, and feather-like quills grew upright from its swaying tail. The crest behind its head fanned out like a sunburst, and on its face were three massive horns, one curving up from the nose of its beak and two curving forward from above its eyes.

This terrible creature was not at all like a bull nor an eagle nor a lion but was instead unlike any creature Elsinore had ever seen, though it partook of the nature of many. The three horns of its face were pointed toward the girl, and though every muscle in her body urged her to run, she knew she would never escape the beast's enormous stride.

Instead, she maintained enough presence of mind to sheath her sword. It was clear the trader had been right; the blade was unlikely to do any good against the griffin's scaly hide. With her hands free, she stood ready, her feet set apart and poised to fly when the moment came.

The colossus bellowed again and lurched forward in a charge. Elsinore had barely a moment to prepare; though it seemed lumbering, huge, and hardly graceful, its muscular legs and long stride gave it all the momentum it needed to outpace the smaller woman. Standing her ground, Elsinore kept her eyes focused on the creature's head and the long, sharp horns that protruded forward like the spikes on a siege engine.

In an instant, it was upon her; in an instant, the girl was ready. The beast lowered its head to strike, to gore and trample her as it had the other victims nearby. As it did,

Elsinore jumped and flipped through the air, catching the horns gracefully in her hands and vaulting her body over like a ritual bull leaper.

She turned as she flew through the air and came down on the creature's back, barely clearing the crest behind its head. She held onto the rim of the crest for stability, desperately clinging for her life as the monster tossed and reared, refusing to be thrown aside and dashed and trampled upon the ground. She held on but lost hope, realizing she had no notion of how she would attain the ground and free herself from the creature's reach. She had dodged one mortal fate for another, and she despaired of attaining safety.

The wind picked up again, as did the whirling of the sand. She felt each grain strike her face, no longer protected by her hood, but she heard something more beyond the now-familiar howling of the air. The ringing of bells tinkled on the wind, growing closer, followed by the exultant sound of a horn.

Before Elsinore had time to speculate, she saw them. Riders hurried forth upon horses sleek and tall, though from where she could not see. There were three, but their features were unclear in the fierceness of the moment. One rode forward, charging the griffin head-on, and at the last moment, fell away to the right as the monster leaned its head in a futile strike. Till the last moment, Elsinore did not see a second rider, a split second behind the first, peeling off to the left and along the beast's side.

"My hand, sister!" the ride yelled, his voice smooth and commanding. "Take it! To me, if you can!"

In the bare instant, Elsinore fell to the side into the man's arms and onto the back of his horse. The riders swung through the field around the behemoth, turning back in retreat. The air rippled through Elsinore's hair, her hood trailing behind.

As they moved farther away from the eggs, the griffin held back at last.

The wind came not only from the speed of the horses but from the rising whirlwind of sand, and the riders dove straight into it without hesitation. Something in the distance ahead sparkled, a flash of light, cold and silver. The world fell away, and all was a sea of sand. Then, as quickly as it had risen, the wall of wind died away, and Elsinore found herself in the canyon once more. The stone figure of the seated goddess loomed above her, the silver object in its lap glinting—now in the light of the moon rather than the sun. The dry air took her breath away, and she nearly swooned and fell from the horse.

"Careful! Don't hurt yourself after all the trouble we went to." The rider laughed. "Here, brothers! Let's stop and rest for a moment."

Elsinore dismounted and leaned back against a boulder to regain her composer as the rider sat beside her. She could better see him now in the calm and the starlight. A thin wisp of a beard grew along his narrow jaw, though he was older than an adolescent; Elsinore guessed he was closer to her own age, surely twenty or more. His eyes were dark, like little pools of wine, his brow and cheeks gently curved.

When he noticed her staring, he raised an eyebrow, though surely not intending to arouse Elsinore as much as he did. She thought she could swoon again, this time for entirely different reasons.

Dark geometric tattoos covered his shoulders and strong upper arms, visible beneath an open leather vest. The patterns reached below his pectoral muscles, where they seemed to radiate up his chest from tattoos in red ink—except the long red outlines along the underside of his pectorals were not tattoos but scars. Indeed, they were scars she recognized from her brothers at the Temple of the Goddess.

She smiled at him, searching for something to say beyond a meager thank-you, when something wet—and rough as the sharp sand in the wind—dragged across the side of her face. As the rider laughed, Elsinore shrank away, only to see Risky perched on the boulder behind her, their rough cat tongue still hanging out of their mouth.

"A lot of help you were!" she accused. "What's even the point of having a familiar if you can't transform into a sphinx for me to ride into battle against a griffin?"

The cat inclined their head quizzically, then dropped to the canyon floor and rolled in the dirt.

The rider and his companions laughed. Taking Elsinore's hand, the rider helped her to her feet, then mounted his horse.

"I would thank the little creature, were I you," he teased. "We'd been scouring the canyon for hours for the visitor we were told would arrive, but we hadn't known where to look till this cat fell upon us, crying incessantly. They didn't stop till we gave them our attention and followed them here, to the shrine of Arnahit."

He looked to the figure of the goddess and bowed before it in thanks.

"The wind rose up, and despite knowing the legends of the Bowl of Arnahit, we wondered to find ourselves in that strange land and you astride the griffin like some hero of old. I've heard of the creatures and even have some companions who tell of encountering them, but I never thought I would see one up close, and I would never have had the courage to attempt such a thing as you did."

He brought Elsinore up onto the saddle behind him, and she wrapped her arms around his muscular abdomen for safety, tucking Risky comfortably into her lap. The man leaned back a little as he brought the horse to a gallop, and she responded by leaning into him, resting her head on the back of his shoulder—for stability, of course, as they rode through the racketing winds.

"I have no doubt of your courage," Elsinore said. "You and your friends rescued me; your boldness in confronting that marvelous beast aside, I had no idea where I had gone or how to get back. For a moment, I thought perhaps I had died and was seeing some fantastic vision of a demon attempting to destroy my soul. I owe you my life, or more than that. My name is Elsinore."

The man replied cheerfully that his name was Masidas.

As they at last rode away from the box canyon toward safety through the maze of the Gate, Elsinore looked back at the corner where she had slipped into the awful vision of that mysteriously distant land. On the floor of the canyon before the great figure of the Goddess, she saw the dark shapes of the stone skeletons: the exposed griffin and the humans half-buried in the unknown ages of ever-drifting sand. The faceless figure of Arnahit overlooked them all and seemed to somehow cast an enigmatic glance from the hollow of its head at Elsinore in the moonlight.

"How did you know I would be here?" Elsinore called to Masidas, trying to be heard over the wind.

"I told you, your friend the cat led you to us."

"You said you were looking already, that you were told

a visitor was coming to your village," Elsinore said. "How could you have known I would be coming?"

"The seeresses told us. The Inarae, the priestesses of the Goddess, the healers and soothsayers of our community—they said that a traveler was coming out of the Gate to find us today."

No sooner had Masidas mentioned the Gate than the riders flew out of the canyon, away from the tall stone walls of the mountainside, at last reaching the grassy rolling hills and woodlands beyond. The riders brought their mounts to a halt for a rest and to get their bearings, giving Elsinore a moment to take in the beauty of the country that spread out before them: the sweeping lowlands, the distant hills, and the trees, darkly green in the bright moonlight.

"Or rather," Masidas continued at last, "they said you were coming to find *them*."

After a rest, the party rode on, down into the valley and toward the tree line. As they drew closer, dwellings appeared, first a hut here and there, then fences, structures, halls. At last, the settlement surrounded them. Most of the windows were dark, the common ground vacant, with only a few lanterns posted and one or two houses lit, as most of the town slept at this late hour.

Masidas tended Elsinore, making sure she was all right after her experience, and offered her soft cushions in a room at his home for her to rest for the night, before she met with the seeresses in the morning. Elsinore accepted gratefully, and if she dreamed at all of mazes and chimeras, of the heat of the sun and the edge of the wind, she remembered none of it—only the peace of a restful sleep after a long journey.

When she awoke, Elsinore was taken to a communal bath-house, where women and men of the village washed side by side. The visitor was a little surprised at first. In the temple of the Goddess where she had studied, and in the community where she was raised, such things were taken for granted. But in her recent travels, she had found that the farther reaches beyond the Great River Valley segregated such activities by sex, under the influence of patriarchal cults to the jealous sun god. By grace of the Goddess, Elsinore was, for the most part, assumed to belong with the women, but she had learned not to take local goodwill for granted and remained cautious and guarded in unfamiliar lands.

Perhaps she needn't have worried. The country of Tabitia was renowned well beyond Elsinore's homeland for its egalitarian community; perhaps this was why the Mother Bodhakes had requested she be the one to make such an arduous journey. And she had indeed come to consult the Inarae priestesses, as they themselves had predicted. Whether they would welcome her, and whether they could answer her questions, remained to be seen.

Once she had washed, she waited for the summons from the soothsayers. She spent time talking with Masidas about the ways of Tabitia and, in particular, about the lives of men like himself and women like Elsinore. Those who transitioned to womanhood were not limited in the roles they could perform, but it seemed as if many felt drawn to the holy practice of the Inarae. This intrigued Elsinore. As a mage and acolyte of the Goddess herself, she felt a kinship with the priestesses and was eager to meet them.

Masidas himself had come to his manhood later than most boys and by his own will, as Elsinore had observed. The horse riders—hunters and scouts—counted among their number men, women, and otherwise, as did most other professions, so it had been no controversy in the community when Masidas announced his manhood and his certainty that the gods were calling him to the life of a scout.

Elsinore thanked the gods for leading him on such a path—and again, she expressed her thanks to the young man for rescuing her from the griffin. This time, he blushed and stammered out something more about Elsinore's own bravery before his awkward tension was relieved by the intrusion of a messenger from the priestesses. They were ready to see Elsinore, and she was to come before them without further delay.

The messenger led her along the central avenue, till they crossed the boundary stones of the village. The further they went from the people and buildings, closer to the tree line, the more doubtful Elsinore grew.

"No temple devised by the artifice of mortals would suit the Ladies of the Gray Sight," the messenger said, as if sensing her question. "Their only temple is a grove in the wood, where the voice of the Goddess may be heard all around them."

The messenger stopped at a place where several trees stood apart; the rest had branches grown so close together, it was impossible to see past them. The trees were evergreens suited to the climate, and the path in the opening was carpeted with fallen needles. The trees reminded Elsinore of the cedars and pines that grew at the foot of the far-off mountain that stood at the gate into Faerie, where she had been blessed by the queen of that hollow land. Her hair was dyed blue green to remind her of those trees and of her devotion to the Goddess. Brushing the locks away from her eyes, she breathed deep and took a step forward.

"Wait," the messenger said, stopping her with an out-stretched arm. "Your sword. No blade, sword or spear, may be brought into the sacred space of the Inarae. You must leave it here, outside the grove." The messenger gestured at a little mound of earth by the side of the path.

As Elsinore drew her sword, Moonstar, its blade flashed white in the morning light. Its hilt was a silver crescent, like the moon, and in the pommel was set a clear crystal that glittered like the evening star. Holding it blade down, she plunged it into the earth of the mound, where it stood firmly, star and moon and blade glowing in the sun.

"None will take it, I promise you this," the messenger said. Elsinore nodded and turned to the opening in the trees.

The needles were soft beneath her boots, and the branches brushed her face gently. She expected the interior of the trees to be dark, shaded from the light, but overhead, the pines gave way to the sky, and light filled the space as if from the window of a stone temple in some great city. The path led farther in, to a deeper circle of trees, and she followed it inward, the light guiding her way.

Within the next grove, she saw them, each kneeling in meditation beneath a linden tree. There were seven in all, and there was an empty space in their midst beneath the last tree. The priestesses wore simple hempen robes of undyed gray, and their faces were hidden beneath wide hoods. None moved, nor did they gesture or beckon, but Elsinore knew the eighth seat was meant for the supplicant. In this moment, it was meant for her. Moving tentatively into the grove, she sat beneath the tree in the same kneeling manner as the others, hands folded on her lap.

For a long time, all was silent.

At last, at a sign Elsinore neither knew nor perceived,

the Inara sister opposite her pushed back her hood and spoke.

"The body of the Goddess Arnahit is the world, and Her mind is the passage of time. We read the words of the Goddess woven in the linden-tree bark, the fibers of Her flesh the braided paths through which She shows us Her memory. That memory consists of what was and what will be, and we are thankful for what She shows us of Herself. It is in this way She told us of your coming.

"You have traveled far, Galla, across the great river and the plains, at last through the labyrinth of the Gate of the Wind and the place of the griffin. What you saw of that creature was many aeons ago; you fell into one of the Goddess's deep memories, which few of us in this late age of the world are shown. You were taken to a place before our people settled these lands; before the long-ago time of the Old Ones, whose hubris poisoned the seas and scarred the mountains with their blasphemous iron engines; and further still, before even the first humans walked upright in the grass beneath the low trees. The Bowl of Arnahit has this power; the Bowl of Arnahit is from a time we cannot fathom, forged by hands we cannot name, even with the visions granted by the Goddess. This we know, for the Goddess has shown us.

"But the cause that brings you here we know not. Your spirit is troubled and your mind ill at ease, but we need no clairvoyance to tell us this."

"Why come to us?" another hooded sister interjected. "Your journey has been long and difficult, but you are yourself. Those who make the pilgrimage to see us come for the secrets of the potion of transition you yourself can already produce. Secrets that your sister Gallae in Sanisa know well. Why does a woman like you—free of the shackles that bind those who have not heard or accepted the calling of the Goddess—come to us? What more does she need of the Inarae? Speak to us, sister, of your need. Speak what you wish of the Inarae."

Elsinore closed her eyes, feeling the sunlight seep through her eyelids. She breathed deep before she spoke.

"I am, as you say, a Galla, a priestess of the Goddess outside and across the boundaries of male and female.

"I have seen places and met forms of the Goddess many others have not dreamed of. I have lost the woman I love, and found her again dancing in the banquet hall of She who rules beneath the Mountain. And my love was returned to me in a form I still cannot understand."

The sisters looked from one to another, breaking their stillness, but none of them spoke.

"She knows more, has felt more, than even I. She remembers her life with me before her death, and she remembers lives before even that. She has knowledge of things far outside ordinary life—things even those strong in the wisdom of the Goddess do not know.

"It is she who has sent me here. She knows you, sisters. She is the Mother Bodhakes of Sanisa, and she has learned secrets that the foremothers of the Gallae knew in the lost ages of the Old Ones. So she has called upon me to ask a gift of you."

"Whatever the Mother Bodhakes needs, we will give it," said one of the Inarae. "But what thing could be in our power to give her that she cannot obtain for herself?"

"You needn't guess," Elsinore said. "You know it."

The sisters exchanged glances again, this time mumbling, more taken aback than before. The sister across from Elsinore closed her eyes, lowered her head to her chest, and shivered.

"What you speak of is not ours to give," she said with finality.

"Perhaps not," Elsinore said. "But then, neither is it yours to refuse."

The Inarae looked at each other, touched each other's hands, and conferred with each other silently, in some way Elsinore could not perceive.

Growing uneasy with the Inarae's occult discussion, Elsinore spoke again, her voice even and confident. "I am told your sisterhood is adept at seeking to know the will of the Goddess through casting lots and reading omens. If it is not yours to give, then it is Hers. We can ask Her for it."

"That is out of the question," the central Inara replied sternly. "This matter is unprecedented. Even our sister the Mother Bodhakes of Sanisa should not have spoken of it. Your request is refused."

"The Mother Bodhakes does not wish this thing for herself," Elsinore said. "She wishes to restore what was lost very long ago. She wishes to put right what was broken and restore what was sundered in ages long past."

"No earthly knowledge can restore this thing!" one of the sisters cried.

"But I have brought the Bodhakes news from another world. I have brought her a secret that she understood, a puzzle that she solved, and with what I ask of you, she will be able to solve a greater puzzle still, one that has lain unresolved since the age of the Old Ones."

Elsinore paused then, and a hush grew over the Inarae as they sat still. The eyes of the sister across from Elsinore grew wide, and she nodded at the girl, urging her to go on.

"The Mother Bodhakes has asked me to tell you this: She wishes for you to allow the Bowl of Arnahit to be sent to her in Sanisa so it can at last be reunited with that which it housed."

"No," the central sister gasped, not in denial of Elsinore's request but in amazement at what she said. "It cannot be."

"Further the Mother Bodhakes wishes me to tell you this: She knows where to find the Acus Matris Deum, the Needle of the Mother of the Gods, the black star that fell from the heavens bearing the thread of the Goddess Herself in long ages past—the thread with which She sews all our fates into the web of the world."

All sat silent for a long moment. Elsinore smiled slightly, and none of the Inarae would look her in the eye. Finally, the sister across from Elsinore spoke again, her voice shaking but stern.

"Leave this grove for now. Return when the sun rises in the morning. As you have said, there are no others on earth more skilled at reading the will of the Goddess than the Inarae. We are Her priestesses, and we shall consult Her for your answer. Go for now. Return to this place in a day's time. Goddess be with you, sister."

Elsinore nodded, rose, and took leave of the grove. She drew Moonstar from the earth as she passed and returned to the room that had been given to her. She tried to meditate, but she shook with relief that her petition was over for now. She could not make her mind stop searching for the meaning of what went on here between the Inarae and Folia.

Meowing, Risky came and curled up beside Elsinore. She scratched the cat until she fell asleep, though it was only midday.

As the sun rose dimly the next morning, Masidas summoned Elsinore from her room right away. Once again, she was brought to the grove, where the sisters knelt in their circle like arcane witches. In the center of the circle, a small bonfire blazed, fueled by twigs and sticks and strips of bark. Elsinore joined them, and one Inara spoke from beneath the folds of her hood.

"We have consulted the bark that grows upon the linden trees, the outgrowth of the mind of the Goddess, woven as the threads of our destinies are all woven into the fabric of the world. We have seen, only dimly, hints of the Goddess's memory of what is to come. It is now the decision—it is Her decision—that you be permitted to follow the threads of the Goddess's thoughts as well. So, too, the Mother Bodhakes."

Elsinore looked around the circle expectantly, from sister to sister, but none made any motion or sound, and the one who had spoken now remained silent.

"So . . . I am to prophecy as you have? With sticks and bark read and then tossed into the fire?" Elsinore didn't try to hide her confusion.

"My sister," the Inara spoke again. "You don't really understand what the Mother Bodhakes has asked of you, do you?"

Elsinore stared, unable to make herself respond. Unable to even know how to do so.

"In reading the omens in the tangle of bark, we see distantly," the Inara said. "We see only records of what the Goddess knows, as if reading the hasty scratches on an ancient document in a language long forgotten."

"But you, sister," added another, "you shall see the Goddess's memory firsthand."

Elsinore shook her head in confusion. "I don't understand," she muttered.

"You shall take the Bowl of Arnahit back to Sanisa, to the Bodhakes. And if what she says is true—and the glimpses granted us by our prophecy hint that it is—you shall unite the Bowl once again with the Acus Matris Deum."

"Then," the first sister concluded, "you shall see exactly what we mean."

Preparations were made the next morning for Elsinore's departure from Tabitia. Masidas saddled horses for himself, two other riders, and Elsinore. They packed supplies: dried fruit, bread, bean butter, and water, more than enough to make it to the nearest settlement on the far side of the Gate.

At the edge of town, Elsinore and her companions met them—the seven, hooded in gray and seated not on mats beneath linden trees but upon white horses with saddles decorated with tassels. Each woman wore a black veil over her eyes, producing a ghostly effect. Upon further reflection, Elsinore realized the veils most likely only served to dim the bright light of the sun.

"Come," the lead Inara said. "We must hurry before the winds of the Gate grow too strong."

The party proceeded out of the town and in among the walls of the Gate, where the sand stirred but did not yet cast about in blinding curtains as it had days before. Led by Masidas and his men, they quickly reached the passage to the Shrine of Arnahit. The priestesses dismounted and approached the statue of the Goddess.

Masidas raised a hand to hold Elsinore back as the Inarae surrounded the shrine.

"We may only watch from a distance," the young man explained. "The ceremony may only be performed by Inarae initiates. Outsiders—men, women from abroad, even the Gallae of Sanisa—may not witness the full ritual or hear the prayers the Inarae will say over the Bowl."

"And what use will it be without this knowledge and without any Inarae accompanying me to share it?"

"I should think your Bodhakes will know what to do," Masidas said gravely.

When the ritual was finished, the Inarae returned to the others. In both hands, the head priestess carried the Bowl of Arnahit.

It was a strange thing, Elsinore realized now that she saw it up close. Less like an ordinary bowl, the object looked like silver that had been melted and poured over something like a stone, molded and taking its shape as it cooled and hardened—but without the molded object, the silver now looked only bent and pocked. Around this interior was a rim that bore a wide bent lip, decorated with scenes the meaning of which Elsinore could not guess: Supplicants or initiates approached a priestess or goddess; men raised spears, perhaps threateningly, at the sun above; griffins flanked a woman standing on the peak of a mountain; an androgynous figure lounged languidly—or perhaps lay dying—on a bed of flowers.

One of the priestesses produced an oiled leather saddlebag, and the head Inara slid the Bowl unceremoniously inside, fastening it to hang on the flank of Elsinore's horse.

Elsinore smiled wryly. "I suppose I assumed it would only be permitted for the Bowl to travel in a palanquin in a grand procession."

"It must go unnoticed. No attention must be drawn to the bowl; its worth is too great."

Frowning beneath the shadow of her veil, the old priestess looked to the others. They nodded.

"Go now," she said. "We will return to Tabitia; Masidas will lead you out of the Gate and accompany you on the road back to your valley for safety. Stop only to sleep and be vigilant. You will return with the bowl to the Mother Bodhakes, and she will protect it." The priestess said this not as a prediction or a supposition but as a command.

Elsinore looked at her horse and the satchel she bore. Sitting on the horse's back behind the saddle was Risky.

"It will be safe," Elsinore said. "That isn't a promise. It is merely what will happen." She smiled. "I hope we meet again," she said, meaning it sincerely.

Then the young priestess parted from her distant sisters. Swinging herself up into the saddle, she followed Masidas as he led her on the safe route through the Gate of the Wind.

Elsinore did not know what would be around each turn. Even once they'd come clear of the Gate—far from the cliffside, free of the sands stirring in the winds, and safe on the road to the Great River Valley—Elsinore didn't know what she and her companions would encounter next.

The possibilities of the world were endless, after all, and the paths the Goddess weaved through mountains and valleys, rivers and forests, were twisting and recurring—unpredictable to even the wisest seer.

THE NEW MOON COAST

The Wand'ring Ocean stirred ceaselessly, wildly, black beneath a starless sky. It was made rapid and anxious by a moon that could not be seen, though the air was clear of clouds. Waves flickered and licked and grasped at a shore that stood still, silent in the face of its slow, long-coming doom. On some distant day, the shore might be pulled into the ocean, or the water might retreat far from the shore to trouble some far-off land or raise islands as mountains lonely in the waves. The sorceress knew only that it would change; in what manner could be known by none but the Goddess who is Mother of all.

The beach was framed by a cliff, a sharp cut of rock that rose high above and sliced through the beach and into the ocean. The waves broke against its side like petty mourners worshipping an ancient god of black stone.

The ship had set anchor too far from the shore to disembark. The sorceress, a stranger among the crew, turned away from where she had been leaning against the top edge of the hull to look at the others on the deck. Much of the crew continued their duties, but others had stopped to loiter and stare at her.

"What are we doing? Why have we dropped anchor?" the sorceress asked whoever would listen.

The captain emerged from belowdecks. "We've stopped because this is as far as we're going." He was a gruff man, voice scratched and deepened by years of salt from the sea, but he had been gracious in taking the sorceress aboard.

He had even agreed, against all likelihood, to detour the ship some ways into the Wand'ring Ocean, away from its intended destination, and had not spoken to the crew of what the sorceress had paid him for doing so. His crew whispered rumors: that she had given him a magic jewel that would grant any wish; that she had looked into his mind and whispered to him a secret she had seen within, which he had long forgotten and was desperate to remember; that she had slain an enemy he had made at the last port, someone who would have pursued him without mercy, till the witch's magic sword slid across his neck and ended the threat he posed.

Others simply said she had sucked on his cock until he agreed to take her wherever she wished.

Picking up a black cat from the deck, the sorceress glared at the captain with a mixture of annoyance and confusion. "And how am I to get ashore?"

The captain clapped his hands to the side, and one of the crew rushed to a lifeboat and two oars hung upon ropes, ready to be lowered over the side. Approaching the sorceress, the captain whispered to her gently.

"I promised the Mother Bodhakes I would take you here, and I did. Any captain from the Great River Valley would do as much for her, and I keep my promise and honor her. But, girl, we cannot approach any closer than this."

Then the captain pulled back, and his tone changed; he roared loudly, bragging to the crew to keep face. "We come any closer, and the empty winds'll becalm us, and the darkness of the land beyond will swallow us all like ghosts! Take your witchery into your shadowland and begone with ye, wench!" He followed this bombastic insincerity with a silent wink at the sorceress, and she smirked.

Elsinore sat firmly in the lifeboat and was lowered to the water.

And she rowed.

For hours, the sorceress trod inland, away from the sea and through the sand of the beach, up away into the highlands of the cliffs. Elsinore Ningala, sorceress and priestess, had journeyed far from her home in the Great River Valley to find this place.

No people dwelt near the New Moon Coast, for the sky was unnatural and the earth, though still, was uncertain and strange. Always it was night in that place, yet neither stars nor moon shone to guide sailors on their way, and the air was always still. The sky was total blackness, even when clear of clouds, and those that hung above were thin and sick.

A few days' walk inland, the sky became clear and natural, and so, too, further up the coast, where tribes had dwelt for generations out of mind. But by ancient taboo, neither they nor travelers from afar would let themselves be waylaid long in this dark place. The stars had fallen from this land, the sun never dared show its bright face, and the whole sky was like the dark of the new moon.

Accounts available to the dwellers of the Great River Valley made no mention of the peculiar nature of this place. Whether this was because chroniclers had felt no need to describe the obvious, they had felt too much fear of some accursed taboo to make mention of it, or they had written records from so ancient a time that the darkness had not yet fallen upon the coast, Elsinore could not tell. But Folia, the Mother Bodhakes, had strange secrets within her reach, things forgotten for generations, including knowledge from the past of lands far distant, lands to which she had never been in life.

Elsinore thought of her lover as she pressed on along the shore to the cliff. Folia, now high priestess of the temple in Sanisa, where both women had studied the ways of the Goddess what felt like a lifetime ago. Folia, who had died, leaving Elsinore alone. Folia, whom Elsinore had found dancing at the feast of the Goddess in the city in the heart of the Mountain, in Faerie, in Hell. Folia, more beautiful than the stars, who had been reborn in the world knowing deeper secrets than Elsinore could understand, even in their most intimate moments together.

"I just don't understand why she has to be so fucking mysterious," Elsinore said aloud. Then she stopped, looked up into the darkness, and let herself fall backward into the soft sand.

After lying with her eyes closed for a long moment, she crossed her legs and sat up. She shook her head and brushed sand out of her long hair, dyed the blue green of a better sea than the one that had rolled silently beneath the ship that had brought her here.

This sea had been black, a reflection of the endless, starless sky above. Yet even though darkness surrounded Elsinore and oppressed her, she could clearly see all around her in an uneasy luminescence whose source she could not guess. Each grain of sand glowed a rich, bright purple, and rock formations here, further inland, cast a shifting blue and green and purple light.

No, not cast, for no light fell upon the rest of this land of darkness; rather, they were simply visible. Elsinore herself even seemed . . . not lit by the black light of the scenery around her but merely able to be seen.

When she focused her eyes on her surroundings, even on her hands, everything seemed to faintly shiver and drift ever so slightly, as if it all were under the rolling waters of the sea. But no seawater could have reached this land, hours inland from the shore and high above sea level. This land could not have been underwater for thousands of years. Yet the land and air around her was strange and shifting and dry.

As she sat cross-legged on the ground she took a handful of sand in her fist, felt the soft minuscule particles part and flow in her hand like water, and let the sand sift and fall through her fingers to the countless grains below. The sand swirled and drifted as it fell, creating whorls like nebulae, each grain a star following the cosmic wind that flows inevitably from the Beginning, ever onward through the worlds, rising and falling, ever changing, the breath of the universe, till in immeasurable aeons finally falling still when all comes to the Final End, the stillness of all breath—before the All shall inhale once again, an eternity of the cycle's repetition.

Then exhalation again, a breath exponentially longer than that which mortals can recognize as Forever.

The sand glittered and sparkled in its own fluorescence, reflecting no light at all, luminous like stars in the dark matter of space. The sand flowed and spiraled like the river of stars, the galaxy Elsinore knew in her heart was somewhere above, though she could not see it.

Then the sand in her fingers ran out, the last of it fallen, only a little left caked on the sorceress's palm. She brushed her hands together, then wiped them on the sides of her skirt, which was a similar purple to the luminous starlight sand. She stood and brushed off her dress and bare legs. She'd grown used to the sand in her tall sandal boots, and left them on; there was no point in shaking them out yet.

Further inland, in the distance, were the cliffs and the rock formations and mesas. Elsinore pressed on.

As she left the sea farther and farther behind, the plant life grew thicker, if plant life was what Elsinore saw. There were tall, straight spreading reeds, stunted shrubs, needle bushes, and gnarled things for which she knew no name, like some unknown hybrid of pine and succulent; they grew tall above the young woman but bent down threateningly upon her. Elsinore saw no path to keep clear of the vegetation, wary though she was. It was unlikely any animal life dwelt in this eerie place to blaze a path through continuous use, much as humans themselves kept far away.

Like the sand and the rock, the plants fluoresced with an unnatural light, deep, saturated colors of every part of the spectrum: purple reds, green blues, and yellow oranges, garish colors that stood out against the surrounding darkness like jewels on a black veil—or arcane sigils painted by the gods on the carapace of a venomous spider.

Brightest of all to Elsinore's eye were clutches of strange plants—or something like plants—that stood in and among all the others. Deep orange pink, with many thin branches that twisted and crept, these things drifted in the air, growing from only a thin trunk in the ground. Like tall reeds in a soft breeze during the Season of Light—or seaweed in the water of a calm sea—these things drifted . . . but there was no wind. There never had been, not for a moment since Elsinore had come ashore to this place of new-moon darkness. Yet still the pink things drifted, and Elsinore kept away from them the best she could as she passed carefully through the scrub reeds.

When the way through became too much, Elsinore drew Moonstar, her glittering short sword—its blade white and its cross guard a silver crescent moon with a crystal-star pommel. Moonstar had been bestowed upon her by her mother Glamis on the last night they had ever seen each other, when last the girl had felt her mother's strong embrace. That night was the last time Elsinore and her mothers had stood together, beneath the soft rainbow light of the Pomegranate Moon in the Season of Shadows, a world away and a generation past. Since then, every time Elsinore held Moonstar's hilt in her hand, she remembered them; every time going forward became too much for her, she tightened her grip and followed Moonstar's white light.

She swung her blade to clear the way of brambles and thorns, making her own path forward.

After progressing for some time, Elsinore held her sword still and listened. In all this dark place, there had been no sound save her own mutterings and sighs. But now a rustle in the path behind her reached her ear, very quiet, almost imperceptible, but terribly loud when surrounded by the silence of the land of the new moon. Another new sound rose, not in the sorceress's ears but in her head and her chest—her heartbeat, racing, drumming, thumping in anticipation of what crept behind.

With her sword at her side, Elsinore turned.

A cat had followed her: her familiar, Risky.

They were sleek and black furred, well-groomed and proud, with their head held high. They looked about with yellow-green eyes that shone with a light of their own, not reflecting the garish black light of the surroundings. The cat stopped when they noticed the young woman looking at them and meowed with something like irritation.

"You took your time. I haven't seen you since we disembarked. I suppose you went around the beach to keep the sand out of your precious little paws?" Elsinore said teasingly.

Risky meowed in response.

"I'm sorry, I'm trying my best to clear a path for us! I hope it's to your liking." She grinned and giggled, and Risky made a hissing cough of dissatisfaction. The entity in the form of a cat approached at last and rubbed their fur against Elsinore's leg. Sighing, the woman returned to her attempts at making progress.

It was slow going through the scrub and reeds, but gradually, Elsinore and Risky drew closer to the mesa ahead. Though all features of this landscape made the sorceress uneasy, she noted that the eerie luminescence of the plants faded not at all when they were cut down; instead, they continued to glow, even lying severed on the earth. Risky tiptoed between the stalks on careful paws, unwilling to touch them—though whether from fear of real danger or the usual fastidiousness of a cat, Elsinore could not tell. She kicked the stalks aside with her boots as she cut them, allowing for a better path.

In her haste, Elsinore failed to notice how close she had come to the pink, twisted, drifting things. The tip of her sword caught a branch on an upswing as the thing drifted toward her on the imperceptible breeze, and severed it.

At once, there came a cry, a piercing terrible wail like a flute-whistle, reminding Elsinore of faun-women in stage tragedies mourning the death of the goddess Galattis. The cry was like a nail in Elsinore's ear; she fell to her knees and saw Risky at her side, howling. The wail from the pink thing was so loud, she was barely able to hear the cat.

A gruesome sensation like warm slime crept onto Elsinore's right leg. A pink glowing branch gripped her leg like a tendril, growing rapidly tighter. Elsinore recoiled but could not pull away. Another grabbed her arm, and Elsinore was pulled up away from the ground. The thing continued its awful cry, but it was not the one that entrapped her. Another had her in its grasp—or several; Elsinore could not tell in the terror of the moment.

With her free arm, Elsinore swung Moonstar up across her body and down onto the slithering branch that held her leg. Of course, the thing responded with another shriek, as loud as the first, which had yet to subside. The shriek matched the other in tone and pitch, such that they blended into each other and Elsinore could not distinguish them.

She swung again at the one holding her arm, freeing herself to fall to her feet, but a third inhuman voice joined the others. Patches of earth trembled, and the roots of the pink things rose and lengthened and grew outward, like the roots of a tree pulled from the ground. The roots connected the thing that had held her to the one that first screamed, then to another, and to another. Waving their branches high in the air, the things rose and grew, connected in a complex branching net, all glowing with the same spectral orange-pink light, stark against the starless black sky. Waving tendrils grew from each nexus on the web.

Though terror darkened Elsinore's heart as the thing rose into the air, she saw a path of hope. As it rose tall upon its roots and consolidated into the net of its unified body, the thing cleared the ground where it had been hidden, leaving wide open paths of dark soil that glittered with stirred-up bits of purple sand. A twisting path to the cliffside ahead now ran clear through the reeds and thorns she had been cutting.

Elsinore sheathed her sword and dashed ahead, careful of her footing in the turned soil. Risky quickly sped ahead of her, finding simple small paths the human woman missed. The screaming, trembling pink thing rose still taller and drifted after the girl, following—but slowly.

At last, Elsinore made it to the cliffs and to a canyon carved between edges of rock. It was wide enough for perhaps a wagon two horses abreast, and Elsinore quickly slipped in, following the cat, who had gone ahead. Running into the canyon, she went about a hundred yards, then turned back and drew her sword. Would the thing still follow her between the rock walls?

As the thing slowly approached the cliff, it halted at the entrance. The mass of its great interlocking net of a body seemed unable to fold into the canyon, though the tendrils at its nexus points reached out feebly. After a few short moments, only brief but that seemed to stretch out in the terror of Elsinore's shaking breath, the thing drew its tendrils back, shrinking down again, and its wailing scream grew quieter, though it still rang in Elsinore's ears even so far off. Finally, the thing began drifting back the way it had come.

But Elsinore was not relieved.

For a moment, before it finally pulled away and retreated, the shape of the thing appeared to have shrunken into the form of a man.

Safe for now from the wounded unearthly thing—as far as she could tell—Elsinore proceeded forward into the narrow canyon. As she went on, the passage widened into a grand gallery, but it was still bound on the sides by the cliff, and there was only one way to move forward.

Half of her wondered if she would find what she sought, but her lover, the Bodhakes, was rarely mistaken in her insights—for reasons obscure even to Elsinore. She trusted the reverend mother, yet doubt crept cynically into her mind.

The Goddess is all things, in land and sea and the depths of space none could ever know. She is our bodies, our movements, our hearts and desires, the wind and the rain and the starlight and time, life and death and rebirth after everything.

But if the Goddess's presence had withdrawn from any place, it was from the black sky of this land, the roiling, unreflecting sea, the bright black light of the sand and the creatures, neither animal nor plant, that grew here. This place was more like a dead world orbiting a distant, forgotten, empty star than a place on Earth—or else a miniature world contained within a shell, separated from the rest of the Goddess's body.

But Elsinore knew that the Goddess was the source of even such worlds as those.

Unlike the fields before, the canyon was devoid of any life she could see. It seemed very much like a riverbed, centuries dry, that had once fed into the sea. Perhaps it had dried up when the shell of darkness enclosed this land, or perhaps it had suffered some other ancient fate. Elsinore did not know.

At last, after a bend in the canyon, Elsinore came upon a wall rising high up to the land above. It seemed to be natural stone; perhaps the earth had moved in a great quake once, cutting off the ancient river and drying the canyon. A recessed alcove had been cut into the wall by human hands, within which stood a colossal figure carved in relief from the living rock.

Twenty times taller at least than the human woman who stood before it, a figure with a female form loomed above the canyon floor. Her right arm was bent at the elbow, hand raised in front of her in an open-palmed ritual gesture of peace. Under her left arm, she carried a wide, flat object like a drum. Carved without clothes, her breasts were bare, and her legs were slightly spread, revealing, to Elsinore's wry recognition, the Goddess's penis. Below this, the space between the legs was darkness into which Elsinore could not yet see.

Atop the neck of the statue was only a wide, empty space. From where Elsinore stood, there appeared to be a concave emptiness where the head should have been. It struck her less as something that had been defaced, hammered and broken as an act of sacrilege, and more as if the entire face had been a separate piece, fitted into the space like a ball in a hand, and the piece representing the face was now missing.

Elsinore stared up at the empty face for a long time. She imagined the colossus as the husk of a seed that had been planted within the wall long ago by some divine gardener—the Goddess Herself—and left discarded once the seed had grown full and ripe and finally been plucked out, all long before this age of the world.

Or it was only a statue missing its head.

Once, long ago, another statue of the Goddess had been set with a strange stone, a stone long lost and forgotten. The Mother Bodhakes had sent Elsinore to this dreadful land to find it.

Since disregarding the warnings at the entrance to the Mountain and returning a lifetime later to the world, Elsinore had struggled to find her place. The life she knew was gone. The people she knew were lost, moved on in the years that had passed while Elsinore spent a single night within the Mountain of Faerie. They had been carried along on the wheel of life that ever spins, adrift in the sea of time that circles life and death, their being dispersed to be reaggregated in some other form, inexplicable to any who live and are reborn.

Except, perhaps, to Folia.

Where Elsinore had been adrift since her return, her temple sister Folia had found clarity, wisdom, and purpose in rebirth. She had studied the history of the life of the Goddess in the realm beneath the Mountain, had learned deep, hidden secrets lost for ages of the world, and had been reborn in the world with an insight into her own many lives that awed and startled those around her. The temple siblings who now considered her their reverend mother looked to her for guidance and counsel. To Elsinore, who had known her in a past life as a shy and awkward girl—a girl to whom she had given all her heart—her new life was remarkable, and Elsinore was still a little incredulous.

But the visions and realizations Folia had that brought Elsinore to this place had been very clear, and something in them rang in Elsinore's mind like a bell:

An object had fallen to earth in ages long forgotten: a black iron star no bigger than a human skull, conical and coming to a point. It had once been set in a bowl-shaped silver frame in the head of a statue of the Goddess, a silver frame that now rested in the temple of Tiranna in Sanisa, awaiting the return of that which it had once housed: the Acus Matris Deum, or the Needle of the Mother of the Gods.

The artifact that represents the cosmic needle with which the Goddess sews each thread of life into the fabric of the world, of life and death and rebirth—the web of interconnected phenomena. Each thread an infinite string of life and rebirth, hung with glittering beads that each reflect all the others, each interdependent on the others, part of each other, originating all at once as the world arises.

Elsinore still doubted she could find any clue to the whereabouts of such an object, so weighty with significance yet so small, ages lost and forgotten long ago by a people who had themselves been forgotten by the countless centuries.

Nor did she know what she could possibly do if she found it.

Elsinore felt Risky curl themself around her feet and purr. Looking down at last from the mighty megalithic form before her, she saw the little cat look up at her, their bright green eyes flashing curiously. Their sleek black fur reflecting the eerie light that suffused the canyon yet seemed to emanate from nowhere at all and cast only faint, edgeless shadows from the traveler and her familiar.

Sighing, Elsinore bent over to scratch behind the little cat's ear, but they suddenly paid her no mind. Instead, they hurried forward, quick but not running, into the darkness between the colossal goddess's feet.

Elsinore sighed again and followed till she caught up, and the two companions proceeded together.

The darkness hid a tunnel, black and unlit even by any fluorescence. The sorceress snapped her fingers and cast a cantrip, a simple spell, sparking a fiery ball of light that floated in the air above her hand. A hall had been carved into the rock ages ago, dry and coated in unknown years of dust, far from the river and the sea. Walking through the passage, the sorceress came to a wide, circular chamber with a low, domed ceiling.

All along the curving wall were reliefs cut from the solid rock, images of stories Elsinore felt she should remember, but whose meaning eluded her in her fear and haste. These scenes of occult legend flickered in the dim magic flame like a paper lantern show:

A pair of women stood together, raising their skirts almost demurely, revealing each to have breasts and a penis.

Another figure brandished a crayfish, driving away a winged lion—or drawing it to her.

A woman in a field of wheat held a pair of balancing scales and stood in judgment over—or perhaps guarded by—a scorpion with the head of a man wearing a tall crown and raising his pincers to her.

An archer with a wide stance aimed his bow at the scorpion-man.

A goat with curled horns and a lower body like a serpent or a fish rose from an unquiet sea and stared out at Elsinore with wild eyes that flashed with deep shadow in the firelight.

Above the passage through which she had entered, there was a bull with its horns lowered as if to charge. On its back rode six maidens, very small compared to the colossal bull. All were waving their arms or holding the bull's mane and horns. The six appeared to be dancers, joyfully celebrating on the back of the animal.

No, Elsinore thought as she looked closer, *not six.* There was a seventh maiden, almost hidden behind another, holding onto her sister's waist.

All the images flickered and changed in the light of the fire spell, growing obscure and then clear, moving and shifting like moments of time, wave foam in the sea, or shapes in the quick-spinning spokes of a wheel. All flashed before Elsinore in moments as she passed, as quickly as the real things in her firelight.

One carving in particular drew her attention. A woman carried a krater of water, which she poured out in waves into a river. A pair of fish swam and danced out of the vase, twisting through the stream. There was something about this image . . .

Reaching out with her free hand, she touched the carving in the space between the woman and the fish. Without warning, the wall shifted and sank back, due to some ancient mechanism hidden in the wall, and the panel slid up into the ceiling, revealing a dark, unlit passage leading further in. Perturbed but no longer wishing to dawdle, Elsinore proceeded with her familiar deeper into the dark.

The passage twisted through the rock—turning, spiraling suddenly, in places bending back—and at many places, it branched off into other halls. Each branch of the path was marked with more images, each more obscure than those in the circular chamber. As before, one specific image stood out to her. She could not say why, but something about it seemed vaguely familiar.

A pair of men—perhaps brothers—embraced beneath a large bell, like those in some of the monasteries of the valley, and were encircled by a river. Across the river, in a barren forest of pine, was a chimerical creature with the hooves and horns of a goat, the front legs and claws of a lion, a tail like a writhing snake, the face of an ass with tall square ears, and the wings of a terrible bird of prey. Standing upright, the creature was surrounded by what looked like chickens. It raised its front paw in an open gesture of welcome, like the colossal Goddess above the tunnel.

The image was a mystery to Elsinore, but somehow, though the sorceress had long since lost track of her direction and the distance she had gone, she felt this marked the correct way forward. She pushed on through the portal, following her light, and from then on, when she came to a turn she knew she must take, she took it. When she knew she must go straight, she proceeded without doubt. The curving, turning halls bent around each other, crossing, recrossing, following other pathways, spiraling inward and then back out. She felt something, followed something, but she knew not what in the conscious part of her mind.

After moving through the labyrinth for some time, Elsinore grew uneasy with the surety of her progress. At last, she stopped and sat on the floor with her legs crossed. Risky stopped beside her when they saw their companion cease to follow and curled up in the crook of her crossed legs.

Elsinore closed her eyes, cleared her mind, and focused as she had when she ran the glittering sand through her hands earlier in the day. Meditating had been difficult for Elsinore her whole life; always, there were thoughts, notions, and endless worries clouding her mind. But since reuniting with Folia, her lover had guided her. Folia knew so much and had grown so wise in the many years she had spent in the world—not only from the wisdom of age and practice and study but from the experience she had inherited through awakening to . . .

To what? To her past?

To the lives she had lived before?

Elsinore gritted her teeth and snarled at herself. Her mind was wandering again. She focused on clearing her mind, this time not entirely but only of everything but Folia's gentle face.

Folia's face as it had been when Elsinore first saw her, long ago in the temple.

Clearing her mind of all but this was easy.

She focused. She focused on Folia's eyes, on her smile, on her cheeks. She thought of her at sunset, as the light grew red and dim, as beautiful darkness on a night of the new moon surrounded them, and she could barely see her lover in front of her. She imagined leaning into her, inclining her face, parting her lips against hers, closing her eyes . . .

Once her mind's eye was closed in this kiss, there was nothing. There was not even darkness, not even nothing. Simply clarity.

Elsinore drifted, her awareness separated from her body, separated from the thoughts that roiled through her mind, all left behind.

This was the trick, wasn't it?

(Elsinore did not think this; she did not think anything. Elsinore, finally, simply was.)

At last, the young woman opened her eyes to her surroundings and saw things as they were. She saw, faintly but truly, the ghostly image of a thread, or a stream, of trailing silver light, leading ahead of her into the darkness, not fading away as it grew distant but bending around the next turn she knew she should take. Turning back, she saw the silver stream leading back down the passage the way she had come.

Only for a moment did she see this before she returned to her mind, before her thoughts and worries surrounded her again. But now she knew.

That was enough.

Elsinore proceeded as she had, her faith in the path she took now supported by her realization. She ignored the flickering scenes on the walls and moved ever forward in the light of her fire spell.

In the stone passage within the cliff, Elsinore's every move echoed off the walls, into the distance, and back again. Even Risky's extraordinary cat paws could be heard padding beside her, and their claws clicked on the stone floor.

From somewhere—behind or ahead or above—Elsinore heard a voice.

With its distance impossible to tell as it reverberated softly in the echoing chamber, she at first couldn't tell what it said. The echoes spun it into rhyme, repeating, twisting it poetically into itself, like the endless halls of this labyrinth.

Nin-ngu . . .

Nin-ngu galla-zu . . .

Nin-ngu . . . Nin-ngu . . . galla-zu . . . galla-zu . . .

Nin-ngu galla-zu imshiresh.

Elsinore's eyes widened in horror, and her heart leaped to her throat. Even Risky, finally moved to urgency rare for their calm cat form, hissed and arched their back. Their fur luminesced with a pale green-yellow glow, and they began to dash forward into the darkness, still ahead, not looking back.

With the light of her familiar to guide her, Elsinore dismissed her fire spell and pumped her arms at her sides as she ran after Risky, praying to the Goddess that they were fleeing the right way, that the now-invisible stream she followed led her away from the voice, away from the hellish poem. Praying that the labyrinth led not to a dead-end chamber but to escape.

Nin-ngu . . . Nin-ngu . . .

As the voice grew louder, it became clear that it was following them from behind. The voice sounded hollow, old, like a drum made of dried skin stretched over some huge, ancient, broken shell.

Galla-zu . . . Galla-zu . . .

The voice spoke in an ancient language, far older than Elsinore's language of the Great River Valley, unspoken for centuries save in rituals or casting spells.

Imshiresh!

Despite how fast she ran and how hard her heart beat, Elsinore's blood ran cold.

Nin-ngu . . . Nin-ngu galla-zu imshiresh!

The voice was closer still, cutting clear through the echo, and Elsinore did not look back, could not look back, but ran, her breath like a knife in her throat, her sides sharp with pain. Risky's light grew fainter, but the tunnel grew no darker.

There was white light ahead. There was day!

But the voice still grew louder, closer. It redoubled in the echo—no, not an echo. Truly, there were many voices— three, four, six—and they repeated their ominous cry in unison:

Nin-ngu galla-zu imshiresh.

The light ahead, too, grew closer. But would the voices follow? What were they? Creatures of the dark, of the defaced figure above the tunnel? Or something stirred from the reeds that glowed by the sea, awakened by the rise of the pink thing?

Elsinore stopped running and turned to face her pursuers. Still unseen in the dark, their awful voices carried before them. Her breath ripped through her lungs, heaving, and she was nearly sick. She bent over, hands on her knees, but only for a moment; that was all she would give herself. Then she stood, snapped her fingers to cast her fire spell in each hand—an orb of glowing yellow flame hovering above each palm—and made with her fingers the sign of casting off evil, her forefingers and little fingers extended in bull's horns.

Her breath still heaving, she controlled herself enough to whisper the rhyme of a spell in the same ancient tongue as the voices that followed her—a spell she had learned only lately at the temple, taught to her by the Bodhakes. Then she shouted the word of power that cast the spell, a word in the old tongue of such magical potency that, once spoken, neither the sorceress nor anyone who heard her speak would remember it—not until she studied the spell once more in the dark shadow of the night between sleeps.

The spell thus cast, the flames in Elsinore's palms glowed green, and she spun her arms in a circle before her, her fingers still in the sign of the bull. Before her, a circle appeared where the flames had traced, and a faint blue-green light rapidly filled the center and expanded from its edge till it filled the space in the tunnel before her like a glass wall. No force—no harmful influence—could pass that wall till Elsinore dismissed the spell known as The Mother's Impassable Shield.

Catching her breath in great gasps, Elsinore stared through the wall of the spell. She could run no more; she did not even know if there would be anywhere to hide if the way forward did lead out of the tunnel. So she faced her pursuers and hoped her magic would hold.

Slowly, through the dim blue light of the shield spell,

she saw them. First, all she saw was their eyes, which glowed not with reflection but with their own inner lurid light, a terrible red. No, not red—the tinted light of the spell was distorting the color.

They glowed with the same orange-pink light as the coral thing that had pursued her in the field.

The young woman stood still with fear as she faced them, watching them glare at her with their frightful pink light, and as they came closer and their bodies should have become clearer, still they were hidden in shadow. Indeed, the shadow seemed to cloak them totally, leaving only their glaring eyes to be seen. They shifted from side to side, up and down and around each other, but by the pairs of eyes, Elsinore could see that there were eight of them. They had stopped, mercifully, at the shield, and shadowy wisps like hands reached out to it but could not pass. Still, they shifted, still they stared, and with a frightful, hollow voice, all eight as one, they moaned again:

Nin-ngu galla-zu imshiresh.

Still dizzy and sore and sick from sprinting, Elsinore focused what energy she had on maintaining the spell. She should be safe for a time as long as she concentrated, even if she turned away, and at last she did so. Turning her back on the shadows that chased her and on the tunnel from which she had come, Elsinore faced the light ahead.

It wasn't daylight after all; it was a pale blue-white artificial light coming from above, from panels in the ceiling. It was a strong light, too strong, stark and unforgiving, and it seemed to make every pore and wrinkle on Elsinore's hand stand out on its own from her skin. But it was familiar, this light. She had seen rooms lit with light like it before—not in the towns of the river valley and not in the great city of Sanisa but . . .

In the Kur.

In the ruined buildings under the Mountain.

In a tomb where she had become trapped.

In a hall of lead coffins and a great serpent from which she had only narrowly escaped.

Piercing her eyelids even as she shut them tightly, the light planted the seed of a faint pain in her head, deep behind her eyes. At first dull and aching, the pain rapidly grew, stronger than Elsinore was able to process. Quickly, she no longer felt the pain but instead felt a profound weight pressing on her head, into her very mind.

She'd felt this weight before, on occasion, since she was a child. When she was little, she would feel it coming on while she played in bright sunlight, and she would go to her mother Milanda, hardly able to speak, weakened and quiet, and moan and tug on her mother's skirt as if she were bored.

Elsie had only been a child and hadn't been able to find words to describe what was happening to her. It was really some profound feeling that she couldn't make herself do anything, not even move; it was a pain too great for her body to endure and understand that it was pain. She would lie on her side on cushions and writhe and lose consciousness, not in sleep but out of the inability to process the world as it existed around her.

Elsie would see things then, things that she remembered very clearly, things that had happened to her very long ago, things that had happened before she was born. Then, just as quickly as they had appeared, they were gone, and she could never remember what she had seen. By then, the pain would subside and become weak enough for her body to understand it as pain. All the vision-memories she saw would dissolve into twirling, scintillating lights that vibrated across her field of vision, and she would be left with a profound ache in her head that would last for hours, before it finally passed and little Elsie was back to normal.

When she tried to describe what had happened to her mother—as she put it in her childlike way, "I can remember things that I can't remember"—Milanda grew fearful that Elsie was experiencing seizures—or worse, that a tumor was pressing on her brain, distorting her mind and threatening her life.

Only once Milanda took her daughter to a nearby city to see another healer who knew more of such things did they learn these were only migraines. Thankfully, they became less frequent as Elsie took medicines and grew older. Only once had Elsinore again been overcome with such an experience as an adult.

It had happened on the night Folia was buried.

On the eve of the Day of Blood, Elsinore had processed with her temple siblings to the Place of the Mound and fainted with visions of the Mountain.

But this time, the migraine was much stronger and more focused. This was like those she had experienced as a child, and she felt the growing pain transform into the pure weight of melancholic lethargy. She tried to move on, still afraid of what pursued her from the dark, but she could not feel her legs, could barely stand, and the way forward became obscured by drifting, sharp hallucinated lights that slowly took the form of memories long hidden.

Unable to make out through the glare where she was going after so long in the dark, and with her eyes blurry with pain her body could not even process as pain, Elsinore stumbled slowly forward. As her eyes slowly adjusted, she saw a door just before her—a simple door, not blocking the whole passage forward but letting in more of the pale, sharp blue light through gaps above, below, and around the edges. It was made of thin, weak metal, a dull brushed steel, held to a frame of the same material by two metal hinges, and shut with a little bolt that seemed to fasten the door with a small knob or dial.

As a wave of dizziness and nausea swept over her, she reached out, unlocked the door, tripped, and found herself in light.

Elsie fell out of the restroom stall and vomited.

She knew it looked like she was drunk, but she didn't care. Or it's not that she didn't care—normally, she would! But Elsie was desperately self-conscious, actually, of presenting herself badly. More that right now, she couldn't care. She couldn't make her body care; the pain from the onset of this migraine was so intense that she didn't care what happened to her in the moment. She didn't care if someone clocked her and kicked her out of the ladies' room. She just wanted the pain to stop.

It would have been a much better idea to do it in the stall, in the toilet bowl. That was why she'd gone into the stall in the first place, actually: to vomit. It had been a pretty good idea she'd had at the time, but Elsie always had kind of a hard time executing her ideas the way she envisioned them. It's something she had been working on as a zine writer and artist and, apparently, also as someone who vomited in the ladies' room of concert venues. There were a lot of improvements Elsie planned to make in her life, and this was going to have to be one of them. Apparently.

Oh my goddess, thank fuck, Elsie thought to herself. It was a trash can. Oh fuck, thank goddess I vomited into a trash can. Like ninety, ninety-five percent of it went into the trash can. Oh my goddess, I didn't puke onto a counter or a sink or the floor in front of four other women in a bathroom at a No Doubt concert in fucking Camden. I only did it in a trash can. Fuck.

If it had to be anywhere, it would probably be better at an amphitheater in Camden than, like, at work in the bookstore in Philly. It would be better, like, nowhere—like, it would be better if it hadn't happened at all—but, I mean. Camden, sure, a music fest at the E-Centre, who gives a shit, right?

All of the Four Other Women in a Bathroom at a No Doubt Concert in Fucking Camden rushed over to Elsie immediately.

"Oh my god, honey, are you okay?" one of them asked, overlapping with another who said basically the same thing. Another folded up a bunch of paper towels from the dispenser, wet them in the sink, and handed them to her. The fourth helped her up once Elsie had wiped off her face and her mouth and let her lean against her shoulder. Thank fuck none of it had gotten on her clothes; she loved this skirt, but if it had, at least the skirt was brown and had a bunch of flowery bullshit on it. Her top was totally white, and that would have been a fucking disaster.

"So, you okay, honey?" the first woman asked again.

Elsie finally worked past the pain and dredged up the nerve to reply, then thought better of speaking and just smiled weakly and nodded. The last woman, the one she was leaning on, asked if she needed help walking back out of the ladies' room and needed someone to sit with her, and Elsie, still thinking it would be smarter not to fucking talk in this extremely fucking precarious situation, sort of shook her head and waved her hand, a gesture she was trying to use to convey gratitude, and congeniality, and that she had recovered, but also refusal? But like a grateful kind of refusal? Like that.

Anyway, you know, idea and execution, right?

"Let's get you out into the fresh air," one of them said.

The woman Elsie was still leaning on, despite what she thought had been an extremely easy to understand hand wave, walked her out into the sunlight. Elsie didn't think she needed help walking, actually. She probably didn't. Did she? Maybe she definitely did. It was hard to tell.

Immediately outside, a crowd of people were cheering, singing along to the opening verse of "Just a Girl." The open-air amphitheater was bright and noisy and grassy, the smell of the nearby Delaware River overcome by the smell of sweat and bodies and beer, people jumping and yelling and clapping for Gwen Stefani. The other women dispersed once they were satisfied that the fourth was taking care of this weird, possibly drunk girl, and they returned to their friends in the audience.

The sunlight, the noise, the smells—it's no wonder a migraine had come on. Elsie suddenly felt dizzy and nauseous again, and the woman beside her could *obviously* tell. She gently led Elsie to a clear area in the grass, away from the people and the stage and in as much shade as they could get. They sat down, and Elsie's peasant skirt spread out on the grass in a way that would have been classical and rustically beautiful or whatever in a different situation, if she hadn't just been in crazy pain and stumbling around puking. The woman propped Elsie up with an arm around her bare shoulders. Elsie felt a little shiver when the woman's hand touched the sunburn she'd gotten around the spaghetti straps of her top; like, she actually felt it over the subsiding pain of the migraine that otherwise took up all the feeling in her body.

That's a good sign, right?

The woman pulled a bottle of water out of her bag, and Elsie drank like crazy. How did she get this thirsty? How long had she been this thirsty?

"I'm Tara," the woman said finally.

Now that Elsie had recovered a little, she realized this chick's voice was . . . a little like Elsie's, actually. She smiled, not weakly but broadly. She couldn't remember—like, not that she'd been checking or anything, she'd been distracted—but she was pretty fucking sure this was the first time she'd felt comfortable all day. Definitely since arriving in New Jersey by PATCO, and *definitely* definitely since the incident back there in the bathroom. This girl's vibe . . . really seemed pretty okay.

"I'm Elisabeth," she replied, suddenly not afraid to use her voice, even if it clocked her. Suddenly not afraid of anything anymore. A lock of blonde hair had fallen loose from her ponytail and she brushed it back behind her ear with her hand. "Everyone calls me Elsie for short, though. Not, like, 'Liz' or 'Beth' or anything."

"Really glad to meet you, Elsie." Tara put her hand softly on Elsie's arm and smiled.

Elsie looked at her—really actually looked at her face—for the first time. Tara's brown skin was framed by curly black hair. Her eyes were hazel, and a ray of sunlight caught them as she turned to Elsie. Tara's eyes were so clear and bright. Elsie thought they shone right at her, only for her, like starlight. Elsie grinned, and suddenly she didn't know what to say. All she wanted to do was get a better look at Tara.

At her beautiful eyes.

ABOUT THE AUTHOR

Emily Wynne is the author of *Princess of the Pomegranate Moon*. She lives with her girlfriend and spends her time writing, editing, watching films, and meditating.